DATE DUE

11/17/07	

PAPER
TRAILS

Pete Dexter

EDITED BY ROB FLEDER

ecco

An Imprint of HarperCollinsPublishers

PAPER

TRUE STORIES OF CONFUSION,

MINDLESS VIOLENCE,

AND FORBIDDEN DESIRES,

A SURPRISING NUMBER OF WHICH

ARE NOT ABOUT MARRIAGE

TRAILS

HarperCollins books may be purchased for educational, business, or sales promotional use. For information, please write: Special Markets Department, HarperCollins Publishers, 10 East 53rd Street, New York, NY 10022.

814.
DEX
4.07

FIRST EDITION

Designed by Cassandra J. Pappas

Library of Congress Cataloging-in-Publication Data is available upon request.

ISBN: 978-0-06-118935-7
ISBN-10: 0-06-118935-9

07 08 09 10 11   WBC/RRD   10 9 8 7 6 5 4 3 2 1

for Millicent

Acknowledgments

Most of these stories originally appeared, in a slightly different form, in the *Philadelphia Daily News,* the *Sacramento Bee, Esquire, Sports Illustrated, New York Woman, Inside Sports,* and *Redbook.* We are grateful to them for permission to reprint, and to any other publication that would have given us permission if we'd bothered to ask.

We would also like to thank Esther Newberg, Dan Halpern, and Dave Hirshey, who conspired to make this book possible. And, of course, Millicent Bennett.

Foreword

Journalism, as all journalists know, is an imperfect craft that can sometimes become art. The ambition is always the same: to make marks on the walls of the cave that will help other members of the tribe understand what lies within. The journalist cannot say that dragons are deep in the darkness if they are not. But he cannot describe a place that is benign and tranquil if he has not gone deep enough to see and smell and hear the dragon. The life of the tribe itself can depend on him.

In this marvelous collection of his journalism, novelist Pete Dexter looks at the American dragons of race, violence, drugs, booze, and hypocrisy during the 1970s and 1980s. His eye is exact. His ear is flawless. He tells us with a chilly accuracy about certain aspects of the dark side of American lives, and yet he hears the dark laughter too. He does not sentimentalize his subjects, but he doesn't judge them either. He knows that all of us are capable of sin, that each one of us, young or old, man or woman, famous or anonymous, can slide into stupidity and folly. He can be outraged by cruelty, but is never surprised.

Many pieces in the collection were originally published as newspaper columns (for the *Philadelphia Daily News* and later the *Sacramento Bee*) or as articles for magazines as varied as *Redbook*, *Sports Illustrated*, and *Esquire*. Such work is always difficult. You interview people and some of them lie and you have almost no way of knowing what is true. Still, you must write with assurance and certainty. You go out in the morning with a notion about a good story and by early afternoon you have reported it out of existence and you still have to write a column. Everything is provisional, the truth always elusive. By 1998, Dexter was writing that "it would be nice once in a while if somebody would stand up and acknowledge the awful truth about the news business: Most of the time, we don't have a clue."

On newspapers, the deadlines are remorseless and the space is rigidly defined. Every columnist believes that the work would have been much better if only he had another hour to write and three more inches of space. But the page is laid out. The delivery trucks are waiting to carry their bundles into the city. Get it written. Magazines have other limitations. Even now, in the age of the computer, their lead time—the gap between finishing the article and actual publication—can be as long as three months. The writer knows that events could change everything. His subject could be indicted. Or murdered. Or found innocent by a jury. The writing demands certainty, but magazine lead time requires a hedge against drastic change. The prose can end up layered with the tentative.

It is most important to remember that Dexter found his voice as a local columnist. Such columns disdain the vast generalizations of political columns, the need to define the Big Picture, the mushy generalities caused by trying to write for as many newspapers as a syndicate can persuade to take the column. The local columnist writes for the guy beside him in the subway car or the bus, the woman in front of him on the line at a supermarket, the teacher crossing the schoolyard. Such columns are built on a sense of place, a feel for the local (not the parochial), and the belief that the best stories might lie right around the corner. As a form, the local column was reinvented in 1963 by Jimmy Breslin on the old *New York Herald-Tribune*. Breslin had been a gifted sportswriter and applied many sports techniques to the fires, homicides, and assorted outrages of life in a big city. Details were everything. So were the words and rhythms of ordinary speech. Breslin's column was so successful that many newspapers looked for their own local columns, and that brought Pete Dexter to the tabloid *Philadelphia Daily News* in 1974, first as a reporter and then, very quickly, as a columnist.

After Dexter came north from Florida, where he was working in a gas station after stints at two papers, a wonderful newspaperman named Gil Spencer gave him a chance to write a column. I got to know Spencer more than a decade later in New York, when he was editing the *New York Daily News*, the country's first and most successful tabloid. Spencer knew in his gut that the essence of a great tabloid story was drama. That is, conflict. Cops vs. robbers, husbands vs. wives, white hats vs. black hats, and, sadly, (this was the 1970s) whites vs. blacks. He had no room in his paper for an analysis of the sisal crop in South Asia. And nobody could write three thousand words on anything and hope to get it in the paper. Even if the analysis explained a murder on the Main Line. This was a *tabloid*, for Chrissakes.

Spencer also knew that a good newspaper needed columnists. They functioned like soloists in a band. They were not, and must never be, the *whole* band. But when they stood up to blow eight or sixteen bars they gave the paper a face, a personality, a voice. And more than one voice, of course. Any newspaper with a single voice is a bore and boring papers die. When I saw Spencer's *Daily News*, I enjoyed the columns of Chuck Stone, who wrote about race with passion tempered by intelligence, and my friend Jack McKinney, himself a superb columnist and a great boxing writer. It was McKinney who first told me about Dexter.

"We got a kid here now who's pretty goddamned good," McKinney said one night in his hoarse Philadelphia accent. "He can punch like hell."

In those days before the Internet, alas, I didn't see much of the paper. If I found myself in Times Square, I usually went into the out-of-town newsstand and bought a few days' worth of the great Philadelphia tabloid, savored its energy, read McKinney and Stone, and then started reading Pete Dexter. As usual, McKinney was right. Dexter could punch.

He had all the basic tools. His nouns were concrete. His verbs were active. He actually listened to his subjects. He described the world he was looking at so that the reader could go there too. And he trusted the reader. He didn't have to italicize his points, or drift into brooding rhapsodies about the Sorrows of Life. He had learned the lessons of Hemingway. Dexter also trained in a local boxing gym, and his education there was surely part of his writing education too. Philadelphia fighters were famous then for their mastery of the explosive left hook, but they all knew that the hook must come off a jab. The jab could be an elegant spear, setting a pace, even lulling an opponent, but ultimately creating a brutal deception. So Dexter could jab and jab and jab, and *then* unload the hook. That rhythm is in many of these pieces.

But reading them now, I see that he had even more unsettling qualities. He understood that the world was often a savage place. Many human beings were nasty and cruel. They had refined gifts for hurting others, with guns and knives and kicks in the head. Like prizefighters, they often talked about "heart," but they used the word in a different way; fighters measured "heart" by the willingness of a fighter to risk great harm in order to win; the street hoods wanted no risk at all. They inflicted hurt, but usually could not endure it. That's why they loved guns. As he moved around, Dexter saw the results of this savage new culture. Bars, predominantly white or mostly black, often seethed with an undercurrent of violence. Too many people lived as if they wanted to die. This was not the city of amiable gangsters out of Damon Runyon. Crack had arrived. Guns were everywhere. Welfare had destroyed most notions of work (in that era in New York, I interviewed many older teenagers who had never known a single person who held a job). Kids with feral eyes were destroying others and themselves and didn't much care. For a year or a month, they owned the night.

Dexter didn't dwell on this savage terrain in every column, of course. As a soloist, he couldn't always play the same tune. He gave his readers scenes of domestic life with Mrs. Dexter that do not at all resemble visions out of Doris Day movies, yet are infused with the unspoken mysteries of love. He wrote about his daughter. He wrote about a cat that moved into their lives one day and refused to leave. He wrote about his dog. All these lighter pieces were written with style and amusement and irony, and some of them are in this collection. But they are played against a larger context: the growing barbarism of American cities.

Along the way, fragments of Dexter's own life emerged in the columns. We learn here a few things about his childhood in Milledgeville, Georgia. "My family moved there when I was four—my father had died and my mother remarried—and left when I was ten, and in the years in between certain things settled in me that never changed." His stepfather taught physics at the local military college, so we assume there were books in the house, and intelligent talk at the dinner table. In 1952, when Dexter was eight, his mother contracted tuberculosis, and he was flown from Atlanta to Detroit to stay for a year with an aunt and uncle. "I remembered that feeling," he writes. "It was the same feeling as being lost." The rural American South, with its loveliness and lurking horror, helped shape his personal template. Dexter implies too that he became a kind of drifter, lived out west, tried various jobs, drank too much, fell in love with the wrong women. He doesn't tell us much more, but those fragments remind me of the words of George Bernard Shaw: "I had a wonderful education, except for school."

There is no account here of the time in Philadelphia when the savagery fell upon Dexter himself. In 1981, he wrote a column about a botched drug deal that left a young participant dead. Dexter explained what happened next in a 2005 interview with Kevin Lanahan of the *Albany Times-Union*: "The kid's brother called me up and said he was going to break my hands. He bartended in Devil's Pocket, which has got to be the worst neighborhood in the city—maybe anywhere. I thought I could talk to him and work it out, so I went down there."

Dexter arrived at the bar alone, and left without half of his upper teeth, thanks to patrons who set upon him with beer bottles. He returned a short time later and brought along a friend, the prizefighter named Randall "Tex" Cobb, a heavyweight contender good enough to eventually get a shot at the title. After all, it took heart simply to walk around Devil's Pocket.

"When we got to the bar about thirty guys with baseball bats came through the back door," Dexter said. "Cobb turned to me and said, 'I hope this is the local softball team.' "

It wasn't. Some of them carried tire irons too. Both visitors took a savage beating. Dexter's back and pelvis were broken. Cobb's arm was broken, and he was never the same fighter again. Dexter took a long time to recover, and parts of his body are still held together with pins and rods. While recovering, he started writing his first novel, and left Philadelphia for good in 1986. In a farewell piece, he talked about some of the

Philadelphia people he cherished (from Spencer to Tex Cobb) and the special events he had witnessed. "One night," he wrote, "I almost saw myself die."

It has been our good fortune that Pete Dexter did not die at the hands of those heroes with ballbats and tire irons. He has gone on to write some of the most original, and disturbing, novels in American literature. And now, in this collection, we are able to look again at some of his first drafts. They are as good as it ever gets.

—PETE HAMILL

Introduction

I was warned before I left the world of personal reportage (a word I've never used before) that I was in for a rude awakening. That the world was not a pretty place for those who had no newspaper column to protect them.

It goes without saying, I was not fazed. First of all, where I come from, men don't take advice. Second, I didn't believe it. The world wasn't that cold and calculating, it just happened to think I was a wonderful guy. Third, even if what they said was true, I'd already decided I was tired of special handling. I wanted to go into the streets again and meet the world on its own terms.

(A Note on Type: The sentence you have just read, like a lot of the sentences you will read in the pages that follow, was never articulated out loud and never even appeared in this form in my head, as nobody is that stupid. It does, nevertheless, represent the gist of the situation, which is, this being journalism, as much as anyone can expect.)

Anyway, long story short, I quit the world of non-fiction for a more down-to-earth life here on my damp little outpost in the Puget Sound. With my damp little wife, my damp dogs, reawakened to the pleasure of simple pleasures. What pleasures? Why, the pleasure of going all winter and never losing the smell of wet Labrador retrievers in the truck, for one thing.

The pleasure of picking up the telephone and getting nothing but

an answering machine on the other end, like everybody else. The pleasure of no one returning my calls. But wait, that's not all. Restaurants
do not fuss over me anymore when I come in; sometimes in tourist
season they won't even give me a table. Salesmen lie to my face, the
dogs chew the butt out of all my favorite sweatpants, and low-life cable network producers, who have never had a thought in their heads
that did not come from something else they saw on cable television,
are so unthreatened by me that they feel safe stealing my stuff and
claiming to have had sudden strokes of genius. I know, I know, imitation is the sincerest form of flattery. That's what they say. And like
most of what they say, it doesn't apply. And yeah, I tried calling a lawyer, but all I got was a recorded message.

But then, as they also say, at least I was warned. Which is an especially pointless thing to say, it seems to me, issued as if there were some
consolation in being warned. It is, in fact, the opposite of consolation. It
is heckling.

Be that as it may, what I was not warned of was the other, larger problem which, as far as I know, has no name and exists out on the periphery
somewhere as a feeling of full-udderness. Full of juice and no place to
shoot it.

What does one do, for instance, with the story of Lucky Al, as he was
known during his short stay here on the island, a fifty-four-year-old
bachelor who got a seven-figure settlement from a drug company and
showed up one spring smoking fifty-dollar cigars? He bought a new car,
the first house he'd ever owned, his first set of Callaways, a membership at
the golf club. He rescued a dog from the dog pound—yes, it was his first
dog—joined the local council for the arts, and volunteered for the garden
tour, and then, a few months into his new life, died in his bathtub, which I
suppose was not unrelated to the seven-figure settlement with the drug
company, and was subsequently eaten by his dog (I think the Mexicans
have a term for preparing meat that way, but I'm not sure). In the dog's
defense, she'd only been with him a month, and it's easy to criticize from
the sidelines when you're not hungry yourself.

Or, moving on, the incident in the adult diaper aisle of the Safeway in
Green Valley, Arizona. What does one do with that?

Or, for that matter, what of the blemish that only recently appeared on one's chest, on the site of a spider bite, and when squeezed, shot a miraculous, *audible* volume of what one can only assume was spider jizzom onto the bathroom mirror, in the form—may the dog eat me if I'm lying—of an inverted question mark?

Actually, I did do something with that. I called Miss Julie Ansell over at Gracie Films about the question mark incident, seeing if she was interested in optioning it for a film, but I don't seem to have much juice left in Hollywood, either.

So, the problem. Where does one go? One who used to relieve himself in the pages of a daily newspaper, and now has no newspaper, and, just as important, no cocked gun behind his ear to obligate him to fill a regular slot. One is not, let me add, the sort of self-starter to write these things down for fun.

Well, in my case, one went to Fleder.

Fleder is as reliable a sympathetic ear as you are likely to find in the dog-eat-dog world of big-time journalism (and I hope Lucky Al hasn't ruined that expression for you). In fact, you could say that he has made a living sympathizing with writers and their problems, and—this is the unbelievable part, if you keep in mind that Fleder is an editor, not an understanding doctor with a prescription pad—often makes things better instead of worse.

So I spelled out the situation in all its gritty detail, the cold, hard truth of what it's like to live in this world without a newspaper column. Presently, I noticed myself starting to repeat the details, which (pay attention, young authors, this is literary advice) is how writers traditionally know it's time to shut up, unless, of course, you're Norman Mailer.

Anyway, in the suddenly quiet room, Fleder mulled over the situation, looking at it from my point of view, from his point of view, from the point of view of the outside world. Fleder can mull with anybody on the planet.

"Well," he said when he'd finished, "what if we got a collection of your old stuff together, from back in the days you weren't impotent? Would that make you feel better?"

I said, "Fuck no, it wouldn't make me feel better."

And thus was born the project.

We began to gather non-fiction. First, Fleder went through as many columns as he could find from all the places that I could remember that I'd worked, millions of words, and then spent nine months winnowing them down to a nine-pound pile of the toxic paper that comes out of copying machines and dries out your fingers. He sent this pile to me Federal Express with a note saying he thought it was a little on the heavy side, and what did I think we ought to cut?

Holding the pile in my arms, I had the distinct feeling of a one-night stand gone wrong. I put the pile into a drawer for nine months, not wanting to give the impression that I wasn't accepting responsibility for it, and then sent it back Federal Express, priority overnight delivery, also with a note:

Rob—I can't pick one column over another because I love them all the same.

Fleder understood, and went back into the pile for a couple of months, added some magazine pieces, and at the same time winnowed off another three pounds or so (does anybody here know if *winnow* is a word? See, this is the kind of nitpick bullshit I didn't have to worry about when I was a newspaper celebrity), and Federal Expressed back what was left, and I kept it two months, correcting the occasional blown syntax to prove I'd actually read it, and also changed all the different names I'd used in print over the years for my wife to one name: *Mrs. Dexter.* I did this to avoid confusion, by the way, not wanting the reader to think that I'd had half a dozen different wives just because the one I have has half a dozen different personalities.

Still, the pile didn't feel like mine. I don't know how else to put it, although abandoning it now was out of the question. To quote an old saying, I have to look at myself in the mirror too.

And in this way did fall Fleder and I into a kind of reverse custody battle.

Fleder would send our pile to me, I would keep it a polite amount of time and send it back. When it was at his house, I was happy; when it was at my house, he was happy. Years passed in this way, in a polite cordiality, the time fluctuations becoming gradually shorter as good manners fell victim to the desire to be free that burns in all our hearts, and then one day Fleder did something completely unexpected.

He called and said he had been giving our pile a lot of thought lately, and perhaps it was time to let go, to send it out into the world on its own. And as the first step in that general direction, he suggested we put the contents in some sort of logical order, and as the second step, find the dates of publication.

Now the truth is, I have never been much of a worrier about logical order. Why can't we just shuffle them? On the other hand, having glimpsed our six pounds of toxic paper out on its own, of course, I saw that Fleder was right about the dates. The dates were crucial, lest some worn-out old whore like Jonathan Yardley over at the *Washington Post* use the opportunity to gratuitously insult the author's work ethic. To head that off, I agreed on the need for the dates of publication, and, the next day, when we saw what obtaining these dates entailed, we simultaneously acknowledged that what we really needed was not the dates of publication, but an inviolate, inarguable, incurable reason for *not* having the dates of publication. Which is to say, finally, I had something to bring to the table:

The author and editor of this project have, from its inception, taken every precaution to avoid compromising the timelessness of these pieces. Thank you for your attention. I can do that in my sleep.

And thus, the little pile, dateless but well traveled, passed to the next stage of its life, a visit to the offices of Miss Esther Newberg, the powerful literary agent, a woman who does not have time for Federal Express—who scorns Federal Express—and instead messengers everything directly to its target, which means, as I understand it, our project was given a daring bicycle ride through Manhattan to a place where it was finally wanted and loved for itself.

Yes, a happy ending.

The manuscript no longer appears on the doorstep every three or four months with a note pinned to its blanket, and the custody issue has been taken off the table anyway, by the kindness of the people at Ecco, and for Fleder and me, civility has replaced Federal Express.

And relieved of my half of our mutual burden, I would like now to acknowledge my affection and gratitude for my old friend Fleder, not only for thinking of doing this in the first place, but for doing all the work. And on the subject of Fleder, and perhaps at the risk of changing the mood of this essay, I would just like to add the following for the record: Who the *fuck* are you calling impotent?

PAPER
TRAILS

1

The man spent a week trying to get rid of the cat on the front porch, then he gave up. For that week, he hissed every time he walked out the front door. He lobbed firewood over her head, let his dogs chase her up trees. He told his wife to leave the cat food across the road in the woods.

None of it worked.

In the morning—every morning—the cat would be there to curl around his leg when he came out the door, and after a week he gave up hissing and lobbing firewood, but he did not give up wishing she would go away.

He said to his wife, "As soon as it warms up, quit feeding her and maybe she'll go someplace else." He said that in January.

Two months went by, and it got warmer. The wife quit leaving food. The cat got pregnant. When she rubbed her stomach against his leg now, he thought he could feel the kittens. He didn't say anything when his wife began feeding her again.

The cat was gentler than the other cats that lived in the woods. They showed up from time to time on the front porch too. She was also cleaner than the others. The man noticed that. He had a year-old daughter, and he didn't stop her when she moved to hug the cat. And he had lost things that mattered before and was not inclined to take chances with his child.

The litter of kittens came in the middle of April. There were five of them, all except one looked like the mother. They were white and had brown and black circles on their heads and shoulders and tails. The fifth one was gray.

The delivery occurred behind a pile of stacked bricks in a neighbor's yard. The neighbor had a German shepherd, and the man's wife climbed the fence between the yards to move the kittens into a cardboard box near his front porch.

As she was going back over the fence for the second one, the mother cat was coming under the fence with the first one, carrying it back to the bricks.

The wife worried about the kittens at night. The man said he was worried too. "I don't know what we'll do if the dog gets them," he said. "Imagine being down to eleven cats again. Oh, Christ, I can't think about it . . ."

But when he looked again one afternoon a week later and there were only three of them left, the feeling he got stayed with him through supper.

A day or two later he moved them to a pile of scrap wood in his backyard. He had been planning to haul the wood away for eight months, which meant—conservatively—that the kittens had another half-year before they had to worry about finding a different place to stay.

That was the way the man was.

The hawk was waiting in a high limb of one of the tallest pine trees in the woods across the road. The man had seen her hunt from there before. She was brown in the face and wings and a redder color across her chest. When she left the limb, her wings would pump the air slowly, and it was the nature of her power that you could see the effect of each of the strokes on her flight.

Tip to tip, those wings were five feet across.

Right now, though, the man wasn't watching the hawk. He was watching the cat, who was moving her kittens away from the wood pile. There were only two of them left, the gray and one that looked like the mother.

The cat picked up the white one by the skin around its neck, walked to a tree. She dropped it, picked it up again to get the right hold, then

moved up the tree and onto the flat part of the roof. She found a protected spot behind a roll of tar paper that the man had left there—
planning to fix a leak—and put the kitten down.

The man was watching all this in the garden, wondering what had
eaten his bean sprouts, and that didn't make him any happier about having a nest of cats on his roof. He began working on the two plans at the
same time, one for the beans, one for the cats. The mother came back
down the tree.

She was close by when the hawk got the gray kitten. It had been nursing when she'd decided to move and it had held onto a nipple for a couple
of seconds after she'd gotten up. The kitten had dropped off in the sun-
shine, a foot or two from the pile of wood.

It was too young still to move without its mother, so it lay in the
grass and waited, half again the size of a mouse.

The mother cat was almost back to it when the shadow blocked out
the sun. She ducked, then looked back. There was the shadow, the sound
of the hawk's wings, pine needles and dust blowing off the ground, and
then the gray kitten was gone.

It seemed to happen all at once.

The hawk carried it in her talons out over the lake, banked through
a long circle and disappeared behind the trees across the road.

The man walked over to the cat. She searched his face, then came up
on her hind legs, asking for her kitten back. He held out his hands to show
her he didn't have it, then started for the house to get her some milk.

As he moved, his shadow crossed the cat and she cringed, and that is
what he would lie awake thinking about that night, and the next.

The man had lost things that had mattered before, and he knew
what it was to cringe at sudden shadows, the ones that just drop on you
out of the sky.

2

I think it's fair to say that women overestimate breasts. More to the point, they overestimate the hold breasts have on men. Men notice new breasts, but by the time they get to know the owner, breasts—or the absence of breasts—are among the things they have taken for granted, like southern accents. This isn't all bad. Like almost everything else, in the end, breasts are more complicated than they look, and too much thinking can ruin anything.

A long time ago, before I knew my way around, I used to get mashed about once a month in somebody's breasts. Every time I walked into a strange room, some woman with blue hair whom I hadn't seen in a while would pick me up off the floor and hug me. I was a wormy sort of kid, but the women with blue hair had powerful arms, and, invariably, I was crushed in their breasts.

The harder I fought to get away, the harder they held on. Breasts, I learned, were designed on the tar-baby principle. The construction puzzled me, though. You could push them away from your nose—or push part of them away—but that pushed another part into your eye. And if on the one hand they were mushy, on the other hand they seemed to have little rib bones and beaks.

A year or two after breasts became a problem, however, I made an adjustment, which after all is what growing up is about. I began to play dead. Every time I got caught in a set of breasts I went limp, and most of the time they'd just let go.

Early on, I learned not to struggle with breasts.

And for a while I thought that was all there was to it. As I've mentioned, this was before I knew my way around. Then one day a couple of years later—I guess I was seven or eight years old—a kid named Kenny Durkin told me he wanted to dive down the front of Martha Horschler's shirt. Now, Kenny Durkin was the biggest liar in Milledgeville, Georgia, but I must have sensed he was on to something because I asked him what he wanted to do that for. He closed his eyes and brushed his lips and the end of his nose back and forth against the side of his fist, making bubble noises.

As far as I know, Kenny Durkin is still in Milledgeville, making bubble noises against the side of his fist, but the confusion he created that afternoon has never completely disappeared, and the thought of jumping down Martha Horschler's shirt won't leave me alone to this day.

The problem, I guess, is that no matter how much I have wanted this or that breast, I've never been sure what I wanted them for. I don't mean to brag here, but I have been with at least nine of them that I can think of, not even counting the ladies with the blue hair, and it always ends up the same way.

Which is to say, in the end, they're dull. No opinions, no moods, very few moving parts. You can't even race them. The words you see used around breasts, of course, *are* interesting. *Proud* breasts, *haughty* breasts, *aching-to-be-touched* beasts, *sullen* breasts, and the ever-popular *nearly translucent* breasts. But no amount of propaganda can invent a personality where none exists, and when the whole truth comes out, Kenny Durkin may have said everything worth saying about it when he bounced his lips and nose back and forth against the side of his fist.

Still, there is my neighbor Hal. More to the point, there is Hal's wife. If it weren't for Hal's wife, I probably wouldn't have even brought this up. But there he is, no more religious than I am, and he didn't have to give up breasts to get married. I think about that on laundry days, when his wife hangs her underthings on the clothesline.

Most mornings I go out and sit by the lake and read the papers, but on laundry days my eyes run right past President Reagan and Jesse Jackson and keep going, off the page, down the bulkhead, and don't stop until they're next door. On laundry days, there is nothing anybody can do to keep my eyes in my own yard.

Hal's lawn is green too. Everything over there seems to grow.

And something else. Whenever we pass on the road, Hal smiles and waves. His hand seems to be cupping maybe a 36C. I make tweezers of my thumb and fingernails and wave back. It looks as if I were feeding BBs to a canary. I don't know how there got to be a signal between us, but there it is.

"Why are you looking at the neighbors' clothesline?" my wife says. "You're thinking about Martha Horschler again, aren't you?"

My wife has very little in common with Martha Horschler—or with Hal's wife—and I have lived with her for six years without ever bringing up the matter in anything but a playful way. I think you could say, considering what there is to work with, that I've had a lot of fun with my wife's breasts.

"I wasn't thinking about Martha Horschler," I tell her. "I was just thinking about breasts."

"I have breasts," she says.

"Yes, and Russia has elections."

My wife doesn't mind. She says, "You wouldn't know what to do if I woke up tomorrow with big breasts."

I think about that a long time—what I would do. And in the end I decide that if that happened, I'd get dressed and run next door. I wouldn't want to miss the look on Hal's face in case his were missing.

3

The first time I wrote a book, Robert Loomis said he couldn't read it. Loomis is the editor who handles my manuscripts.

"Too much blood," he said. This was over the phone.

I explained that the bleeding was a motif, and I was surprised I had to point that out to a man of his education and experience.

"Not that blood," he said. "This is about *blood* blood, on the page. It's so . . . distracting, and so are the stains. How did this thing get so messy?"

I said, "Let me get this straight. You live in New York City, and you're complaining to me about a little blood?"

The truth, if you are interested in this, is that my ear used to bleed when I wrote. I got it fixed, but not, I would point out, for Loomis.

For Loomis, I bought a self-correcting IBM Selectric typewriter, and then one morning when the next book was finished, I sat down with 700 sheets of paper, manually typed and covered with Coke-can circles and blood and slapped flies—the flies were mostly in the two middle parts that were written in the summer—and realized I now had to run all this through the new IBM Selectric.

It was one of those moments you know is coming but you never quite believe will arrive.

But wait.

It turns out you do not just retype pages. As you sit there moving words from dirty pages to clean pages, you begin to think of other words, and then you argue with yourself which words are better, or if you need them at all.

It took fifty-nine days to run that manuscript through the new IBM Selectric, working every morning from nine to eleven-thirty. Toward the end I was haunted by the idea that somehow Joyce Carol Oates had finished two books while I was retyping *Deadwood*.

Anyway, on the sixtieth day I delivered the manuscript to Loomis's office personally, dropping it from maybe a foot onto his desk. "I don't care if you find somebody's head in there, Bob," I said, "that is as clean as it gets."

He looked as if he did not understand why I would be like that. He said, "I'm sure it's fine," but it is a mortal lock he checked for the head after I left.

It didn't really matter. Later that night, driving out of the city, I made some decisions about my life. There is something about leaving New York that makes me feel as if I have beaten some charge on a technicality, and so I decided to go straight. To get my ear fixed, and buy a computer.

Now here is where it gets interesting. It turns out that the price of a hard-disc Leading Edge computer with a printer and soft floppies and surge suppressors and all the other stuff that Stanley down at the computer store said I needed to write a novel about Georgia in the early 1950s came to just over $2,930, and—are you ready for this?—the cost of having the bad part of one ear lopped off and replaced with tissue from the back of the other ear was exactly $2,915, not counting fifteen dollars' worth of the pain drug Percodan, which is as much as the plastic surgeon said I would need. He did not realize, of course, that I was buying a computer.

But the similarity does not stop there. Ears and computers take the same number of visits (four), and none of the names of things in either store are in English. And so, admitting I could be wrong, I am going to submit here that the only difference between getting a computer and an ear lop is that Stanley down at the computer store won't take Blue Cross.

All right, I brought the computer home and plugged all the parts into each other. There was one extra plug and that went into the wall. It felt like a miracle. And then I sat down and began to write the novel about Georgia in the early 1950s.

As my novels go, it wasn't too bad.

Esther Newberg, who is my agent and knows about these things, read the first three parts, maybe 200 pages, and said, "You are a seriously sick man."

And then, meeting Loomis over lunch, she pushed the pages—which, I might add, were flawlessly typed—across the table and told him what she thought they were worth. And then she said something like, "As you read this, Bob, I think you should ask yourself if you want anybody capable of writing it to be mad at you."

While negotiations went on, I resumed work. The fourth part of the book is where characters are stretched beyond what is comfortable, and the stretching sets things in motion the rest of the way. It is the longest part and the hardest to write, and it took two and a half months to finish. On the day it was done, I reset the computer's margins and spacing, and then hit the pagination button.

My guess was 130 pages, but, of course, we'll never know.

I can tell you it was at least twelve, because it was that far when it stopped. The little red light that means the machine is thinking went on, and then a sentence appeared at the very top of the screen that said, GENERAL DISC FAILURE. USE BACKUP TO REPLACE.

I put one hand on each side of the computer, and began talking to the screen. "You know there isn't any backup," I said. "Remember? We couldn't get the backup to work."

The machine sat, blinking its cursor.

I hit keys, exiting out of part four, and then tried to get back in. The message printed out across the screen again.

I sat very still, thinking of all the flies that had died for just walking across my pages, trying to come up with something appropriately large to kill, and settled finally on Stanley down at the computer store. I called to make an appointment, and was very annoyed when Stanley turned out to be completely understanding. Perhaps he did not know what a Sicilian necktie was. "I know how you feel," he said. "My uncle's a writer, and this happened to him too."

I said, "Oh really? What does he write?"

He threw out some title I'd never heard of, and I told him the book was plagiarized. He said, "Why don't you bring the machine down and let me look it over and see what we can save?"

And I did that, but first I had to make sure nobody was on my side. I began by calling Loomis. He was at his house in Sag Harbor for the weekend. I said, "Bob, I just had a general disc failure and lost a hundred and twenty pages of the novel. I am never writing another word, and I'm not giving you any of your money back."

Loomis took a historical perspective. "You know, Pete," he said, "the most famous case like this was when Thomas Carlyle lost the only copy of his completed manuscript of *The French Revolution* in a house fire. He had to do the whole thing over."

I thanked Loomis for his insight into the way I was feeling. A house fire was exactly what I had in mind.

Then I said something that amazed me even as I said it. Yes, I told Esther Newberg, who took those red-eye flights between cities in order to see every game, that I was glad the Mets had beaten the Boston Red Sox in the World Series. Which is as close as you can come to committing suicide in New York while you're sitting in your room in California.

After that, I walked into the kitchen and hit the stool. It is satisfying stuff, of course, to hit a stool anytime, but especially right after your computer just ate 120 pages of your book. You will notice that I did not hit the computer itself, still not completely satisfied that what was inside it was gone.

When I turned around, my wife was standing in the door. "What in the world are you doing?" she said. She hates it when somebody picks on her stool, and always has.

"I am trying to write a damn book," I said, "if you don't mind."

Then I went back into the office, unplugged the computer, and carried it out to the truck, and, driving over a garbage can, I went to see Stanley. The front of Stanley's store is all glass, sidewalk to ceiling. The truck bumper stopped close enough to press Stanley's only outdoor plant right up against it—but wait, allow me to pause a moment here to tell you the meaning of life. Life is a constant process of learning. Every year, every month, every week. And with knowledge, we mature. And as close as I can calculate it, if Part Four had been finished and then lost, say, thirty-six hours earlier, I would have been immature enough to drive through the glass. We are speaking of perhaps two inches.

Anyway, Stanley and I took the computer into the back, where he set it on a table and plugged it in and read the message about general disc failure for himself. He got into Part Four, and pulled up the first twelve pages, and then the last three. Everything in between had been replaced by a line of happy faces that stretched all the way across the screen.

Happy faces.

It was quiet for a minute, and I tried to find something in my experience that resembled the feeling that was settling over me now that I saw it was really gone.

Thomas Carlyle or not, when it's gone it's gone, and you never get it back. It may come out better or worse next time, but it won't be the same. Trying to get it back is exactly like trying to get the trash man to take a smashed garbage can away with the garbage.

Except *that*, of course, is the opposite problem. It feels a little like when the doctor comes in and says, "Why don't we try an extra week in the hospital, see if we can't get that swelling down," and it feels a little like losing your wallet. But that isn't it. It's like driving out across the country, getting to Boone, Iowa, and realizing your wallet is lying in your pants back on the floor of the Holiday Inn in Sioux City.

There is nothing to do but throw your tantrum and then go back to Sioux City and start over. Except now that I have done that, I see there is a flaw with that analogy too.

There is no map that can show you how to get back to page 130.

4

The last I'd heard of Low Gear and Minus, one of them had shot the other one in the leg, trying to kill a pig that they'd raised from a baby in their backyard in Florida. "That scream," Low Gear had said later, "it sounded so human."

The plan was for the pig to end up bacon. Like most things Minus and Low Gear touch, the pig ended up in the want ads, damaged but alive, and Minus and Low Gear ended up sellers in a buyers' market and lost $60, not counting labor and the medical bills. It didn't do much for the friendship, either.

A month after Minus stopped limping, though, he and Low Gear bought a rug-shampoo business. They found it in the want ads. It came with shampoo, a shampoo machine, a 1968 Ford van with "Flash Rug Cleaners" written on both sides and a list of twenty-five loyal clients who, Low Gear said, were "warrantied not to see dogshit on their feet before they halfway to the kitchen."

They felt so good about going into business again that they decided to take a vacation. They loaded an undetermined number of cases of Busch beer into the van, found some hopeless teenage drug addicts with names like Jennifer and Stephanie, and headed south for Key West.

Low Gear had found the girls, and Minus studied them in the rear-view mirror. "Nobody back there is married, is it?" he said.

Minus had been shot twice in his life, and now there were two things he was afraid of, married women and pigs. He had been married once himself, and sometime, if the right song was on the jukebox and he had enough beer in him, he'd tell Low Gear that he still loved her.

Low Gear used teenagers and never told Minus a thing. And after the drinking was over, Minus always felt a little ashamed and wished Low Gear would confess something too.

The boys never made it to Key West.

They stopped just short at the Saddle Bunch Keys. By the time they got there, it was the middle of the morning and two cases of beer were gone. The empty cans rolled across the floor every time Minus pulled the van over for somebody to go to the bathroom. One of the girls thought they sounded like church bells.

They found a spot on one of the beaches. Low Gear had to carry the cooler because Minus said it hurt his leg to put weight on it. The girls sat in shallow water, feeling the sand moving, and every now and then one of them would scream, "I'm falling."

Low Gear and Minus stayed close to the beer for an hour, and then Low Gear got up to swim. It was a clear, calm day, and he swam a long way out and a long way back. He was about a hundred yards offshore when the jellyfish got him.

The tentacles went around his hand and arm, they touched his neck. He'd never been hit by a jellyfish before and he was surprised how much they stung. He was more surprised a minute later when he noticed it was getting harder to breathe.

There were other people on the beach, and some of them had seen it happen. By the time Low Gear got his feet on the bottom, several of them were waiting there to rub sand into his arms and neck.

By that time Low Gear was weak and dizzy and white. He was bent over the arm, fighting a middle-aged woman for his hand. "The only way to get the sting out is to urinate on it," she said. "Really, it is."

Low Gear was pulling for his air now, it sounded to the woman like he was crying. "I know it hurts," she said, "but the thing is to urinate right on the burns . . ."

The beer can on Minus's chest fell over and woke him up. He shaded his eyes and saw a small crowd walking Low Gear up from the water.

He fell twice getting there, and when he looked into Low Gear's eyes, they weren't focusing. "What the hell?" he said.

The woman said, "A jellyfish stung him. The only thing that helps is either vinegar or somebody has to urinate on it . . ." Minus leaned in to help him and Low Gear talked in his ear.

"I'm in allergic shock," he said, "and someplace around here there is a woman who keeps trying to piss on my arm."

One of the teenagers drove the van across Seven-Mile Bridge to Marathon, where the hospital was. Flat out, eighty-five miles an hour, dodging traffic. She never blinked until she got there, and then she passed out.

Low Gear was dying and he knew it. Minus was holding him against his shoulder in the front seat, and slowly, Low Gear made a sentence. "You tell . . . if this doesn't work out . . . you tell Mona . . ."

The van was off the bridge and coming to the emergency room entrance, still going eighty-five miles an hour. Minus leaned closer. "What?" he said. "Tell me who the fuck is Mona . . ."

Low Gear said, "Tell Mona . . ." and went to sleep.

The emergency room doctor and two nurses ran outside to get him. They'd run inside a second before that when they'd seen a Flash Rug Cleaners van coming at them sideways, forty miles an hour.

They gave him oxygen and put adrenaline into his chest, and Low Gear lived. He spent the night in intensive care, and the doctor told him that being drunk had probably slowed down the allergic reaction and saved his life.

In the morning they let him go. He walked across the parking lot to a 7-Eleven store and bought a six-pack of Busch, and was half through it when the van pulled into the parking lot.

The girls were asleep in the back. Minus drove back over the Seven-Mile Bridge, and they stopped for a while and looked at the pelicans. "Tell me something," Minus said. "Tell me, who was Mona?"

Low Gear looked at him and smiled. "You know what the doctor said?"

"No, what?"

Low Gear reached back into the cooler and found a cold beer. "He said this shit saved my life."

5

For ABC newsman Bill Stewart, it ended at a roadblock in Nicaragua. You probably saw it on television. A Nicaraguan national guard soldier forcing him onto his knees, then onto his face, Stewart still holding the white handkerchief and his press credentials in his hand.

The soldier kicks him in the side, steps away, then closer again. He says something and Stewart's hands go up behind his neck.

The rifle jumps, and the body on the street jumps too.

And a voice from inside the press van—where the end of Bill Stewart's life is being filmed—says, "They've killed him."

And then the film clip ends and you are looking at Ron and Beverly or Jim again. And they make the practiced gestures that acknowledge, yes, what you have seen is grim stuff.

And coming right up is Jim O'Brien with the weather—a lot of good guys in our area tonight—or Hank Sperka eating out, behaving like any other fourteen-year-old kid behaves when he suddenly finds himself in front of a TV camera, or Bill Currie all dressed up funny to say he doesn't care who wins Wimbledon.

Which, of course, is only part of the news business. Bill Stewart is dead. There are other stories to cover. But it seems to me that before we put Stewart's story behind us, we might tell something more about it than the way it ended.

It seems that we should say something about why he was in Nicaragua, and why the Rons and Beverlys and Hanks and Jims weren't.

The thing is, Bill Stewart was a newsman. He worked with a television crew, but he could have just as easily written for a newspaper. The people who remember him from his years here at WCAU all tell you that.

John Facenda anchored the Channel 10 news while Stewart worked in Philadelphia. He said he loved him. "I looked on him more or less as a son. He was fair, articulate, gentle. He asked the tough questions. He knew when he was being snowed.

"But more than that, he wanted to have some meaning to what he said. I was only hoping that someday he'd take my place . . ."

For a while, Stewart considered that, too. But somewhere in the years here, things began to change. Not just at Channel 10, but at all the stations. And not just in Philadelphia, all over the country.

What happened was local news became a big-money proposition.

And the people who knew the most about making money—the guys from sales and promotion—became the station managers and they ran the news.

And being from sales and promotion, they didn't know anything about news. And they still don't.

They do know about what sells. That would be even teeth.

So before long, all the anchormen began to look like each other, and if the ratings weren't high enough, come five-thirty one afternoon, a new set of even teeth would be modulating you the local news.

The station managers plugged them in until one fit. They still do. In fairness, of course, that's not all there is to it. You also have to be able to read.

Also in fairness, there are some good local television reporters. Just not very many of them.

Anyway, Bill Stewart didn't look like an anchorman. He was small, he had a high forehead, there was nothing dramatic about his voice. And he had another drawback.

He was a newsman.

One of the cameramen he worked with at Channel 10 said, "He was the last type of guy we had around here who would see a story and just go out and do it. He'd keep going until he'd found what he was looking for, you know, till he had his answers. Now they just go into the office in the morning and take whatever somebody tells them to do.

"He was a considerate man, a decent man. He never flew off the handle like some of them now. At his crew or the people he was interviewing. He didn't think of himself as a star, you know, he just wanted to go out and do the story."

So Stewart went to Minneapolis, stayed there three years, and then went to work for ABC's national news.

It probably ought to be pointed out that a network reporter usually makes about $40,000 a year. A local anchorman in a major market will usually make at least twice that. Stewart took a pay cut to join ABC.

Ron Miller worked with Stewart at WCAU, and is now with ABC national news in Chicago. He was Stewart's friend. "He could have been an anchor in Minneapolis," Miller said. "But he decided he wanted something more than that. He took his work very seriously, but fortunately that wasn't the way he took himself . . .

"I'm sure if this thing hadn't ended the way it did in Nicaragua, after he got over being mad he would have smiled about it. He accepted the bullshit—that's part of this job."

Miller thought for a minute. "There are too few good men, you know that?

"He didn't have to get out of that van, you know. He didn't have to go talk to those guys. Who would have known, who would have given a shit? He didn't have to be in Nicaragua for some asshole war either."

He said, "I don't want this to sound stupid, but he made me proud of being a television reporter."

Yesterday morning, a Channel 10 cameraman and a sound man on the way to a job talked about Bill Stewart.

"We were talkin' about what happened," the cameraman said. "And we wondered why is it the good ones it always happens to. Why are they the ones that get killed?"

The answer is that the good ones will follow a story out where the shooting is.

The ones who pay their dues with voice lessons and capped teeth will read the story of a reporter's death over the eleven-o'clock news and say they have lost a colleague.

6

There was a peahen in the garage one day last week. It stayed four hours and left. A peahen, of course, is a female peacock, and the way you tell a peahen from a peacock is that a peahen is less ornamental and a peacock doesn't lay eggs.

The one in my garage was sort of dull green—at least it would have been dull for a peacock, but being a peahen, I supposed it was about average. It was standing in front of the trash compactor, staring at a small red light that stays on while the compactor is in its "extra-pack" mode.

I saw the peahen as I came into the garage on my tractor, and while no exotic bird had ever wandered into my garage before, I was not in the frame of mind to appreciate it. While I'd been cutting the grass, the tractor had begun making horrible noises. I am close to my tractor; I depend on it emotionally. And until the day this happened, the tractor itself had always been so loud that I'd been unable to hear anything else while I was riding it. Or, now that I think about it, for a couple of hours afterward.

It seemed to me this was big trouble.

And not just the noise. The tractor is an Allis-Chalmers, a company that went into bankruptcy immediately following my purchase of the machine, and whose closest authorized dealer, as far as I know, is in downstate Illinois.

Worse still, I do not live in downstate Illinois. I live on an island in the Puget Sound, and 2,000 miles is a long way to push a tractor to get it fixed. Not that anybody in Illinois could fix it anyway. The engine is a 920 diesel Lombardini, made in Italy, a country famous for—and proud of—its heritage as the manufacturer of the most temperamental engines and transmissions in the world.

I suspected the problem was either in the engine or the transmission, because the noise—an unearthly scream, something that perhaps would sound healthy to your Rolfing therapist—occurred half a dozen times just as I was climbing the steepest hill on the property.

And after the sixth time it happened, I drove my Chapter 11 tractor with the Italian background into the garage, to think for a while about why I couldn't have just bought a John Deere like everybody else, and then maybe to burn myself touching some stuff under the hood.

And there, standing in the dark, was the peahen.

If she was bothered by the noise of the tractor—it had stopped screaming now that it wasn't climbing hills—she kept it to herself. She stared at me a minute; I stared at her. When I killed the engine—with a Lombardini 920 diesel, by the way, you do not just turn a key, you pull a lever that strangles it—she went back to watching the trash compactor.

I walked over to see what she thought she was doing in my garage, and while you couldn't call her friendly—there are no friendly birds— she did sidle over a step or two to make room so I could watch the light on the trash compactor too.

And so we stood there a while, the peahen and me, enjoying the "extra-pack" light, and when I began to imagine us as a married couple watching the sunset, I realized it was time to go back and look at the tractor.

The peahen stayed where she was. I guess she knew what she liked when she saw it.

I lifted the lid off the engine, got the metric wrenches, and began, as they say, at the beginning.

Meaning, I started with Mussolini and worked my way forward to the Sawyer Brothers Allis-Chalmers dealership in Maryland, where I bought this thing. I used terrible language, language so bad that at one point I stopped and went into the house and called my old friend Mickey Rosati in South Philadephia to apologize for what I'd been saying about the Italians.

Mick accepted the apology in the name of Italians everywhere, and hearing my description of the scream, he suggested the problem might be in the tension of the belts. I went back outside to check.

The bird didn't even stir as I walked past. She was completely involved in the compactor light.

I reached underneath the tractor and fingered the belt that connects the engine to the lawn mower. It seemed all right—it gave about as much as a brassiere when you pull the strap in back—but still, it was hard to say for sure. I couldn't really get at it, which, going back thirty years or so, was always a problem with brassieres too.

I have never been good with these things. In the end, some of us are Italians and some of us aren't.

Anyway, I thought it over a long time, and then reached for the wrenches, dropped the lawn-mowing deck off the tractor, and then slid it out from underneath.

It weighs about a hundred pounds, and I distinctly remembered one of the Sawyer brothers telling me how easy this thing was going to be to take off for sharpening. A couple of bolts, a couple of linchpins, and it's done. In fairness, I am not sure he said anything about putting it back together.

Three hours later, sweating, arms shaking, I finally got one of those pins back in place and was able from there to reassemble my lawn mower. I had found nothing wrong with it, but I had dropped the mower deck on the same hand twice, and to even the casual observer it was clear that this hand would never unhook a brassiere again.

I got up off the floor and noticed the peahen still standing in front of the compactor, staring at the red light.

"Show's over," I said as I went past and switched the button to "regular-pack," and a moment later the red light went off.

The bird stared at me as if she couldn't believe what I'd done, and then, as I headed up the stairs to the house to call Mickey again and report it was not the belts, she opened her mouth, and in a moment the walls seemed to shatter, and I understood in that moment that the noise had not come from the tractor.

7

This is the story of a failure of education. Of two thirsty minds that were denied the wellspring of knowledge.

Everybody else in the story gets all the drinks they want.

It actually begins six years ago in a New Orleans bar, where an argument developed over the probabilities of throwing a football across Canal Street. Bad Peter, one of the two thirsty minds, was there but expressed no opinion.

Now, Canal is maybe the widest street in America, probably sixty yards across, and among the faction at the bar that thought a football could be thrown across it was a thin, unimpressive kid with thick glasses who, it turned out, was a second-string quarterback for Tulane University.

It took most of an hour and an unknown number of bottles of Dixie beer—which you don't ever want to taste—for the argument to take on meaningful proportions. It took another half hour to locate a football.

Then, with a pile of small bills waiting thick on the bar, Bad Peter and the rest of the place all went outside and watched the thin kid with the thick glasses let go a throw that surely was destined for eighty yards, except he threw it into a light pole. Which is probably why the kid was second-string.

Anyway, Bad Peter was telling his friend John about that throw the night this failure of education occurred. They had been socializing for some time, and John was not impressed.

"Listen," he said. "Forget Canal Street. I can throw a football across *Pine Street*." John and Bad Peter stared at each other a while, letting that settle in, and everybody in the place knew it wasn't over. "Except we don't have a football," he added.

Bad Peter said, "We got a case of beer."

The bet was this: Bad Peter said John could not throw a case of full sixteen-ounce bottles of Rolling Rock beer sidewalk to sidewalk across Pine Street.

John said he could.

Whoever was wrong had to pay for the beer and any other damages, which have a way of coming up. There were a few side bets among the spectators, but not between Bad Peter and John. They keep their sport pure.

Bad Peter grabbed the beer and together they walked outside. Right away there were complications. Being employed, responsible members of the community and almost veterans, they did not want to take any unnecessary chances of damaging innocent citizenry.

"The trouble with throwing beer," John said, checking the grip his wingtips had on the sidewalk, "is if it opens up you get bottles flying all over the place . . ." Bad Peter looked at John again, beginning to wonder. It sounded like experience talking.

They decided they needed a belt. Bad Peter's wasn't close to long enough. Neither was John's. An overweight kid came out of the gathering spectators and offered his. It went around almost twice.

"Damn, is that a beer belly," said John. There was more praise from the bystanders. The people of Pine Street admire those who do things all the way.

Modestly, the kid allowed as how he was on a diet. John tightened the belt around the case, then picked it up, looking for leverage. Then he looked across Pine Street. "You better go over to the other side," he said, ". . . catch it if it's gonna go through any windows."

Bad Peter walked over and waited. His condition at this point was such that while he still believed nobody could throw a case full of beer bottles—which weighs as much as three shot puts and isn't as handy sized—across Pine Street, there was absolutely no doubt in his mind that he could catch it.

That is when the sergeant showed up, driving his cruiser fast the wrong way down Pine Street, and pointed his spotlight at John.

John put the evidence down and sat on it. He assumed a casual posture, crossing his legs, as if that was where he always sat down. The sergeant was not fooled. He got out of the cruiser, looking disturbed.

"Trouble, Officer?" John said.

"We got a call," he said, taking in the situation. "Where'd you get the beer?"

"I got it at home."

The sergeant asked where John lived, got a South Philadelphia address. "You carried it all the way up here," he said, not sounding convinced.

John said he and Bad Peter were going to a party. He couldn't remember where it was. Neither could Bad Peter. The sergeant sighed. "At one o'clock in the morning," he said, "you're gonna walk three miles with a case of beer at one o'clock in the damn morning to go to a party and you don't know where it is at ONE O'CLOCK IN THE DAMN MORNING."

Somehow sensing disbelief, Bad Peter stepped in and tried something he had never done with a policeman before. "You want to know the truth?" he said.

The cop looked from John to Bad Peter to the spectators. *He* told the truth too. "I don't know," he said.

But Bad Peter and John told the sergeant the whole story anyway, starting back in New Orleans and including the trouble they had taken to find a belt and how Bad Peter was going to catch the beer so it wouldn't break any of the innocent citizenry's windows. They said they were employed and almost veterans.

"I'm going on a diet," the fat kid said, holding on to his pants.

The sergeant felt Bad Peter's muscle. "You," he said, "you were going to catch the beer." Everybody nodded.

The sergeant put his hands over his face, maybe thinking of explaining this to a judge. Finally he made the kind of decision every good cop has to make every day he's on the street. Damn if he was going to do the paperwork.

"In one minute, I don't want to see that beer anymore," he said. "And I don't want to see you two guys anymore. And I don't want you to do this again in my district . . ."

So John and Bad Peter and the spectators all went back into the bar and watched the sergeant drive off. John bought Bad Peter a drink and asked how he'd ever thought to tell the truth. "Brilliant," he said.

But it was too late for congratulations. Bad Peter was already *philosophical*. "It's always the same," he said. "Every time you're about to find something out for sure . . ." Bad Peter and John shook their heads.

For children of the city, sometimes a thirst for knowledge is not enough.

8

They had just closed the door when the kid next to me suddenly stood up, said "excuse me" as he stumbled over my feet and out into the aisle, and then ran toward the front of the airplane.

I sat very still. I am not irrational about flying, but I'm not crazy either, and I know an omen of doom when I see one.

He was a blond kid, small for his age, and I watched him as the flight attendant kneeled in front of him, listening and nodding, and then brought him back to his seat. By the time he was climbing back over my feet, she was telling him he could have extra cookies once we got in the air, and he had begun to cry.

He was trying to hold it back, but it spilled out all over him, his lips trembled and his breath caught in his throat, and there was nothing he could do about it. "Hey," I said, "they wouldn't let you drive or what?"

He shook his head and looked out the window, embarrassed, and a moment later the truck that pulls the planes away from the gate had us and we were backing out toward the runway. The movement set him off, and his shoulders shook and he stared out his window as if he were looking for something, and cried without a sound.

"Is this the first time you've flown alone?" I said.

He shook his head and wiped his face with his hands. "I wanted to say good-bye to my mother," he said. And then he put his face in the window again, looking for her. "I didn't get to say good-bye."

He didn't mention his father; maybe he wasn't around anymore.

"Does she live in Seattle?" I said. "We can call her from the phone on the plane."

He shook his head again and said he lived in Friday Harbor, which is a town in the San Juan Islands, and we would be in Sacramento a long time before his mother was home.

"What are you going to do in Sacramento?"

"Visit my grandparents," he said.

"For how long?"

"A month," he said. I remembered being this kid's age, and what a month looked like then.

I also remembered the first ride I ever had on an airplane, flying from Atlanta to Detroit to stay for a year with my Aunt Helen and Uncle Bill because my mother had to go to a tuberculosis sanatorium in Alabama. I remembered that feeling; it was the same feeling as being lost.

"What's your grandfather do?" I said.

"He's retired," the kid said. "They were supposed to drive up and get me, but I got sick. That's what I'm doing on this airplane."

"Myself," I said, "I usually get on the plane and *then* get sick." A glimpse of a smile crossed his face, and passed. The plane taxied up the runway, turned, and then the engine pitch changed until the plane shook, and a moment later the pilot released the brakes and we were on the way to Sacramento.

Assuming, of course, the kid was not the omen of doom. Otherwise, we figured to crash in downtown West Sacramento, destroying the entire business district with damage possibly in the hundreds of dollars.

That is every flier's worst fear, of course, going down in West Sacramento. If it's going to happen, it ought to be someplace scenic.

The plane's nose lifted, and a moment later I felt that curious thump from behind—what is that noise, by the way, if it isn't the tail bumping against the ground?—and we were in the air.

"So," I said, "you want a couple of beers or what?"

"I don't drink," he said.

"How old are you?"

"Ten," he said.

"You smoke?"

He shook his head no.

"Women?"

He shrugged.

"How about the stewardess? I think she likes you."

The kid looked at the stewardess, then shook his head. "She's too tall," he said.

I said, "Listen, the short ones are bossy. Take my word for it . . ."

The plane went out over Puget Sound, then banked left and headed south. The kid stared out the window until the city was out of sight. Then he took a newspaper, giving him a little privacy, but the next time I looked he was blinking tears.

"The thing I always remember when I go away," I said, "is how happy I'm going to be when I come home. You can picture it . . ."

"I just wanted to tell her good-bye."

"She must have been at the gate," I said.

"But I forgot to tell her," he said.

And I knew what was pulling at him; the same thing pulls at me too.

The worry that things have been left unclear, that someday you will leave home and not be able to find the way back.

Later, the stewardess brought him three packs of Oreo cookies, and he put them in his pockets, holding them until his grandfather picked him up at the airport and he could go back to being ten years old.

9

The following was one of a series of columns entitled "Dr. Dexter's Sex Clinic," which ran for several years in the Philadelphia Daily News, *until the author had imparted to his readers all he knew or could invent on the subject.*

I am a 19-year-old virgin, going into the Army in July. I am going to live in a barracks with a bunch of other guys and I know they all have experience in this area. I don't want to look like a kid when they talk about it, but the chances of me getting any firsthand information seems slim at this late date.

The guy I work for tells me that it's just like learning to ride a horse. Do you know what he means by that? Can you give me any information that will help me get through basic training?

Thank you,

Bob from Newtown Square

Dear Bob from Newtown,

Your boss is giving you good information, and I couldn't agree with him more. It is exactly like learning to ride a horse.

The first rule, in fact, is that you always get on from the left side.

Before you do that, though, make sure she is friendly. Rub her nose, feed her a carrot. Coo in her ear as she eats it. Say, "Nice girl, nice girl," until you have her confidence.

It is important at this point to watch the ears. They should be perked, even twitching. If for some reason she suddenly lays them back against her head, get out of there fast. Later you can come back with another carrot and try again.

When you are sitting around the barracks this summer and the other fellows say, "Hey, Bob, tell us a good sex story," you can always be sure that a tale about laid-back ears will ring true. The story should end up with you keeping most of your carrots and going for a ride anyway.

There is some argument—even in the scientific community—about the optimum length of the ride. There is one school that says, "The longer the better," and another school that says, "The less time you spend in the saddle, the less chance you have of falling off."

(Needless to say, if you do fall off it is vital to get right back on and try again.)

In my research I have found that most people are happiest with the middle distances. That usually means a mile and a quarter, which—without getting into track conditions—should go in 2:05 or so. If your time is more than eight seconds off either way, something is wrong.

The last thing I can tell you—and possibly the most important—is to be sure you know where the finish line is. We all remember Willie Shoemaker standing up in the saddle a sixteenth of a mile too soon on Gallant Man and blowing the 1957 Kentucky Derby.

That is the one thing that people may someday forgive but nobody ever forgets.

Dear Dr. Dexter,

Is there any way to test yourself for venereal disease?

I get a burning sensation whenever I urinate, but I am afraid to go to my parents and I am afraid to go to the family doctor, for fear he will tell them. If they ever found out, they would kill me. My name is Norman Lieberman, but please just sign me Dutch Cleanser.

Signed,
Dutch Cleanser

Dear Dutch,

Glad I can help. The first thing you should do is check to see if you are smoking at the same time you are urinating. Ask yourself, "Where is my cigarette right now?"

If that isn't it, another good test is to wait 20–30 years and see if you go criminally insane.

Finally, I would recommend F. Dougherty's personal account, *One Hand Clapping—The Ordeal of a Man Who Gave It to Himself*. The book is available through Phantom Paperbacks, or at your local 7-Eleven.

Dear Dr. Dexter,

I'm an eighth-grader in a mess. My grades are terrible, my father caught me smoking pot, my mother found my birth-control pills. My mother said if I screw up anything else she would tell my father about the pills. My father said if I screw up anything else he'd tell my mother about the pot. Once they start talking to each other, I'm grounded. So if you could help me it would really mean a lot.

The term paper is due next Friday, so if you could hurry that would really mean a lot too. What I need to know is, how do trees do it? This is for biology class, so if you answer in the paper, please keep it clean.

Signed,

Judy M.

Society Hill

Dear Judy,

I will help you with this, but I certainly hope you pay more attention in class from now on. After all, some day you may be a doctor yourself.

It is a fundamental principle of science that all living things— creatures and plants—reproduce in the same basic way. And that way is called the "missionary position."

The exact nature of the union depends on what kind of trees you mean. Oaks get together one way, elms another. I do not think it would be appropriate to get into a more graphic description here. Without violating the rules of good taste, however, I feel I can tell you this mating accounts for thousands of squirrels being crushed in their homes every year.

Unlike humans, trees mate for life and continue to reproduce into old age and even beyond. That's right, even chairs and tables. Dr. Joyce Druthers has written a paper saying this occurs because trees have no stereotyped notions about their sexual processes.

She is supported in this by a group of women called the Bend Don't Break Coalition. Sexually, these women imitate dead trees.

The reports are that some of them are better at it than the trees.

10

The cat was gone half the day. I saw her across the street in the woods once, but by the time I got there she'd run away. I thought she was bleeding.

I went in and got Mrs. Dexter. The cat likes her better than me, and she feels the same way about the cat. Of course, they've had the same operation. I said, "I think there's something wrong with the cat."

Mother is the cat's name. My wife went into the woods and a few minutes later the cat came out, walked across the street on three legs, and hid under the car. Bleeding from the shoulder.

Fifteen minutes later Mrs. Dexter came out of the woods too and crawled under the car after her. They talked it over under there a while, and then they came out together.

"It looks like something bit her," she said.

I didn't say anything then, but it wasn't a bite. It looked like somebody had shot her. When I tried to get close enough to look, though, the cat tried to run again. I gave her some room, wondering why somebody would do something like that.

The cat came with the house. The day after we moved in she came by, dirty and thin and hungry, nursing four kittens, and she moved in too. That was five years ago. I liked the way she took care of herself without getting in the way, and I liked how she was around my daughter, and how she was around me.

She never pushed herself on you. If you wanted to play, she'd play, and if you wanted her to get off the couch, that was all right with her too. She never made any noise, she never asked for anything.

In five years, the only temper she ever showed was when she caught something in the woods and brought it home for Mrs. Dexter. All I know about the victim was that it was brown and little and had a tail.

Mrs. Dexter got whatever it was out of the cat's mouth and let it go, and then carried her inside so she couldn't get it again. Mrs. Dexter is an ingrate, of course.

Anyway, the cat stood by the door and nobody let her out. She stood there about five minutes—I guess figuring how much head start the brown thing with the tail was getting—and then she did a curious thing. She crawled up on the back of the sofa and urinated all over the Sunday *Inquirer.*

Mrs. Dexter, of course, put the cat outside, which I believe is what the cat had in mind. Needless to say, I felt closer to the cat after that.

And so perhaps you can understand that I wasn't happy to see her come out of the woods bleeding and shot. The woods there are narrow, and there is nothing on the other side but marsh. The road is a dead end, and strangers don't come by. So it was somebody who lives on our side of the lake, I thought. Probably a kid. And I had another thought. My daughter plays in front of the house, ten yards from the woods.

Mrs. Dexter took the cat to the veterinarian and I went to work, where the story was developing that somebody had put cyanide in Tylenol and killed seven people. And that sounded like a kid too. A kid, or somebody who never loved anybody but himself.

And I had a picture then, of the kid. A smart kid, sitting alone in a dark room, and realizing suddenly that he'd made a mistake. That he'd left something that could give him away.

I thought of John Hinckley. I thought of a man I knew in Minneapolis who worked in his father's store and wanted to be a poet. He kept glass bottles under the seat of his car, and would throw them at night in front of animals he saw beside the highway, spraying them with the pieces at seventy miles an hour.

I was still thinking about him when I finally got my wife on the phone. She'd been at the veterinarian's place four hours. The pellet had broken the cat's leg and damaged some nerves. They'd put her in a cast and said she might lose the leg.

In that moment I could have broken legs myself.

And then I remembered the man in Minneapolis, and the last time I'd seen him. He was sitting in a bar on Hennepin Avenue, telling a fat Indian woman that he'd been cheated out of his life. He was crying, she was holding his head in the folds of her shoulder and stealing his money off the bar.

And the justice in this world is that you don't have to break legs because somebody's broken yours.

The justice is, what you are is what you become; all you have to do is wait.

Her husband built the new house in the fall of 1968, up the hill from the old place, away from the feed yard and the road. He built it for her.

He had grown up in the old house outside Carroll, Iowa, and farmed the half section it sat on with his father. They'd farmed it through the thirties—the years when the earth turned to dust and nothing would grow—they'd stayed when their neighbors had sold out and moved to Sioux City or Chicago or Omaha. The year it began to rain again, his father had died.

He'd married her before the war and brought up his own sons in the house, and no strings of good crops would ever let him forget the years when nothing would grow. He carried his money in a change purse and saddle-soaped his work boots at night before supper.

"I never saw him waste nothin' but prayers," she said. "If there was an extra piece of two-by-six from fixin' the porch, he'd make me a flowerbed out the bathroom window. That's why I couldn't believe my ears the night he set down at the table and told me about this . . ."

She was sitting in the front window, a sleeping child's shoes hung off the outlines of her leg under the dress, and you could hear his breathing against her neck. The shoes were as long as her own, he seemed too big to be in her lap. The sun was dropping behind an elm tree near the road. She turned, turning the child with her, and looked at the place he had built.

A ranch-style brick house. Four bedrooms, two baths, carpets. A kitchen with a built-in dishwasher. "I told him, 'Mac, we *got* a good house.' But it was somethin' different about this. Some of the neighbors was buildin' new houses that year, and it was like he'd decided we was gonna have one, too. It was like he was payin' a debt. Mac couldn't never stand to owe.

"'It's time we moved up the hill,' he said. I didn't mind where we was—I liked the animals, and I liked the trucks come by at night. Some of the neighbor wives said it kept them up, but it soothed me. I could feel the vibrations, don't you know, just like the boy here can feel when I talk."

She looked at him a minute, smoothing his hair back. "He's stone deaf," she said.

The child stirred and she pulled him back into her neck and began to rock. "I could see he had his mind made up," she said, "and I knew we had the money. I never knew how much till after he died, but this is some of the best soil on earth right here, and it was good to us a long time.

"So he built the house and the boys come over from town one Saturday and we moved everything up the hill. Took most of it by hand, all except for the kitchen. Mac wanted everything in the kitchen brand new.

"The boys was good workers, but neither of them ever wanted the farm. They had enough of it when they was younger, I guess. This one here," she nodded at her arms, "he belongs to the oldest. Him and his wife both work in town, and I watch the baby."

The sun was gone now, the sky to the west was the color of peaches. A hundred yards below, the old house looked emptier than it had. "It wasn't long after we moved up here, his health failed," she said. "It was the same thing as his daddy had before him, and for a while, we'd sit here or on the porch most of the day, and sometimes he'd say what a shame it was one of the boys hadn't wanted the farm.

"He died August 1970, at the age of fifty-seven, and I almost moved back down the hill. I think I would've, but the house was his present . . ." She smiled. "The neighbor ladies would still be talkin' about what was wrong in my wig if I'd done that." She shifted the child's weight. "The thing is, we wasn't together here long enough for it to feel like home. The things I remember are all down there."

She looked out the window a long time, fixed on the old house. She looked until she found something she wanted, then she closed her eyes around it and held it and began to rock.

And the only thing to mark the passing of time was the sound of a deaf child breathing against her neck.

12

Whenever I think about baseball—as I tend to do in the spring—
I think about Tim McCarver. That does not necessarily mean,
of course, that whenever I think about McCarver I think about baseball.
There was a night several years ago, for instance—I think it was night, I
don't remember seeing the sun—when a McCarver thought put itself
together in my head, concerning some pigeons that needed to be shot off
the giant clothespin statue that sits across from City Hall in the city of
Philadelphia.

That's right, we've got a statue of a clothespin. And we've got pigeons. Back then we had McCarver too—this was before he went to
New York to broadcast the Mets games—and I called him up. He wasn't
the only person I knew in the city with a shotgun, but at that time of the
night, everybody else would be using theirs.

"Tim," I said, "what do you say to driving over to City Hall and
shooting some birds off the clothespin tonight?"

Tim didn't think we ought to, but he thanked me for thinking of him.

I walked back to the seat at the bar and spoke to a woman in the
next seat who claimed to believe hunting pigeons was morally repugnant.

I said, "Lady, you never saw a pigeon in your life that didn't look like
it was losing a contact lens."

"That is *exactly* the point," she said.

"The point," I said—please, Jesus, don't let them always tell me what the point is—"is maturity. And graciousness." And hours later, lying next to my sleeping wife—moonlight fell across her hair on the pillow and just a hint of a whistle rose from her lips—I was still struck dumb by the same thing. "I just can't get over how mature he is," I said.

She opened one eye, but I could see it wasn't a bedroom eye, even before she spoke. "You're shit-brained drunk, aren't you?" she said.

Allow me to speak to that now, in public, where there are no pillows to hide under to avoid the answer.

It is a fact of life, I think, that some of us are born with talent and some of us are born with shit for brains. Maturity comes into it later, when you try to figure out which way you are.

From my own experience, I can tell you that there are mornings when you sit down at the typewriter and knock out three pages in forty-five minutes, and you look at yourself in the toaster over breakfast and your head's all misshapen and pointy, and you say, "Son, you were born with talent."

And there are other days, often the following day, after you have read those three pages, when you say, "Son, you were born with shit for brains." And if you happen to say that out loud, by the way, there will be a woman in the room who believes hunting pigeons is morally repugnant, and she will say, "That is *exactly* the point."

But don't listen to her. The point is that it takes a maturity and a graciousness to appreciate what you were given, even on days when it isn't working, to appreciate your failures as well as your success. Baseball is a good place for that. The game—and more to the point, the season—plays itself out in a rhythm that resembles life more than the other sports do. You lose yourself, you find yourself. And Tim McCarver understands that better than anyone I know.

I guess I ought to say right here that McCarver is a friend of mine. Not a close friend—obviously we're not hunting buddies—but somebody I have liked and admired from the day I met him, and even before.

I think he is the best color man on television right now—baseball, football, politics, or anything else. Of course, I also think, sincerely think, he was a great baseball player, better than his numbers show, so what do I know about anything?

Going back to the day I met him, though, he was sitting in a dressing room full of sullen Phillies, staring at his toes. I was looking for something to put in the newspaper the next day, and I'll take sore toes over sore losers any time I can get them.

I said, "You hurt your toes today?"

He said, "I didn't play today." By then he was backup catcher, pinch-hitting once in a while, and only taking a turn behind the plate when Steve Carlton pitched.

I said, "Well, if you did play, you think you would've done any good?"

He rolled it around a while. "One for four," he said, "a meaningless single."

Tim McCarver came to the major leagues in 1959, right out of Christian Brothers High School in Memphis, Tennessee. He was seventeen years old, an all-state football player and one of the most promising and promised high school baseball players in the country. His father was a Memphis policeman, and every school he'd ever gone to was segregated.

"That first year," he said, "down in spring training in Florida, we got on the bus after a game and I was sitting across the aisle from Bob Gibson. He was already a great pitcher, later he would become a great friend. I was a seventeen-year-old kid with a bottle of Nehi orange pop who'd hardly even spoken to anybody black.

"Gibson saw it right away, where I was from. He said, 'Hey, kid, let me have a swallow that . . .' I looked at his mouth and then at the lip of the bottle. I said, 'I'll save you some.' "

McCarver played for St. Louis the last month of that season, and spent the next four years in and out of the minors. He became the Cardinals' regular catcher in 1963, and the following year, twenty-two years old, he found himself hitting .478 in the World Series against the

Yankees, driving in the winning run in game five with a three-run homer in the tenth inning.

There were two more World Series in the next four years.

"For a little while there," he said, "the horizon looked vaguely ownable. Ever since I was old enough to notice, I knew I was different. I never said it, but if you're always hitting a hundred points higher than anybody else on the team, you know. When you're faster than the kids your age, and you can throw better and hit the ball farther, you've got to know it."

The thing you don't know is how far it goes, if there is some level—maybe the major leagues, maybe before—where you won't be special anymore. That can be a fearful thing to a professional athlete who has been special since he was twelve or fourteen years old and understands, as he gets older, how fragile it is.

But that never happened to McCarver; he never let it. Even at the end, when some of the talent was slipping away, he played with integrity, every day they'd let him, as well as he could. He wasn't showy about it—he didn't sprint to first base on walks like Pete Rose, for instance—but he made all the everyday plays, he never cost anybody a ball game being lazy. And given the length of a season, that's as rare in baseball as it is anywhere.

And there was something else, too. McCarver was happy on the field. He was—and is—competitive in a way that ordinary people aren't, but he wasn't afraid of losing, and that freed him to enjoy the playing.

And when he quit baseball—the only modern-era catcher to play in four decades—and went into the announcing booth, he wasn't afraid of that, either.

There has been a lot said, of course, about jocks in the announcing booth. Much of it has been said by announcers who were never players themselves. Often they remind you how silly they would look putting on a uniform and trying to hit Steve Carlton's slider. They say it is the same thing for Carlton to try to step into the booth with them and call a game.

I turned on a radio last year and heard one of them explain it like this: "Just because somebody went to college once doesn't make him a brain surgeon."

I am going to hurt some feelings now, but this needs to be said. Announcing a baseball game on television—play-by-play or color—isn't anywhere near as hard as hitting Steve Carlton's slider. It probably isn't even as hard as brain surgery.

You are, after all, telling people who are watching the same thing you are watching what they are watching. Baseball, for all its intricacy, is a repetitive series of situations, and by the time most children are old enough, say, to break into a bank's computer—oh, nine years old—they are also old enough to tell you 90 percent of what an announcer is going to say on television.

What that leaves an announcer with, then, to separate himself from a nine-year-old, is his personality, a sense of perspective, and the other 10 percent of the time.

Often this is not enough.

McCarver, however, manages to remind you that he is an adult without offending you. I know this from experience.

He explains things you might not have known—"The reason he's not on third base," he said once, after Mike Schmidt hit a ball off the top of the wall, "is that he thought it was going out, and he stopped running to admire it"—without reminding you of all the other things he knows and you don't, the most crucial of them being that there are things about professional baseball you will never understand because you never played it.

And he is forgiving at the microphone, consistently more forgiving than the announcers who never played.

"I never forgot how difficult baseball was to play," he said. "I don't talk down on a player, although I'll criticize what he does. I'll tell the truth, but I keep it in the context of the game. And I'm down in the clubhouse every day, so if anybody's got a bitch, we can clear the air. I'll always listen. Shit, maybe I was wrong."

Shit, maybe I was wrong.

I look at those five words and have to smile, remembering the night I got pigeon urges in Philadelphia, and the way my wife looked at me when I tried to explain maturity and graciousness. Of course, she never says, "Thanks for thinking of me, but I don't think we ought to." She says, "You're shit-brained drunk, aren't you?"

She certainly never says, "Maybe I was wrong."

But Tim does. And that's why I am forgiving him for not coming with me that night.

And not her.

13

About four-thirty Monday afternoon, someone in the permanent-resident section of the downtown YMCA dropped a bottle of Thunderbird wine out his window, and in so doing broke an old unwritten law of that Christian establishment.

Yes, somebody actually threw away a bottle that still had wine inside it.

The Thunderbird was delivered to the sidewalk on the east side of Fifteenth Street, inside a brown paper sack. The noise it made when it hit said it had fallen fifteen or twenty floors, and it had nothing to do with the sound of broken glass.

It was more like what a caterpillar might hear as the bottom of a tennis shoe turns the lights out on him for good. Sort of a muted explosion.

The person closest to the explosion was an old woman wearing a straw hat with artificial flowers and moving—a few inches at a time—up Fifteenth Street on metal crutches. She was thirty or thirty-five feet away, another ten minutes and she could have been killed.

She stopped for a moment and looked up. She scowled into the glare of the sky and said something about bums and hoodlums and perverts. She seemed to know the neighborhood.

Then she took off her straw hat with the artificial flowers, tucked it into her armpit to protect it, and started up the street again.

Myself, I was preoccupied at the time. Earlier that same day I'd gotten out of bed, walked into the bathroom, and torn the nail half off my favorite toe. Then I'd been to the dentist. Then I'd gone for a walk and bought a hot dog and a can of Pepsi. The ring broke off the zip-top can, so I pushed the aluminum tab in with my finger.

I cut the finger once going in, once coming out. The blood got all over my hot dog. I threw the weenie part away and squeezed the finger in the bun, trying to stop the bleeding. The bun got wet, the mustard turned orange.

While this was going on, I was limping down Fifteenth Street toward three men who may have been bums but didn't seem ambitious enough for hoodlums. They were standing and sitting near the corner of Fifteenth and Arch, moving a half-inch cigarette butt around a three-way circle, following it with a quart of beer.

Just before the Thunderbird hit, the oldest of them looked over at what had started out as my hot dog and said, "That's the ugliest sand-wich I ever saw."

And then the Thunderbird exploded on the sidewalk.

One of them covered his head and ducked. He was wearing a shirt without buttons, pants without a zipper. No shoelaces. Clearly a man with no use for accessories. He protected the quart from danger with his body.

The other two men looked up at the sky. The oldest one said, "They's only one of them, whatever it is."

The third one had a scar where somebody had once cut his throat. "Don't make no difference," he said. "I'm covered. I got in-surance."

Presently, the oldest one crossed the street and looked down at the bottle and the wet brown bag. Then he leaned back and looked up the side of the YMCA, wondering who would do such a thing.

When he got back he said, "A whole bottle out the window."

The man with the scar said, "All I know is I got in-surance."

The old man gave him a look. "What the fuck you talkin' about?" he said.

"Just what I'm talkin' about is what the fuck I'm talkin' about," said the man with the scar. "I'm talkin' about in-surance. I'm covered."

The old man said, "You covered in shit."

"He throwed that whole bottle out the window?" said the man who had no use for accessories. There was no answer, and he crossed the street to see for himself, ducking his head into his shoulders all the way there. The other two continued their discussion of insurance.

They were still at it when the man who had no use for accessories sat down between them and began smoothing back his hair.

"Goddamn," he sighed, "I hate waste."

14

Old Pete had worked construction since he was eleven. He'd never laid brick or run the heavy machinery, he'd never been the foreman. He was fifty-six years old and he looked seventy, and he'd never wanted to be anything but common labor. He'd been good at it, and it had used him up.

He came to the job on time, he left on time. He didn't say much while there was work to do, and he sat alone at lunch, eating a sandwich made out of Wonder Bread and bologna. He always shaved before he came to work, and he'd had the same lunch pail as long as anybody could remember. Everybody liked to work with Pete because he pulled his share.

The foreman was twenty-seven years old. He'd been shot up and left for dead in Vietnam, and he'd killed men there too. Some of his crew were kids, some of them were men in their thirties and forties, and there were days—mostly when his legs hurt—when he felt older than anybody who worked for him.

He thought he knew everybody he had—he could tell you who would steal and who wouldn't, who would work if there wasn't somebody there to watch him—but he's been around men and fighting all of his adult life, and he also knew he could be wrong.

The kid carried a straight razor in his back pocket. He's been on the job two weeks and the foreman hadn't liked him when he'd come on, and nothing the kid had done in the time since had changed that.

He was a narrow-faced kid who never sounded right when he laughed. He dropped a word about the razor into everything he said, and sometimes, in a move so practiced you almost couldn't see it, his hand would go into the pocket and bring out the razor, and when that motion had ended, the blade would be open and waiting, a few inches from somebody's face.

And the kid would be laughing in that way that never sounded right.

The foreman had watched it and let it go. The only time he spoke to him was when the kid was talking instead of doing his job. The razor had given him a standing with the other kids on the crew, and when he talked, they stopped work to listen.

When that happened, the kid would say, "Yessir, Mister Boss Man. I gets right back to work in the field now."

The foreman watched it and let it go. Some of the men thought he was afraid of the kid's razor.

It didn't matter to him at all.

From the first day, the kid had been after Old Pete. He had tried to talk to him that day, and as soon as he mentioned the razor, the old man had just walked away.

After that the kid had talked in front of him to the kids on the crew. "You get to be old like Pete," he'd say, "you gone get hard of hearing too. Maybe somebody gone cut off your ears. Maybe they cut off your prick—hey, Pete, that how come you so mad? They cut off your prick? Hell, I be mad my own self."

Pete never acknowledged the kid was there. The foreman stayed out of it. He understood that he couldn't protect him without hurting him.

On the day it happened, the old man was sitting on cement blocks, eating his sandwich. The kid was talking and showing off the razor. Some of the others had gotten bored with the razor and had gone back to talking about women.

The kid said, "I think I gone cut Old Pete." He moved his hand into his back pocket and half a second later the razor stopped against the old man's cheek. He had just bitten into the sandwich. He stared at the kid until he took the razor away. Then a thread of blood took its place. It collected almost into a kiss, and then washed down to the old man's jaw line, where it collected again, and then dripped into the Wonder Bread.

The kid tried to laugh and apologize at the same time. The old man stared. He stared until the kid turned around to get help. Everybody was dead quiet, and while the kid was laughing in a way that would never be right, Old Pete stood up behind him and crushed the back of his skull with an iron pipe.

The foreman didn't bother trying to restore the breathing. He knew the damage almost without looking. The pulse stopped before the police arrived. Old Pete sat on the cement blocks and looked at the body while the foreman told them how it happened.

He said the twenty-pound piece of steel came loose from a cable and hit the kid in the back of the head. The police asked if anybody had seen it happen.

"We all did," one of the kids said. "It happened while we were eating lunch."

15

The old woman was sitting at the bend in the bar near the pinball machines at Doc Watson's on Vine Street, working on her third martini, straight up. No olive. She had a glass of water beside the martini for when she choked, and a day-old *Daily News* on the bar beside that.

Her name was Marjorie and she hit me in the head with the *Daily News*.

"Why didn't you tell me you work for the newspaper?" she said. "Don't they pay you enough to buy a comb?"

Marjorie had been looking at my hair a long time. I said some days I couldn't do a thing with it.

"Oh, I know, I know. I got up this morning and found gray hairs . . . I thought I'd die." She patted at her head, which she's covered with a dark-blue turban. "I pulled them out, of course, but imagine the shock. I thought I'd die." I looked at Marjorie and imagined the shock.

"You don't believe that, do you, Petey-Peet-Peet?" She gave me a nudge that spilled my drink. I said of course I believed it. "You're too gracious," she said.

And I had no idea at all how to take that.

Marjorie was in town on failed business.

The girls back at the retirement home had sent her out to do some shopping for them at the Rite Aid Discount drugstore. "I was supposed to get something for sore toes," she said. "And I was supposed to get two bags of Rite Aid butterscotch candy . . ."

She looked up at the clock, which said five minutes to six. "I'm quite sure it's too late now. I'll just have to tell them I was held up. I don't think anybody will die, do you?"

She drank about half of her martini while I thought that over. She was wearing white pearls and a blue-and-white print dress and brown loafers. She had a plastic purse that she kept on her lap, the straps looped over her arm at the elbow, where they seemed to be cutting off the circulation. When she used her handkerchief, she put it back in her purse, not down the front of her dress. She was seventy-five years old and there weren't any wrinkles in her hands.

"No," I said, "I don't think anybody is going to die . . ."

It was Friday afternoon and Doc Watson's was fairly crowded. Nurses and people watching nurses.

From time to time somebody would get it in his head to come over to Marjorie and smile or introduce themselves and ask her how she was enjoying the bar, sort of the way you might ask an immigrant how he likes America.

Marjorie would say, "Who cares who you are?"

Or she would turn to me and say, "What sort of creature is this?"

Or, if they tried to make her laugh, "I don't think you're a great jokester, you know."

And pretty soon people didn't stop by to smile or make small talk anymore, except for one heavy bald man who kept coming back to play pinball. Every time she saw him, Marjorie thought of something new to say.

"Here comes that big, fat slob again, Petey-Peet-Peet." She nudged my arm and I spilled my drink.

"I don't know," I said. "His hairdo is about right . . ." Which got Marjorie's attention back on my hair again. It seemed to hurt her to look at it.

"Couldn't you do *something* with all . . . that?" she said. Then she sighed and I bought her a martini. "Well," she said, "it's *your* head, but I'd use a hairnet if mine looked like that."

Marjorie said her father had been a newspaper reporter with a quick temper, and because of an inherited interest in the business she read all the local papers every day—although usually a day late because that way she got them free—and had strong opinions about what she liked.

"That girl with the column in the *Inquirer*," she said. "That [Dorothy] Storch girl confuses me. I saw her on the *Joel Spivak Show*, and her hair comes over her eye . . ." She pulled her smooth hand across one eye to show it. "And she picks at it, pick, pick, pick all the time. I think it's terrible.

"The one I like is Kiki [Olson, of the *Journal*]. I think she's so interesting, what she writes. Her hair is so nice and curly . . ."

The heavy bald man walked by again, smiling at her on the way to the pinball machine. "How would you like to have something like that around the house and have to look at it all the time?" she said.

I am sorry to have to report this, but about two-thirds of the way through the fourth martini Marjorie dropped the sweetness act.

"Let me tell you something, Petey-Peet-Peet," she said, hitting me on the arm, "getting old stinks. Everybody thinks it's so cute, little old hundred-year-old ladies, so sweety-sweet.

"You know what I think when I see a cute little hundred-year-old lady?" She leaned in again to make sure nobody else would hear. "What I think is I'd like to take a gun . . ." She made a pistol out of her hand, cocked it, pulled the trigger. "Pshhew," she said.

Then she got up and headed slowly to the back of the place, where the bathrooms are, glaring at unkempt hair. "It's that one," somebody said, pointing to the door marked Women, or Ladies, or Cowgirls, or whatever it's marked.

"I can read," she said, and reached for the door.

The door was locked. And the old woman took the side of her fist and beat on it. You could hear the pounding all the way to the front of the bar, even over the pinball machine.

Some people looked away, some people watched her, smiling. The way I saw it, a seventy-five-year-old woman's got as much right—and probably more reason—to be a mean drunk as anybody else.

I just hope the girls back at the home had enough sense not to press her about what happened to the butterscotch.

16

Mummers Day on Two Street:

The body is laid out on the corner. The pink dress is pulled up around the neck, which is painted green. The eyes are partly open; but when you look into them all you see is white.

Four or five young girls make half a circle around the body. "That's Mark's brother," one of them says. "I think he's dead."

"He's not either," another one says. She takes the gum out of her mouth and holds it over the body's head, threatening. When the body doesn't move she drops it. The gum lands on the forehead, rolls down over the eyes, past the nose, and stops in the mustache. The mustache is green too.

The girl studies the face a long time. "Somebody better go get Mark," she says.

The boy's right hand is full of dress ruffles, the left is still wrapped around the neck of an empty bottle of vodka. A couple of cops drive by in an unmarked car. They tell the girls the body is just sleeping it off. The girls wait until they pass and then call them jerkoffs. They step over the body and walk up Two Street.

As they leave, the last one bends over to get her gum back. Just as she touches it, the body moves. Almost nobody turns to see why she screams.

Everywhere you look people are drunk. A teenage girl stumbles down the middle of the street, giving away vacuum-cleaner kisses to anyone who grabs her. Her face is smudged at least four different colors. She has kissed somebody red, somebody green, somebody blue, and somebody black.

She is carrying a bottle of beer and a Kleenex. After each kiss she wipes her mouth with the Kleenex and swallows more beer.

One of the boys who kisses her is fat. He is wearing a blue dress and has painted his face white. He mumbles, "My California baby," and pulls her against him. The kiss lasts about a minute and a half, and the last thirty seconds or so is accomplished lying on the street where they fall.

An eighty-year-old woman watches it all from the curb. "I believe he's going to have his way with that girl," she says.

But just when it looks like she's right, the girl uncouples from the fat kid and slowly gets up. She pulls at her tongue with her Kleenex, washes her mouth with beer, and heads up the street.

The fat kid pushes himself up to his hands and knees and watches her walk away. Then, falling once, he gets to his feet and sees another girl. She is walking with her mother. The fat kid tries to grab her. "My California baby," he says.

But the girl ducks under his arms and the kid comes face-to-face with the mother, who's wearing an expression that resembles a grizzly bear. She-rips, they call them back home. The mother slaps at the kid's hands. "Don't you ever," she says. "You touch her and I'll kill you . . ."

The kid sways, blinks his eyes a couple of times to help him see. Then he smiles, a little drool darkens the paint below one corner of his mouth. "My California baby," he says and plants one on the mother's mouth.

The bars, of course, are packed. People drinking and people coming in from drinking to use the bathrooms. In one of the bars, the bathroom door isn't working. You can get in but you can't get out.

The owner of the bar has white hair and a gold neck chain and is dancing slow and romantic with a woman who seems to be asleep when the banging starts. He lets go of the woman, who lies down on the bar, and begins threatening a fifteen- or sixteen-year-old kid who is standing near the door.

"There's somebody in there, jerkoff," he says. He puts his finger under the kid's chin and begins to push him with it. "You don't go poundin' in the doors when somebody's in there doing their own business . . ."

The kid has a bigger friend. The friend steps in front of the owner to explain. "The door is broke," he says. "You shut it and it'll lock you out . . ."

The owner says, "I'll show you who's gonna get knocked out." And he throws a long punch that misses because the kid has half an hour to get out of the way.

Then the kid tackles the owner, they rock the cigarette machine, knock over a table, a customer. As they wrestle on the floor, a girl turns to a man she has never seen before. She says, "My New Year's resolution is to have the best body in Philadelphia by June 15th."

Back out on the street, boys as young as ten and eleven are drinking beer and smoking dope and throwing firecrackers under each other's feet. Some of them are in doorways, kissing ten- and eleven-year-old girls.

One of these boys is Mark, who has heard that his brother's body is lying on the sidewalk, probably dead. The children standing around the body move to let him through. Mark is carrying a can of Schaefer beer and smoking a cigarette.

He stands over the body a long time, looking down.

"He ain't my brother," he says.

17

S unday is Father's Day, and I'm going to be in Chicago, probably red-eyed and sorry and starting a brand-new drunk with my brother Tom, instead of sitting out on the lake with my wife and Casey. Casey is two now, and she dances when I sing her songs.

Mrs. Dexter, of course, is from a different era, and won't dance because nobody can Charleston anymore.

There it is again. Four sentences ago I started out to write something I meant about my family, and I'm already saying Mrs. Dexter is seventy-six years old. I swear there is something in me that has to tease that girl, and every time I do it, I get letters from people who say she ought to slam the door on my testicles. Two years ago one group of ladies formed a "Free Mrs. Dexter Group," and a woman in New York wrote that I needed "a rude awakening."

Of course none of these people know Mrs. Dexter.

The year I came to Philadelphia I lived in a second-floor apartment on Eighth Street. I was getting divorced, and everything I had was a mattress and a dog. My friend Fred came from South Dakota to spend the summer and take care of me after an operation, and for a while I had two mattresses.

Fred and I and the dog never spent much time at the apartment. We went to bars or we drove to the ocean, or visited Mrs. Dexter over in

Jersey. Sometimes when we came home we threw soup cans through the windows.

And one night I looked around and there were newspapers all over the floor and broken glass on both mattresses and three months' worth of Pepsi bottles and dog-food cans lying around, and I decided to move to a nicer place. I called the landlady and told her I was breaking the lease.

"Thank you," she said.

And I moved in with Mrs. Dexter.

We lived for a while on the top floor of a little house in Barrington, New Jersey. There were chairs and windows and food when I came home from work. Then we bought a television set and a record player and moved into a bigger apartment.

And that place had air conditioning, and Mrs. Dexter kept the broken glass off the floor, and I taught her to cook, and in the way things happen we got comfortable with each other. Next door there was a go-go dancer who beat her son all the time.

We rented a house, we planted a garden, we bought a house. We got married, Mrs. Dexter got pregnant—all of this is not necessarily in any particular order.

The baby was a month early, and Mrs. Dexter had enough complications that for a while nobody was sure she was going to live. She was lying in the recovery room when I saw her, no color, dead still, with tubes running into both arms and out from under the sheets.

They took her away and I went into the nursery to hold the baby. She was less than a day old. I felt her breath against my neck, her head wobbled into my shoulder, tiny fists.

Mrs. Dexter recovered, and I taught her to ride a bicycle. She taught me not to throw food at the dinner table. Together we got scared every time Casey got a fever or choked on food.

We still do.

And sometimes, at night, we walk out by the lake, and I thank Mrs. Dexter for the dancing baby.

It's Father's Day, and I'd like to be home.

18

It is Sunday morning on Toronto Street, and Red Peak is sitting on the sidewalk out in front of his home. Red's real name is Haril. He is sixty-four years old, and he's put twenty years of Sunday mornings into the sidewalk there.

He says, "I just set here lookin'. Sometime it's somethin' to see, sometime it ain't."

Either way, Red is there. He is wearing bedroom slippers, checkered pants, and a baseball cap that says COPENHAGEN SNUFF.

The home is on the 1300 block of Toronto—a steep canyon through beat-up, three-story brick rowhouses. It runs one block, from Broad Street to Park Avenue. Park Avenue is ten feet wide. Behind that is a cement wall.

Kids jump rope, other kids bounce a basketball across the cement.

Red has just bought a day-old *Daily News* from the paperboy. He settles into his chair, opens it, and hears the gunshots. Three of them, coming from around the corner.

Then he sees the cab. By this time the driver has already been shot in the wrist, neck, and forehead with a .22-caliber pistol. He is leaning out the window—away from the eighteen- or nineteen-year-old man in the backseat—trying not to get shot any more. His car slides into the cement wall and stops.

Red Peak will say later, "Before that car stop, the back door flyin' open, and one in back, he come out so fast I can't see him good. All I know is he jump out of that cab and start haulin' ass up the street. By the time the driver get out, the one that shot him gone clear the hell out of there."

The driver of Yellow Cab 936 will be identified by police as Ronald Wooten, thirty-one, of the 4500 block of North Broad. He opens his door, gets out, falls in the street. Then he gets back up and begins running up the street toward Red Peak.

"He's jus' a little brown-skinned boy," Red will say. "Short, not much to him at all. He comes runnin' up the street yellin', 'Help me, help me.' Blood comin' out like a waterfall. Couldn' even see me. Blood runnin' all down his eyes, all down his shirt.

"Man, I was scart. I wanted to run myself. You see somethin' like that, at first you don't know what it is. You think two, three times. Sometimes they try to trick you, you know. I can't take no ass-whippin' no more, too old for that bi'ness.

"But there he was, bleedin'. He say, 'Please, call the police.' Then he tol' me to take the bullet out of his throat. You could see it there all right. There was a big hole and you could see the bullet.

"I said, 'Man, I'll get you a towel, but I can't be messin' wich your throat. I ain't no doctor.'

"Then I invited him to set on the bench."

Red goes into his house, gets a towel, and calls the police.

"They got to know ever'thing on the phone," he will say. "They ast me all kinds of questions. They ast me did I shoot him myself. Hell, if I shot him I ain't gonna call the police. I gonna be haulin' ass up the street like that boy come out of the back of the cab."

Red finishes with the police, gets a towel, and comes back outside. He tries to wipe some of the blood out of Ronald Wooten's eyes, but Wooten stops him. "He says he do it hisself. I must have been pressin' it too hard. Then he ast me to go turn off his car.

"He wants his keys, and he tol' me to get him his paper and the change in the front seat. I did that, give him his stuff, and after that he didn't do much talkin'. He jus' sat there on the bench. Weak, you know. Sometimes his eyes was open, sometimes closed. He didn't say nothin' about how it happened, he didn't say nothin' after that at all . . ."

Red Peak stands beside the bench and waits for the police. "They don't come and they don't come," he says. "Now and again the boy looks up at me. I tell him, 'They on the way. They comin' soon now.' I go back inside and call them again. All the neighbors out in the street now, watchin' him sittin' there on the bench, bleedin'. I hate to look at anybody sufferin' like that. It took somethin' out of me to look at that. I couldn't stand it.

"Then he's lookin' at me again. I say, 'Man, what you want me to do? I can't put you in my own car and drive you to the hospital. Then I be involved in it . . .' But then his eyes was gone somewhere else again."

It is about twenty minutes from the time the cabdriver is shot until the police get to Toronto Street. At least that is what Red Peak and the neighbors will say later. The police chase some of them back into their houses, make room for the rescue squad.

They lift Wooten off the bench and put him on a stretcher. They take him to Temple University Hospital, where later—after surgery— he will be listed in stable condition.

The police will begin looking for the man who tried to rob and kill him. They will not have much of a description to work with. Young, black.

Most of the neighbors will go back into their houses. The kids will go back to jumping rope and bouncing a basketball across the street.

Red Peak will sit down in his chair and open his paper. After a few minutes he will close it and get up. He will walk into his house for a bucket of water and a mop.

Red Peak finds that he can't sit in front of his home on Toronto Street until the blood has been washed away.

19

The Tinsley brothers had been in the motel business in a small way for a long time, and for a long time they had been trying to get into it bigger.

That means they didn't want to have to rob the Coke machine for drinking money anymore. The Coke machine and the small motel both belonged to the old man, I. W. Tinsley, Sr.

For the last three or four years, I.W. Sr. and the boys have been talking about building the sweetest motel in Sevier County, Tennessee. Two hundred rooms, Olympic-size swimming pool, a restaurant that cooked everything with onions, and a courtyard with a waterfall. They would all be partners.

They had blueprints, they had the land. But every time they talked to a bank vice president about lending them $8 million or so, the vice president would think a while, rub his eyes, and ask them what they thought was wrong with the University of Tennessee's football team.

Even Bob began to get discouraged. When he sold the El Dorado his father had given him for graduating college, he said to I.W. (Jr.), "Brother, I have this terrible feeling I'm never going to drive one of those again."

And I.W. felt bad too, even though all he'd gotten for graduation was a Buick.

Earlier this year, though, the boys finally caught a break. A motel for sale. It wasn't 200 rooms with a waterfall in the courtyard, but it wasn't $8 million either. It was about half that, and the same day Bob found a banker who didn't want to talk about the University of Tennessee football team.

The plan was to buy the $4 million motel, and then in four or five years use it as collateral to build the $8 million motel.

I heard about it and called Bob to congratulate him on the plan. He answered the phone up in the motel's executive offices, making the kind of hard decisions a man who owes somebody $4 million has to make. "I don't want to see any more yellow mustard on the restaurant tables. Brown mustard only," he said before he said hello.

"You actually borrowed $4 million?" I said. Bob said yes, but it was only a start. I said, "Is it easy to sleep with your eyes open?"

Bob said it wasn't the right time to worry.

"The way I look at it," he said, "if you owe the bank four thousand dollars and you can't pay them, you've got a problem. But if you owe the bank four million and you can't pay them, then *they've* got the problem."

He said once I learned that, I'd be ready to buy a motel of my own.

He invited me down to help celebrate, but I couldn't go. I'm sorry I didn't, I would have liked to have seen the partnership take form.

They started in the afternoon on the way up to Knoxville. Knoxville is about forty miles and fifteen bars. The trip took four hours. They stopped the car in front of one of the best-known hotels in that city, and Bob fell out.

I.W. picked him up, kicking beer cans, and walked him toward the door. There was a sign outside that said: WELCOME SOUTHEASTERN STATES SHERIFFS CONVENTION. Or words to that effect.

"Now, Bob," I.W. said, warning him.

"Now, I.W," Bob said.

And they walked into the hotel together. And right away Bob bumped into somebody's chest with his nose. The chest came with a name tag. Carson somebody from Macon, Georgia. Bob grabbed Sheriff Carson's hand and pumped it up and down.

"Well," he said, "I guess we're in the same business. Sheriff Tinsley from Sevier County."

The sheriff said, "Looks like you boys got a head start on us." There were a half a dozen other sheriffs standing around in the same circle as Sheriff Carson.

Bob slapped him on the shoulder. "Now, Sheriff," he said, "we'll catch you up, don't worry." And he took them all into the bar and started a tab.

An hour later, I.W. and Bob fell in love with the same girl. That happens to partners sometimes when there's only one girl in the bar.

She invited them up for a drink. She said, "Do you have a bottle?"

I.W. didn't think so, but Bob went out to the car and found one. They drank straight shots of tequila in her room, waiting for each other to pass out. Finally Bob lay down on the floor and closed his eyes. Which should have told I.W. something, because Bob has all the luck.

The girl sat next to I.W. on the bed and ran her hands over his shirt. She said she liked his chest. He said he liked her chest too. She said did he like it $50 worth. He said he'd just borrowed $4 million but he didn't have it on him.

She said she was sorry but I.W. was wasting her precious time.

I.W. carried Bob a little ways up the hall, then put him down. He found one of those carts the bellhops use to carry luggage and coats and lifted him up on that. He wheeled him into the elevator, then through the lobby.

On the way out, people called to them from the bar. They said, "Good night, Sheriff Tinsley."

On the way home, Bob woke up and asked about the girl. I.W. said she was a good time, all right.

They talked about the motels and the money they would make.

Bob said, "If we do this right, someday we're going to owe somebody twenty or thirty million dollars."

I.W. smiled and sat back. "That old girl was sure good," he said.

Bob said, "Hell, I.W., we get this thing rolling, next time you'll *have* the fifty dollars."

20

The cat never had a name, we just fell into calling her Mother. She came out of the woods, nursing four kittens, late in the fall of 1977. It was the same day we moved into a little house by a lake near Cecil, New Jersey, and she moved in with us.

It never for a minute seemed like she didn't belong.

I don't want to say much more about her now than that—it never seemed like she didn't belong. She was a gentle cat and a quiet cat and she found out-of-the-way places in the house or the garage to fill. That's a lot of what a cat does, fill your out-of-the-way places. She would find a spot in the bookshelf, or in a shoe box, or curl herself around the stem of a potted plant, and she'd use that place on and off for a week and then find someplace else.

My daughter was born in February of the following year, and almost from the time she could walk, she was carrying the cat. She would pick her up under the front legs—an involuntary reflex would push them straight out—and her belly would hang with the hind legs, swinging as my daughter walked.

She was gentle, and she was patient, and in all the happiness and good luck I have had since my daughter was born, that cat has been some constant, quiet part of it.

Of course, nobody is happy all the time.

There was a day, three years ago, when some neighborhood kid with a pellet rifle shot the cat in the leg and broke it, and Mrs. Dexter had to crawl under the car to coax her out.

She limped around the house for a month, maybe longer, dragging her front arm and the sling it was wrapped in, and that got to me all over again every time I saw it.

And if what had happened seemed inappropriate to the way she'd always been around us, it was also in some way heartening, watching her accept the sling, and whatever discomforts went with it. I would never presume to know what is going on inside a cat, but I saw something during her mending that I understood, and that reassured me that I had mended too—sometimes when you have been banged up too much, you lose your confidence about healing—and in that way a cat will fill your out-of-the-way places too.

Anyway, a couple of years later we moved to a house with a few acres of weeds and woods down in Maryland, and the cat found herself new places in the same house, and places in the weeds.

Two weeks ago, my wife picked her up off the floor and a mouse ran out from underneath.

And that is the kind of cat she was, and that was the way we knew her.

And then Christmas morning, we all got up early, and my wife let the cat out along with the other animals, and she followed one of the dogs a few hundred yards across the meadow and disappeared into the woods, and she never came back.

It was a windy, bitter day, the clouds were blowing in off the bay right over the tops of the trees. It was somewhere around noon when my wife mentioned that the cat hadn't come home. She wouldn't have mentioned it then except she'd heard some dogs earlier in the woods, and they'd sounded excited. There are half a dozen other houses on that part of the cove, and strange cars and strange dogs had been up on the road visiting for the holidays for three days.

I told her not to worry, that the cat could take care of herself around dogs, that she would wait in a tree until they got tired and left. Nothing is as patient as a worried cat.

Somewhere around eleven that night, though, I took the flashlight and walked out into the woods to look for her. The sky had cleared by then, and in the trees the wind was only a sound from outside. I walked all the way to the edge of the cove, calling for her, and then stood still a minute, listening to a can blow across thin ice—after the visitors, there are always cans and bottles—and then I turned around and walked back to the house, without calling her again.

My wife found her in the morning. She got up to let the dogs out, and saw something white on the lawn. She put on slippers and ran outside and picked Mother up—mauled and stiff, even her fur, where the saliva of dogs had frozen. She wrapped the cat in a towel and put her in the garage, and then came upstairs to tell me; she could barely get it out.

The cat came to us out of the woods, and the woods took her back.

21

There was trouble with the dogs, and every night you could hear Roy in there, slapping Ethel around in the bathroom.

There was no lock on the bathroom door and that's where he always caught up with her. Roy was from Macon, Georgia.

It was a cold winter, even for Minnesota, and I was twenty years old and I didn't have a job. It cost $8 a week to live at Ethel and Roy's, but they let me stay because I'd run errands for Ethel and pick up the trash every morning after the dogs had knocked over the cans.

I don't know how the other citizens at Ethel and Roy's came up with $8, except for the two Indians upstairs who took turns holding up the same liquor store a block and a half up the street. After the arrests, Ethel would say she didn't care what anybody said, they paid their rent on time.

The errands I ran for Ethel were no trouble—I mentioned the liquor store was only a block and a half away—but the dogs were everywhere. They roamed the city, mostly in packs, getting more and more aggressive. They ate garbage and attacked a couple of children. Sometimes their bites were poisonous.

And every night they'd knock over the goddamn garbage cans outside the back door.

One of these dogs, an old black one, belonged marginally to Roy. Not exactly belonged to him, but the dog would be outside every morning at six-thirty or seven to walk with him to work. Nobody knew what Roy did, but when he'd come home at noon, the dog would still be with him, both of them walking head down against the cold.

At the door, Roy would scratch at the dog's scarred head, then go inside to deal with Ethel. The dog would watch him get through the door, then disappear until the next morning, business of his own to see to.

Sometimes I'd toss the animal a piece of bread—he wouldn't take it from my hand—and he'd swallow it almost without chewing. Roy would shake his head. "Dawg's gettin' fat," he'd say. I never knew for sure which one of us he was talking to, but the dog was fat the same way the dog was friendly, which was not at all, except to Roy.

Which is more than you could say for Ethel. While Roy was at work, Ethel would send me to the liquor store for medicine. A new fifth of Calvert's blended whiskey every day. Smooth as glass. She said the doctor said to take it for her chest pain.

She would lie in her robe on the couch, watching television, taking her medicine. On top of the set were four pictures of her when she was young, and she always wanted to talk about how beautiful she used to be.

One of the pictures was Ethel and Roy helping each other cut a yard-high wedding cake. It didn't show now, but Ethel was a lot younger than he was then.

It didn't show, except maybe to Roy. He'd leave the dog, come inside, and Ethel would start on him. You could hear it everywhere in the house because none of the walls had any insulation.

"I was a beautiful woman." She began by yelling, and gradually raised her voice. "A beautiful, gorgeous woman, and you brought me here . . ."

It would go on and on, Roy only mumbling. A glass would break. Ethel would tell him he didn't know what she did while he was away in the morning.

Long silences. Ethel would ask if he wanted to know.

More long silences. Ethel would ask if he'd noticed how strong-built the colored boy upstairs was.

Which, most nights, was when Roy, who after all was from pre–Allman Brothers Macon, Georgia, would chase her into the bathroom and slap her around. Sometimes the process would take a few hours, sometimes all night. But it always ended in the bathroom.

The dog got killed the day before Christmas. The police came to get the second Indian. And one of them drove over the curb and got the dog while he was standing on the sidewalk, watching Roy go through the door.

By the time I got outside, most of the police were inside, guns out, looking for the Indian—who wasn't there anyway. Roy and one cop stood over the dog, the cop looking away, Roy just looking.

The dog's back was broken, part of his insides had come through his stomach. And he was still alive. "These things happen," the cop said. Nobody answered. "Doesn't look like he belonged to anybody . . ."

Roy didn't say anything.

The dog stopped screaming. Its sound now was hollow and low. I told Roy to go in the house, that I'd take care of it. He walked away, wordless.

I asked the cop to finish it. He wouldn't. I asked him to let me use his gun. He said he'd like to, but he couldn't. The dog got tired of this and died on his own.

I walked into the house, looking for a place to throw up. The police were asking Ethel and Roy about the whereabouts of the second Indian.

Roy leaned back against the wall, answered their questions—yes-sir and no-sir—not really paying attention. Face as calm as warm water.

Ethel said she had no earthly idea where such a person could be. She patted her hair, straightened her robe, and asked them into her living room. She wanted them to see the pictures of when she was beautiful.

22

The town of Grand Marais sits on a small bay of the same name on the northern edge of Michigan's Upper Peninsula. There are two bars, a gas station, a pay phone, a lighthouse, an IGA store, and the Superior Hotel. All those places except the phone booth and maybe the lighthouse sell rifle shells.

The hotel is owned by an old woman and her daughter, who is only a few years from being an old woman too. The mother came to the town from England before the turn of the century. In those days Grand Marais was the last stop on the train line. There was logging and trapping and 2,000 people.

In those days it was the biggest town in Alger County. Now it is almost the only town, and since 1910 the nearest train stop has been Seney, twenty-five miles south, down in the middle of the peninsula.

And when the train stopped coming, the town died.

It was the daughter who came to the desk. "We don't get many people coming through this late in the year," she said. She handed me a registration book, and beside the last name on it was the notation "Sept. 29."

It was Oct. 24.

I wrote my name and slid the book back across the counter. "That'll be four-fifty each," she said, "unless you boys want to look at the room first."

I gave her $9. I said to my cousin, "That's all right, Bill, you got it last night." I think the Holiday Inn had been $42.

She told us how to get to the room. It was through her living room and up the stairs. "Don't mind my mother," she said.

For a long minute we stood there looking at each other. She began telling us how to get to the room again.

I said, "You didn't give us the key."

That made her smile. "Key?" she said. "We haven't used keys in years."

The old woman was sitting in a reclining chair, next to the piano, feet up to help her circulation. Doctor's orders, she said. She was wearing dark glasses and staring at a television set that seemed to be between channels.

The pictures of her family covered the piano. School pictures, pictures from World War II, pictures from before that. The daughter came in behind us and told us who they were. Most of them had died or left town.

"The storm blew something loose in the antenna," the old woman said, "and the repairman from Newberry said he can't get up to fix it until it quits blowing. I just leave it on so this place won't seem so dark and awful . . ."

Outside, the wind was a steady forty-five or fifty miles an hour, and the rain was sharp with ice. And even inside the hotel, you could hear Lake Superior tearing into the breakwater on the edge of town. Earlier we had driven by, and the spray was exploding thirty feet into the air.

It was six o'clock in the afternoon and it felt like midnight.

"Newberry?" my cousin said. That was in Luce County, an hour and a half over unmarked dirt roads. Roads you couldn't use six months of the year because of the snow. Miles don't mean much in the Upper Peninsula, neither does time. It's the weather that counts.

"That's right, and he says he can't fix the set until it stops."

The daughter sighed and showed us the stairs. "Don't mind her," she said.

The last thing I heard before I closed the door at the top of the stairs was the old woman. "A couple of odd birds there," she said.

There was no answer.

There were fourteen rooms to the hotel. Two toilets, one shower at the end of the hall. It was the coldest place I have ever taken off wet clothes.

Bill looked around the room, at the ceiling and the walls. Everything was made of wood. He looked out the window, judging the distance to the ground. "You think this place is a firetrap?" he said. I could see his breath and the light wasn't even on.

I grabbed a Moose Head beer and jumped into bed. "Christ, I hope so," I said.

He grabbed a beer and settled into the other bed. It took a couple of minutes for the springs to quiet down.

After a while Bill said, "Look, we can't just go to bed at six o'clock in the afternoon . . ."

I said, "It's either that or get up."

Somewhere a beagle was howling. Bill got out of bed, went outside to the phone booth, and called his wife. He held the phone so she could hear it. He told her it was a bear.

The dog lasted about an hour. I drifted in and out of sleep the rest of the night. Once I woke up and heard the old woman snoring or sobbing, it was hard to tell which. It came to me then that she and her daughter hadn't spoken to each other the whole time we were downstairs.

The next time I woke up there was only the wind and the lake.

In the morning, the old woman and her daughter and the beagle were all in the office. Outside it was still storming.

The old woman sat at one end of the counter, her daughter at the other. The old woman told us what had happened to her television again and how the man from Newberry couldn't come down until after the blow.

She said there had been a couple of odd birds come in last night.

The daughter told us which bar had the best breakfast.

The whole time we were there, they never spoke to each other, never looked at each other. It wasn't that they didn't love each other, I don't think. I think there just wasn't much left to say. They'd been a long time at the end of the line together, and the train didn't come through there anymore.

23

About two o'clock in the afternoon, the recently retired heavy-weight boxer Randall Cobb, looking red-eyed and awful, walked into my office, smiling a red-eyed, awful smile underneath the ugliest cowboy hat you ever saw.

"I thought you were in California with the beautiful people," I said.

"No," he said, "I'm here with you. But don't ask me, ask the guard. He called you on the phone when I came in and said there was a gentleman to see you in the lobby."

I said, "The guard meant *you*?" Safer-looking people come in all the time wearing ammunition belts.

Cobb smiled and sat down on an IBM self-correcting Selectric that happened to be where he sat. He caught the space bar, and the typewriter worked its way from one margin to the other. He reached behind himself and turned it off.

"I saw a commercial once," he said, "where they gave one of those things to a gorilla and let him throw it around the cage to prove it couldn't be damaged. I remember because it made me want to buy one."

I said, "I think that was a suitcase."

Cobb shrugged. "It was something I didn't need, I remember that."

He smiled at me again, and I didn't like the way it looked at all. "You in town on business?" I said.

"I got to go up and see some people," he said. "It's business. Can you get me a car for a couple of days?" At the word *car,* my whole body felt like somebody had turned on the hot water downstairs while I was taking a shower. Look, Cobb once put an automobile in short-term parking at the Cleveland airport and left it there seven months. He retrieved it, pulled up to the cashier's window, and handed the lady his ticket and she rang up *thirty-seven hundred dollars.* He said, "You mean that was eighteen dollars a *day?*"

Anyway, I looked at him and said, "Your idea of business is to get in a car and go drink beer with some Texas promoter until he talks you into buying him a bar or you think of somebody you haven't fought yet."

He said that wasn't it at all. He swore there were no Texans involved, and it probably didn't have anything to do with getting back in the ring. Beyond that, there was no plan.

"That's it?" I said. "It doesn't have anything to do with Texans?"

He said, "That's as far as it got." Then he shrugged. "I realize how offensive this must sound to one of America's great planners . . ."

I said, "Well, I can't give you a company car, because they frown on that, and you know how I hate an absence of cheerfulness, and I can't give you my car, because I'm not crazy. I guess that leaves rentals."

He said that was exactly what he had in mind. "I could've done it myself," he said, "except nobody ever gave me a credit card."

"It's a strange world, all right," I said.

And so we walked into the car-rental place and talked to a woman in a uniform about getting a car. "All I have is a mid-size," she said. She looked at me and looked at Cobb—who still had that red-eyed, awful smile on his face—and you could see she liked me better.

"This is for how many days, Mr. Dexter?"

"A couple of days," I said.

And she checked my license and my credit card and ran a contract through her computer, doing all this without ever taking her eyes off Cobb. "Do you take collision, personal injury?" she said.

I said, "Do you have something if it just disappears?"

And she looked at Cobb again, but she turned over the car. When I saw it, I realized why. It was a beat-up Renault Alliance, they couldn't have sold it for what it cost to rent it a day. I gave the keys to Cobb and said, "Is there any chance you are going to return this to the airport?"

"Absolutely," he said. "There is always a chance . . ."

Three or four days went by and I hadn't heard a thing. It makes me nervous not to hear a thing. If it's in a lake, I sleep better knowing that than I do wondering *if* it's in a lake.

On the fifth day, I called the car-rental company and asked if the car had been returned. The woman looked into some files and then told me no. "The contract is still open," she said, "and I'm afraid you're responsible for the charges."

I said, "Forever? Is it sixty dollars a day for the rest of my life?"

"Perhaps you could call your associate," she said, "and locate the car that way."

So I got on the phone and eventually located Cobb out in California. It took about two days. I said, "Is it in Cleveland?"

He said, "Oh, God. The car."

I said, "Is it in Cleveland?"

"I swear," he said, "I gave it to this good friend of a brother of somebody I know, the man's got a business and everything. . . . Yeah, I know his name. I think it's Pete. He swore he'd take it to the airport."

"Is it in Cleveland?"

"No," he said, "I am almost positive it's not in Cleveland. I've screwed this up, haven't I?"

I said, "Randall, you've got to quit being so hard on yourself."

But that same day I found the car. The man Randall gave it to took it to the airport, it just didn't happen to be *our* airport. He'd left it in Allentown.

Which, in the overview, isn't bad at all.

I am telling you the truth: It *could* have been Cleveland.

24

The last time I saw Jack Walsh his head was level on the table with half a dozen empty beer mugs in a bar in Trenton, New Jersey, and he said he was going to do something special for me.

"Here's what I want to do," he said. "I want to come to Philadelphia and let a four-ton truck sit on my stomach for ten seconds. How would you like that?"

I am not normally a sentimental man, but this offer came very close to bringing tears to my eyes. I was sitting behind a few drinks of my own. "Aw, Jack," I said, "you don't have to do that . . ." But he wouldn't hear it.

"No," he said, "no, I'd really like to. I'd like to do that for you." And we shook hands.

Jack Walsh will be forty-eight years old this month, and he still calls himself the strongest man in the world. For all his adult life he has been traveling around, trying to prove it.

He has lifted elephants, small cars, and football teams. He has pulled a 600-pound motorcycle a foot off the ground using only the middle finger on his left hand. He has killed a 700-pound bull with his bare hands. He has kept a CD-3 airplane from taking off, he has pulled railroad cars with his teeth.

On the other hand, he has also very nearly been cut in half by the props after a tugboat jerked him off a pier in New York City. He has failed to pull railroad cars, only to discover later that he was on an uphill grade. This, of course, in front of cameras.

Then there was a fight with an 1,100-pound bull that Jack let a bunch of Mexicans promote all over the country before he slipped out of a motel room the night before and disappeared. "The reason I did that," he said, "was that unless that animal was awful sick, it was gonna kill me."

And once in Philadelphia as part of his nightclub act he allowed a large black man to come out of the audience and hit him several times in the stomach. Nobody told him until later that the man was Sonny Liston.

"My real ambition in life," he once said, "is to lie on my stomach, let them build one of those Levittown houses on top of me, then stand up."

This is all to say that Jack Walsh is more sincere than most people who come up to you in a bar and offer to let a truck sit on their stomachs.

Still, I was not sure he meant it until he showed up in the office Friday with a bad wrist and his friend Dennis. "I need somebody I can trust," he said, explaining why he'd brought Dennis along. "You'd be surprised how many guys are afraid to drive a truck over you . . ." Dennis smiled modestly, looked down at his nails.

The wrist he had damaged weight lifting earlier in the week, trying to jerk 500 pounds over his head. "You know how that kind of weight can flip back on you, Pete," he said.

Oh yeah, that.

"But all we need for this today is this . . ." He patted his stomach and we all went outside, looking for an 8,000-pound truck.

Anticipating photographers, the company had washed the closest thing they had—a 7,100-pound step-in van—on one side, and Jack and Dennis and my friend Brian and I and maybe half a hundred company truck drivers waited in the cold while a secretary typed up a two-paragraph release saying Philadelphia Newspapers, Inc., was not responsible for anything that ever happened again, anywhere in the solar system, including but not limited to, the nine known planets.

The truckers seemed impatient. They may have had mixed feelings, but there wasn't much doubt that after years of "safe driver" awards, everybody wanted to see somebody finally get run over. Jack signed the release.

Dennis got in the truck and tried the clutch. Jack started to get himself comfortable on the cement, and my friend Brian—who was keeping time in the event of a world record—Brian noticed something then that probably prevented the most memorable moment any of us would ever have.

Brian said, "Excuse me, Jack . . ." and now nobody will ever know what it is like when a 7,100-pound truck runs over a man with a half-pint of vodka in his back pocket.

Jack took the bottle out, gave it to Dennis—who, after all, he trusts— and lay down. He put a three-foot piece of lumber on his stomach to act as a ramp and motioned for the truck.

Now, to tell the truth, the truck was a little more than Jack had expected. The trouble was that even though the van weighed only 7,100 pounds, most of that was right in front, where the engine sits sideways over the axle that would run over Jack.

"A step-in van has always been my nemesis," he would say later.

Nevertheless, Dennis inched the truck to the ramp, then tried to get up on it. Skidding Jack across the cement, Dennis tried again and again. Four times Jack slid across the cement. Later he would show me his back, the skin hanging off it like so much peeling paint.

Somebody found another piece of wood to use for a ramp and Dennis tried again. The truck went up. Jack Walsh's face turned a color you only see coating the tongues of people who are very sick. A pack of Marlboros shook out of his pocket.

After eight seconds he waved the truck off and said he wanted to try again. Even closed, his eyes watered. His hands shook.

The truck went back up. Walsh lasted another eight seconds and change. "That's it," he said, almost apologizing. "That's all I can do."

It took a quarter of an hour, a couple of cigarettes and a half a dozen pulls off the vodka for Jack to settle down.

"You might not realize it," he said, "but that really hurts."

I said that had occurred to me.

That's when he showed me his back. "What matters, Pete, is that we got the record . . .

"Some Hindu sumbitch held a five-thousand-pound Cadillac in

Atlantic City for eight seconds and claimed it." He shook his head, disgusted. "A Cadillac. Jesus . . ."

He puckered for another kiss of vodka. "If that Hindu wants the record now, let him come here and use the same truck," he said. "Let him use the same truck, the same driveway, the same everything." He shook his head again.

"Let's see the Hindu do that."

25

The woman was sitting in a five- or six-year-old Cadillac—the air conditioning blowing one stiff piece of her hair that had somehow broken away from the rest—and honking at a man in a red Buick when the smoke started coming from underneath her car. It was two-thirty in the afternoon and the Buick had blocked off the intersection at Eighth and Pine, trying to follow a bus through a red light.

First there was smoke, then the smell of antifreeze, and then the stuff was leaking green puddles all over the street. The woman who owned the car steered it onto the sidewalk and got out to take a look.

Her friend got out from the other side and looked too. They were both maybe thirty-five, both sunburned. "It's the radiator," the friend said.

The woman who owned the car looked around, nodded. The wind caught some of the smoke and blew it, wet and smelling like acid, into her face. She fanned it away.

"Either the radiator or the carburetor," the friend said.

The woman who owned the car nodded again. "I think Nick did something to it," she said.

"I wouldn't put it past him," said her friend.

"It never happened before, and three months after he splits it starts doing this." She shook her head.

Her friend said, "I wouldn't put it past *any of them.*"

A man who had been sitting on a fire hydrant, watching, lit a cigarette, walked over, and asked if they needed help. The one who owned the car had legs that were pale and bruised on one side and bright red on the other, but her friend didn't. And her friend's shorts stopped at a place where, if she'd had bruises, they would have shown.

He said, "You girls need some help?" He was wearing a dirty T-shirt and looked like the kind of guy who could sit comfortably on a fire hydrant. The weather turns warm and they are everywhere. He scratched at himself and looked at the friend.

The friend made a face that indicated she was disgusted. She began the face as soon as she heard the word *girls*, and stayed with it until he quit looking at her legs. "We don't need anything," she said. Then she stepped around him and looked under the grille for the hood release.

Then she looked under the bumper. Then the woman who owned the car looked and said she thought she saw it. She reached under, screwed up her face with the effort, and before too long there was a banging sound and the hood popped open a couple of inches.

The guy who could sit comfortably on fire hydrants stood by, smiling.

It took a couple of minutes more to locate the second latch, then together the women lifted up the hood. Everything was dripping. Steam poured out of the radiator cap, and you could feel the heat a couple of yards away.

They both stepped back and stared. "I could kill the bastard for this," said the one who owned the car.

"We need a rag or something to get the cap off," her friend said.

The one who owned the car walked back to the driver's-side window, leaned in, and came out with a scarf, the kind women sometimes use to tie around their hair after they've been to the beauty parlor. This one was blue with red and white stars.

She moved toward the radiator cap.

"I wouldn't do that if I was you," said the man who could sit on fire hydrants. By this time, the steam had calmed down.

The friend said, "Why don't you go play with yourself?"

"I don't wanna miss none of this," the man said. He crossed his arms, leaned into a wall, and smiled wide enough to show he didn't have teeth on the sides.

Then the woman just did it. She ignored the man who could sit on hydrants; she ignored me. I'd said, "At least turn the engine on," but she took it for some macho insult. She and her friend were way beyond telling one of us from another.

She pressed on the top of the cap and turned. The cap didn't quite come off but the antifreeze sprayed on her hand and arm and got on her blouse. Her friend held the arm while the stuff boiled and spit out of the radiator.

The arm was already sunburned, and it seemed to turn white where the antifreeze touched it. The woman who owned the car had been scared, and now she was trying not to cry.

"I know Nick did something to the car," she said.

Her friend protected her arm, putting her body between it and the man who could sit on hydrants. She gave us both dark looks. I said, "Let the car cool off a half-hour and you should be able to get it to a gas station."

She said, "We don't need your help."

The man who could sit on fire hydrants comfortably began to laugh. "Why don't you shut up too?" said the friend.

"Yo," said the man, "what'd I do? I didn't do nothin'."

The friend looked at the woman's arm, and the woman began to cry. "No," the friend said, talking to us both. "You never do nothing, do you?"

Then she asked the woman if she wanted to walk up the street to the emergency room at Pennsylvania Hospital to have them look at her arm.

The woman said, "What am I going to do about my car?"

"It's only the radiator . . ." said the friend, "or the carburetor. We'll call the station and they'll send a man out to fix it."

26

The geese come in the morning, after bad weather. The wind blows the bird feeders in the backyard, and they show up underneath them, eating spilled corn and sunflower seeds. The cat stalks them from the fence.

He drops his body to be even with the bottom rail and moves a muscle at a time toward the tree, stopping when they stop—the paw a half-inch off the ground—waiting until they begin eating again to move closer. Seeing him coming, they gossip.

The cat is not quite a cat. He is nine or ten months old, still breaking in. He has two verified kills—a mouse and a sparrow—that he brought home and gave to Mrs. Dexter. The mouse was still warm. He also brought her an eyeless catfish. Call me a crazy romantic, but there is something about the woman that makes you want to do things like that for her.

The rest of it he is picking up faster. He lies in the sun well, he can climb trees and urinate in houseplants. He will jump a bare foot from behind curtains, and he can toss a hair ball with anybody.

But the hunting is slow in coming. The problem, I think, is mental—related to a batter who can't get the hitch out of his swing. The cat will spend all afternoon stalking a jaybird, and then, a second before he is ready to make his rush, his tail starts to twitch and the back feet jump. His front feet aren't ready to move yet—there is nothing as stubborn as the front end of a cat—so the part that does move goes up in the air.

Before it comes down, the blue jay is gone.

The cat will stand in the spot then, staring at the ground—the batter refusing to leave the plate, refusing to believe he has struck out on another change-up.

But things get better for him when Mrs. Dexter hangs the bird feeders. There are more birds to stalk, and less time between them to sulk.

And then the geese show up. Two white and two almost brown, they come every morning after bad weather, and from his first look, there is something in the cat that shows new confidence. He knows something that big with feathers has to be easier to kill than a jaybird.

And every morning he seems to get closer.

He stalks the birds, always from the fence, moving like poured syrup, until he gets to a place five yards from the bird feeder. Then his back end jumps and the air fills with beating wings and webbed feet. And when his back end comes down, he chases the geese all the way to the lake, and the noise hangs in the air with the feathers.

And even though he never kills one, there is something about them all running away that he seems to like. And he walks back to the porch and falls asleep in the sun, smiling.

Today, though, the geese are different. The older male is chasing the others all over the yard. He is an old, beat-up renegade and he has decided it is mating season. The others know it isn't, and bite at him and shame him and refuse to go near the water, which is where geese have their way with other geese.

They stand together, two ganders and a liberated goose.

The male tries again, he gives up. He picks at his food while the others eat. The cat is moving beside the fence, getting closer all the time. The old male watches him, the others see him and gossip.

The cat gets to a place five yards from the tree and flattens himself to the ground. His tail begins to twitch, his back legs jump ahead of the front legs, the geese beat their wings and run for the lake.

All except for the old male. He is still there when the cat's back end comes down, and he is there when the cat arrives.

He comes up off the ground, his wings pounding the air over the cat's head. He hisses and bites, a piece of fur floats in the air.

The cat backs up, the goose follows him. The cat turns, flattens against the ground again, and runs for a tree. The goose chases him to the tree and watches him climb into the branches.

It is a half-hour after the goose leaves before the cat will come down, backwards and checking every few feet.

He sits on the porch, cleaning himself off. Then he lies in the sun, sleepless, looking out at the spot under the bird feeder.

Wondering where it all went wrong.

27

The two old ladies had dressed like sisters. Black dress, freckled cleavage that started low and ended up Jesus knows where. Gold jewelry hanging off anything that would support it. They were talking about operations.

The women were standing together, each with a hand in the small of the other's back, between an imitation Chagall and a man dressed in a tuxedo holding a tray full of mushrooms stuffed with melted liver. The trays always have liver at art-gallery openings. That's one of the reasons you become an artist.

The man with the mushrooms and liver asked if either of the ladies would care for an hors d'oeuvre. The women looked at him for a moment, then looked back at each other. "Eleven days," the older one said, "the doctor told her eleven days to two weeks for the stitches to dissolve . . ."

"Poor thing," said the younger one, shaking her head. "I just know she won't go out. It's like when I fell . . ."

Which the man with the tuxedo and the liver recognized was "No thank you." He smiled and moved his liver through the crowd, looking for takers.

The place that was giving away the liver was A. J. Wood Galleries, on the third floor of a building at Seventeenth and Locust, and by the time I climbed out of the elevator yesterday afternoon and located him rocking beneath a fake Modigliani, David Stein was looking nervous.

Stein is the artist whose paintings A. J. Wood Galleries is trying to sell.

He used to sell his own.

As a matter of fact, in the middle and late 1960s, he sold hundreds, maybe a thousand of them. The other thing he did was sign them. Picasso, Cézanne, Miró, Degas—names like that. And art experts all over the world and people who thought they were art experts looked at the paintings and believed Picasso, Cézanne, Miró, and Degas had actually done them. (Stein, by the way, did forgeries, not copies. He created new work that looked like the masters.) They thought that because Stein was a genius forger.

Nobody knows how many of the forgeries he sold—sometimes he did two or three a day—and if a lot of art experts testified against him at his trials, a lot of other experts and people who thought they were art experts were not inclined to admit that the little Picasso drawing hanging casually in the corner wasn't a Picasso at all.

And at $2,500, it wasn't that casual.

There were enough of the ones who did admit they'd been taken, though, to put David Stein in the slam about four years, here and in France.

He got to Philadelphia a year ago, and now a gallery was opening to sell his paintings—both his works "in the style of" other artists, and his own stuff. All, by the way, carrying the signature "Stein." And now he stood, hands clasped behind him, rocking beneath a long, sad, fake Modigliani, waiting to become a trend.

And if there was a group to oblige a man like that, this was it.

"I think it's important, both as art and anti-art." I heard that and turned around in time to see a man with a pipe in his pocket talking to a man with a pipe in his mouth. Then the second man took the pipe out of his mouth and put it in his pocket. You couldn't tell who had said it was important, because they were both nodding yes.

I watched them for a while, but nobody's pocket started to smoke.

Behind the two men with the pipes were two more men and their wives. The wives were talking about which paintings they wanted. One wife liked the one for $3,500, one wife liked the one for $3,000. I don't know how they knew what cost what. "Lemme get this straight," said one of the husbands. "Are these copies or not?"

From the other side of the pipe-in-the-pocket set: "Of course I'm right. Who else could it be but van Gogh?"

"Of course, Bob."

And in back of that happy couple: "Nineteen attacks in eight years, and you wonder why I gave it up?"

And then the guy with the liver came through, this time with vegetables, followed by a guy with champagne, followed by a guy with little sandwiches, and everywhere you looked women were touching cheeks, kissing air, holding hands. Perfume thick enough to make your eyes water.

Another man—ascot but no pipe—had David Stein deep in art talk, asking when he worked (early till late), how he worked, maybe why he worked. After every answer, the man would tell Stein that was how he did it too, or this was how he did it differently.

While that guy was making the unnecessary point that he was also a painter—after all, I said he had an ascot—a lady knifed through the gray hair covering Stein's ears with her nose and shouted it was all fantastic. Just fantastic.

An overweight kid pushing through the crowd toward the guy with the little sandwiches missed the lady's hair by two inches with the cigarette he was holding over his head. Christ only knows what would have become of Center City if that had gone up.

The lady never knew it. She was hugging David Stein, now kissing his plump cheek hard enough so most of it got pushed into his nose.

He stood there, taking it, smiling, not knowing what to do with his hands. He looked confused and nervous.

All to say, the greatest faker in modern history comes to Center City and finds himself out of his class.

28

Louie the Dog Boy says he is reformed. Doesn't have sexual intercourse with dogs anymore. Doesn't choke them or tie them up and beat them with sticks or make them fight each other like he used to, either. Or torture them with broomsticks.

"I don't do that no more," he says. "The little kids do that now, and I try to stop them. That's why ever'body sayin' I do that . . ."

The Dog Boy's mother stands in the doorway of their living room, nodding at everything he says. "Who say all that?" she says. "I know . . . I know who. Two people, I know them now . . ."

"Yeah, man, I know who it is too," the Dog Boy says. "I know that lady who say that. It be funny if I get a rope and go over and choke her, put a stick up *her* ass, man . . ."

The Dog Boy begins to laugh.

In the room with him are four or five younger children, brothers and sisters or cousins. They all laugh too, all except the smallest boy, who is probably too young to understand what that means. He stands barefoot and shirtless in the middle of the living room, sucking on half of a pale-blue popsicle that melts down his chest and stomach and leaves crooked, narrow lines through the dirt all the way to his underpants. Someone has scribbled blue ink all over his legs.

Louie says it again. "Yeah, man, put a stick up her too." The smallest child looks over to the doorway while the brother and sisters and cousins begin to laugh all over again, and he finds his mother there.

"Put that stick in her," she says. She thinks it over and begins to giggle.

Seeing that, the small one laughs too.

Everybody in the neighborhood knows the Dog Boy.

The old man stands in the shadow of St. Peter's Roman Catholic Church, Fifth and Girard, sweeping dust off the sidewalk. When he sees the Dog Boy, he stops, stops and watches him walk north up Fifth Street until he turns left at Frank's Hard Luck Lounge and disappears around the corner onto Thompson.

"What that kid needs," he says, beginning to sweep again, "is for somebody to break his hands and somebody to break his feet and somebody to break everything in between."

A neighbor who used to feed him: "I like the kid, but he's mean. He's mean, and he's sick, and what he's doin', it ain't right. He's seventeen or eighteen now, and it ain't nothin' new for Louie. My boy told me what he was doin' three, four years ago.

"After all, those dogs is a living thing. You see them afterward, so sore they can hardly walk, sometimes bleedin', and you know some human person had somethin' to do with it.

"And all those little kids who follow him around now, I guess doin' the same thing. They came to my door and threw matches in the house. You know, they wrap a bundle of them together. They threw 'em in my vestibule. I was lucky my dog heard them. He barked and I went out there and there were six of them sittin' on bicycles, waitin' to see the fire . . ."

A neighbor on Fifth Street: "You see him mostly after midnight, always got three or four dogs on a string. Either that, or he's goin' to one of the abandoned houses around here where he's got them locked up.

"He and his friends go in there late at night, and then you hear those dogs screamin' like they was bein' murdered . . ."

Part of the problem is that there are so many abandoned houses. On Wednesday, there were dogs on the roof at 1239 North Orkney. Thursday they were in a used-car office on Fifth Street. Friday neighbors saw them in the third-story windows of a house on Randolph Street. Last week they were on the fourth.

Most of the neighbors are afraid of the Dog Boy. They say he might burn their houses or break their windows.

One person who says she is not afraid is Wilma Liger, who is fifty-three years old and works a concession stand at the post office. She found a dog she says Louie or his friends—she's not sure which—had abused on her doorstep one morning. "I called him Lucky," she said. "I called him that because he was lucky to get away.

"For the first two days he was too sore in the hindquarters to even get up those steps . . ." She points to some steps leading up to a district health center across from her house.

"Next time I saw him, I said, 'You better quit abusin' them animals,' and the little screw threatened me. There was three or four others with him, and he said, 'Lady, you don't know who you're messin' with.'

"I said, 'You don't know who *you're* messin' with,' and waved this under his nose . . ."

Mrs. Liger moves a pudgy, short-fingered hand into the pocket of her cardigan sweater and comes out with a small pistol. "It's a gasser," she says, "can't do much damage. But it's a repeater, yeah. I carry it everywhere I go. I'll kill that kid if he makes me . . ."

Louie the Dog Boy sits on a plastic-covered couch in his living room on the 1200 block of North Randolph Street, and it is hard to see how most of a neighborhood could be afraid of him.

He is small and thin and nervous. The neighbors say he is seventeen or eighteen; he says he is fifteen. When he says that, his sister, lying across a chair on the other side of the room, begins to laugh. "Fifteen," she says.

Immediately he is furious. "Fuckin' shut up," he shouts. "Ma, how old am I? Ain't I fifteen?"

The mother is leaning in the doorway, arms wrapped around her thin chest. "*Sí,*" she says, "sure, you fifteen."

"See?" he says, "fifteen." The anger is suddenly gone.

If he is fifteen, it is safe to say most of the people in the neighborhood would just as soon he didn't get to be sixteen.

Most of the neighbors have never seen the Dog Boy do what they say he does, but their children have. "I see Louie through a window," says one of them. "I see him beat the dogs with the stick, and then he chokes the dog. I seen him fuck the dogs too."

Louie says that is all behind him. "I like dogs," he says. Which is why he keeps locking them up in abandoned houses. "I don't want them to go away."

But at night the neighbors see Louie the Dog Boy go into the houses, and then they hear the dogs.

Neighbors say they have called the police and called the Women's SPCA, but they are always told that nothing can be done unless Louie is caught in the act. "That kid is smart," says another neighbor. "They're never gonna catch him, sittin' in some police car. He sees that, he just goes somewhere else."

With the exception of Wilma Liger, none of the neighbors are willing to have their names used here. They are also, according to police, not willing to sign the formal complaints that would lead to Louie's coming under the jurisdiction of Family Court.

"Somebody has got to stand up," says a source in the Police Department. "Somebody has got to have the balls to say, 'You are a sick kid, and I am going to see to it that you get some help. I am going to stop this.' But until somebody is willing to do that, we can't just railroad him. He's got rights too.

"The neighbors call and complain, all right, but when morals goes over to investigate, nobody has anything to say anymore."

I ask Louie why the neighbors are afraid of him.

"Nobody's scart of me on the block, man."

I ask him again.

"Well," he says, "they might worry that I break their windows. I done that before.

"If I get mad, I do that. I break the windows here too. And the roof. When I get mad I lose my mind. I just go ahead and do what I do . . ." The brothers and sisters all nod. Louie smiles, pleased with that.

"I can't help myself," he says.

29

The first course I ever took from Mrs. Selz was Nineteenth-Century American Literature. I was eighteen years old. Walt Whitman, Edgar Allan Poe, and Nathaniel Hawthorne were dead. Myself, I wanted to be an electrical engineer. Someone had said they made a lot of money.

The first time she gave an essay test, I wrote that all of "those kind of writers" were "provincial." I didn't know what that meant, but I'd heard the word thrown around the English Department. She gave me the test back without a grade. All it said was, "Learn to spell very soon, Peter."

Instead of learning to spell, I went to the bookstore where they sold pamphlets for $1.25 that summarized anything you might ever be forced to read. They summarized it, they told you why it was important, they threw in some stuff about light and dark imagery and motifs and where the author was born.

I saw those pamphlets and knew I was an educated man. In one night I learned to compare and contrast the Hawthorne school of fiction with the Poe school of fiction. "Although alike in their provinciality," I would write in my next exam, "the two schools represent vast differences in different ways."

Mrs. Selz held me after class. "Peter," she would start, "I find a real flair in your writing . . ." She was forty-five or fifty then, a narrow, soft face that blushed when she smiled. She wore her hair in a bun. "But sometimes you seem to be, uh, *uncomfortable* with some of the material we cover."

It would take me fourteen years to figure out she was telling me I was full of shit. I thought then she was just trying to say she knew that Hawthorne and Whitman and I didn't see things eye-to-eye and she wasn't taking sides.

I began skipping Nineteenth-Century American Literature, which was at nine o'clock in the morning, dropping an occasional dark hint about "personal matters" that had to be cleared up at home.

And she took me at my word and asked if she could help.

I got a B in Nineteenth-Century American Literature, signed up for Twentieth-Century American Literature, and quit school. I went to California. Most every spring after that I quit school and went someplace I hadn't been before. I would send Mrs. Selz postcards, and she would write me letters asking what I was reading, was I writing? She always told me not to give up writing. I never told her I'd never really tried.

I'd find a college bookstore and buy a pamphlet on *Moby Dick*, then write her another postcard about depth of imagery and intricacies of subplot. I'd say I was working on something in that same line myself.

In the fall I would be back, sleeping through her classes. She didn't like to do it, but she'd give me C's, sometimes a D. I missed the first eleven weeks of classes one semester before she stepped in front of me in a hallway in Old Main. I said, "Where in *hell* have you been?"

She punched me in the chest.

There was a student protest at the school. Berkeley had one to protest the war in Vietnam, in South Dakota they wanted an extra day off for Thanksgiving vacation.

I happened to be sitting in Mrs. Selz's class the afternoon one of the football players ran in shouting for everybody to get up and leave. I knew the football player and he was an idiot. He was also huge.

Mrs. Selz stared at him a minute, her face turning all colors of red. "You get out," she said finally. "If anyone in here wants to leave with you, that is his choice." She stepped toward him. "But you have no choice."

And then she backed him out the door and then she picked up her book and started reading Vachel Lindsay or somebody, like it never happened.

Somewhere in here a couple of things changed. I began to read poetry and I found out what an electrical engineer was.

Then one afternoon Mrs. Selz came in, closed her books and her eyes, and began reciting Robert Frost's poem "The Road Not Taken." The last part of that poem goes:

> Two roads diverged in a wood, and I—
> I took the one less traveled by.
> And that has made all the difference.

She got all the way through it and forgot the last line. And I sat there with a whole class of girls to impress and didn't say a word. I didn't even know why not, I just didn't. I'd been going to school about five years, on and off, and that might have been the first sign I'd learned anything at all.

I called Mrs. Selz this spring and she had a cancer they couldn't cut out.

"I hope I didn't make this sound too dramatic," she said.

I said, "Oh, Jesus."

I visited her in July. I brought Mrs. Dexter and the baby and some columns I'd written about South Dakota. She apologized for scaring me on the telephone. "The treatment is working right now," she said. And she said that dying was only part of living.

Then she bragged over the columns, held the baby, talked about teaching with Mrs. Dexter. It bothered her that the university was becoming too practical. "The students don't seem to care," she said. "They just want to take courses and graduate and get jobs and not be bothered with learning after they get out." She shook her head. "It kind of makes you feel like you aren't doing your job."

She asked what I'd been reading, I asked about her cancer.

"At first I was frightened," she said. "But I talked with people, I thought about it. I'm fine now. I'm really all right. It's part of things."

The last time Mrs. Selz went to the hospital, the cancer was back, and spreading. But she'd known that before.

I think she probably knew it in July.

30

As distressful as this is to me personally, it's become necessary to discuss menstrual cycles again. There has been a huge misunderstanding, and somebody's got to correct it.

Like a lot of men my age, I grew up under the constant threat of menstrual cycles. It has been a part of daily living, like knowing the Russians have missiles aimed at Washington. I have learned the early warning signs—it starts usually with a simple foaming at the mouth, then the eyes glaze over and there is excruciating pain, signifying the transformation, and then claws grow out their fingers, and muscles and hair sprouting all over, the eyes turn yellow and fangs replace their teeth—and I know from experience when that happens it isn't the time to talk about quitting my job and moving to Australia.

And like a lot of men my age, I have always felt that, except for staying out of the way, it wasn't my problem. To me, it was like those signs you see in the Smokey Mountains that say *RUNAWAY TRUCKS EMERGENCY ROAD 1 MILE AHEAD*. I mean, you can figure out what the guy driving the truck feels like when he sees he's headed down a four-mile grade without brakes, but unless you're in front of him with the gas pedal on the floor, and he's still closing a hundred yards every thirty seconds, you can't *appreciate* it.

I was thinking about that on the way out of the house yesterday. I'd packed some shorts and tennis shoes and hand wraps in my gym bag and was headed out the door when she came running out of the bathroom. "Oh no you don't," she said.

"What?" I said, scared. I had that old feeling that an eighteen-wheeler was about to blot out my sun.

"You know what," she said. And she took the gym bag out of my hand and opened it.

"All right, all right," I said. I took two towels. I am only supposed to take one towel to the gym, because that way I only lose one towel.

"That's not what I mean," she said. She took out the towels and the tennis shoes and the shorts and everything else in there, and then found them on the bottom, under a pair of socks. Two Johnson & Johnson mini-pad liners. The last ones in the house.

I ought to explain that a mini-pad liner looks about like a Band-Aid, except it's bigger.

It is big enough, in fact, to exactly cover all the knuckles on your hand. One side of it is sticky, so after you wrap your hands you can put it across your knuckles before they go into bag gloves, and that way you don't tear up your hands hitting the heavy bag.

In fairness, there are people who don't need mini-pad liners. My friend Mickey, for instance. Mickey owns the gym, and there is a ninety-pound blue Everlast bag up there. If you bump into it, it feels like a corner of the building. Mickey can throw punches at the bag all day and never hurt his hands. Our knuckles have nothing in common, Mickey's and mine.

"My hands are my livelihood," I said to my wife.

"Let go of my mini-pad liners," she said.

"Be reasonable," I said. "There are other things you could use . . ."

Her expression changed. "Like what?" she said. "What else can I use?"

I said, "Well, there's an extra pair of sweat socks in the closet. I could let you borrow those for a while."

She threw what I would like to think was a playful punch at me then, and having been trained in these matters, I stepped away and watched the punch go past me and land on the corner of the door.

Before she grabbed her hand, I could see she had skinned a knuckle.

She bent over it and hissed. I said, "See? That's what real pain is all about. Here we are, dead in the middle of menstrual transformation, the apex—if you believe Phil Donahue—of suffering and anxiety possible in this world, and one skinned knuckle hurts enough to make you forget all about it."

She looked at me then, but there was no answer. "What I think," I said, "is that menstruation is a conspiracy between Phil Donahue and every woman in America. I don't think there is such a thing."

"Peter," she said, "give me those pads."

And so I compromised, which of course is what makes marriage work. I took the flaps off the sticky side and put one of them over her knuckles. "See?" I said. "Isn't that better?"

Then I saw the shadow of the eighteen-wheeler coming after me, and I put my arms around her and held her at the door like that for half a minute. "Don't worry," I said before I let her go, "you'll feel better before long . . ."

And I held her and told her she was a good cook and all that, and asked if she wanted me to bring home some pickles or chocolate ice cream or something. And all the way to the gym, I was thinking that I had to be sensitive now for two days and that it was like this every month.

And it came to me before I got to Mickey's that I was wrong. There *was* such a thing as a menstrual cycle. I'd just misunderstood whose cycle it was.

31

The name of the book is *Experiencing Life (of a Young Man)—A Candid Story about the Life in the Ghetto as Told by a Native*. It begins on page 9 with this sentence:

It started when I was born, moving from one ghetto to another, as far as I can remember, at the age of 5.

It ends twenty-three pages later, without improvement. There are blank pages between the chapters. It took Vernon Cummings a year to write it. "It's not the length, it's the merit," he said, repeating something he'd heard from Ms. Edwards.

"This book was s'posed to get me recognition as a writer so the next one wouldn't cost me nothing . . ."

Ms. Edwards told him that too.

Ms. Edwards is publications director at Carlton Press, Inc., in New York City. Carlton Press published the book in July, after Vernon had paid $2,860. He sent Carlton money orders for eighteen months.

"I was s'posed to pay them $3,324, but they said the book itself would pay for the rest," he said. "Now they askin' me for the money for my second book, *Lyra the Great*, but I don't know. It's science fiction . . ."

Right now *Lyra the Great* is handwritten, every third line, on notebook paper. It begins like this:

Suddenly in the sky, a beam of light huddles down swiftly into the sea of California.

The people of the city thought it was a meteor right.

But little did they know as it plunged to the bottom of the sea and cracked (out came a jittering form).

Vernon Cummings was sitting in his sister's living room in North Philadelphia, holding a briefcase full of his writing on his lap. Outside, kids were screaming; a tow truck was hauling off Vernon's Chevy for repairs. Inside, the shades were pulled over the window, and the only light was coming from the next room, and from the cartoons on the television set.

He said he read about Carlton Press in the want ads. "I sent away for their information," he said. "They told me I'd get autograph parties and television interviews and newspaper stories 'bout the book. They said they'd get me the copyright for the Library of somethin' . . ."

Vernon looked around the room. Broken furniture, torn linoleum. "And then I'd get forty percent off the sales. Dollar-sixty a book. S'posed to be four dollars a copy.

"They give me a list of all these stores where the book was going to be on sale. I went over to the one on Fifty-second Street, and all they had was one book. I bought it because I don't have no other copies, and they charged me two dollars and ten cents. I know I'm not gonna get no dollar-sixty out of that."

Vernon shook his head, flipped through his book. His picture is on the front cover and on the back cover. He is older on the back. "They said it was published on July 16," he said, "but I sure don't see no autograph parties."

The book moves from being born to Carver Elementary School:

I went to Carver from 1960 to 1965. During these years, a lot of things happened. For instance, when I was in the 1st grade, we had a lot of recess periods . . .

To an accident with a childhood friend:

I ran across [the street] and then Thomas, only to be struck by a car. This was a freightening event, for he was lying there with his eyes wide open. Well, I didn't see him anymore afterwards . . .

To leaving home, being hungry, transporting (but not using) drugs, to being around girls with "shapes that wouldn't quit."

He said, "They changed the names and all so it couldn't be libous."
On the jacket cover, someone at Carlton Press has called this work "a
modern Odyssey."

I leave Vernon and call Carlton Press to talk about modern Odys-
seys. The telephone lady says, "Are you one of our writers?"

When I say no, she hooks me up with Alan George, who cannot
keep a tone of faint amusement out of his voice. Alan sounds like he is
twenty-two years old, like he almost graduated from New York University, and like he laughs with his friends after work about people like
Vernon Cummings.

I don't want Alan. I want Ms. Edwards or Thomas Carroll, the executive vice president, who took the time to encourage Vernon too. All the
people at Carlton seem to have two first names, by the way.

It develops that Alan George doesn't know anything about it, and
nobody is there who knows anything about it either.

I ask Alan a couple of questions, anyway, so he can pass them
along. I ask what kind of people would steal $3,000 from a semiliterate
kid because he wants to be a writer.

I ask if they didn't have some kind of bottom line.

When I finish, Alan George says, "My, that's quite a mouthful."

Speaking of which, after I hang up, I call Vernon to read the jacket
cover to me again.

The last part of it goes, "the pursuit of experience was the leitmotif of
the '60s . . . and *Experiencing Life (of a Young Man)* is a book that might
well serve as a metaphor for a past decade."

Vernon says, "I like that last part. That's what it's all about."

32

The Saturday before Easter, Mrs. Dexter took the day off without so much as a note from her doctor. She just up and left the grocery store and the laundromat to have a good time, deserting her family, leaving me alone to make breakfast for Casey. I tried to keep the resentment out of my voice.

I said, "Let's have some fun today, okay?"

Casey said it was okay with her.

"What do you want for breakfast?"

She said apple juice, ice cream, and olives. She is beginning to say things that sound like sentences, either that or I am picking up a new language. At least I'm understanding about two out of three words now.

Anyway, I said, "What are you, pregnant?"

She said it was okay with her.

"You can't eat that for breakfast," I said. And, being a responsible parent—one, I might add, forced to be a mother and a father both—I fixed her something with a little more balance. Bacon, ice cream, apple juice, and olives.

I fixed that, and while she ate it—everything but the bacon—I was figuring out how to fix Mrs. Dexter. And suddenly it came to me. "You want to go get an Easter puppy?" I said.

She said it was okay with her.

I went through the *Daily News* classified advertisements and found a farm near Salem, New Jersey, that had puppies for sale. "That ought to do it," I said, and we got in the car.

The farm was on a little road between Salem and Elmer. There were sheep and lambs and dogs and roosters in the front yard. More of that in the back, with a horse and some cows and pigs. The farmer's wife saw us at the fence and came over to sell us a dog. Casey looked at her, then at me. She said, "Pig?"

"She doesn't mean you," I said. "She means the pigs."

The farmer's wife's smile got tight and unfriendly. That is something I should stop doing—explaining what the child means.

She said it again. "Pig."

The farmer's wife invited us into the house anyway. There were two cats, about half a dozen dogs, and a baby goat walking around the living room, smelling each other. And an aquarium. "We love animals," the farmer's wife said, "and we donate dogs to the blind."

There were four puppies left and Casey and I took the one that was rolling in mud and grabbing at pant legs. "Wait till it gets a hold of your mother's nylons," I said.

Casey said it was okay with her. And we named it McGuire, after my friend the famous police reporter. He and I sometimes have cocktails together.

Casey and McGuire slept most of the way home. I stopped at a grocery store to get some puppy food and a Dodge van with one of the baldest, meanest-looking brothers you ever saw pulled into the next parking space.

McGuire began to growl, Casey smiled at the man on the way into the store. She said, "Hi, boy."

I said, "She doesn't mean *boy* that way . . ." I have got to quit that.

Anyway, when we got into the store, there was a table full of tulips next to the dog food, and I bought some of those too. I mean, how mad can you be at a well-meaning fool who has such a good heart he goes out and buys a puppy and flowers for Easter?

By the time we got to the house, though, McGuire had bitten the tops off the flowers. I carried him inside, along with a pot of flower stems, and handed it all to Mrs. Dexter. The other two dogs were screaming and jumping on her to see what McGuire smelled like, and one of them knocked over the laundry.

"Happy Easter," I said.

One of the first things McGuire did after he got in the house was knock Casey down. He jumped in her face and licked her. For two days after that, every time McGuire would come into the room, Casey climbed on a stool.

All that night McGuire howled. He tore up the carpet, he knocked pans out of shelves, he fell into walls. He left teeth marks everywhere he went. There was something haunting and familiar about his behavior. Mrs. Dexter and I lay awake all night, and finally I realized what it was.

"I should have known better than to name him McGuire," I said.

At six o'clock in the morning, Mrs. Dexter got out of bed and took McGuire into the other bedroom. They slept together, and while I'm not going to make a lot of accusations here, Mrs. Dexter certainly seemed to like him better when they got up than she had when they went to bed.

Meanwhile, my dog Harry came up with a plan. Harry is fifteen years old and bone thin. You can be around him a week and never see him eat, but in the morning after McGuire kept everybody awake, Harry began eating puppy food. No matter how much we put down, Harry ate it. His stomach swelled, he walked around the house burping.

But you cannot starve something that can eat rugs.

It went on like that for a week—it is still going on. Nobody sleeps a whole night, everybody has lost plants or shoes or toys, or found electrical wires chewed in half. Harry walks around looking pregnant.

This Sunday I took Casey out for a hamburger. That usually makes her happy, but once we got in the car I could see there was something bothering her. "Don't you want to go to McDonald's?" I said.

She said okay, then she held up her finger. "No more 'Guire," she said.

I thought of all the editors who have said that before her. I said, "No, no more McGuires. One is enough."

It is the nature of the McGuires of this world, though, that by the time you have said that, it's already too late.

33

One night about three weeks ago I was lying in bed when it came to me that I had to fix the bathroom faucet. It was 3:35 in the morning, and the faucet had been dripping cold water probably since 1964, long enough to have worn a groove in the sink anyway.

Now, I don't mean I thought, *The bathroom faucet has to be fixed*, I mean I had to fix it then. Nothing like that had ever happened to me before, even during daylight, and I was frightened.

It seemed related to Son of Sam getting his orders from a dog.

I woke up Mrs. Dexter and told her what was going on. I said, "I'm not sure, but I think I'm going crazy." She sensed I was afraid, and the compassion she showed then is the kind of thing that happens sometimes in thirty seconds between married people, but stays there holding them together for a lifetime.

She listened to everything I said, then she nodded. "Yeah, it sounds like it all right."

And then she went back to sleep.

I got up and found my toolbox. I took out all the wrenches, a hammer, two kinds of screwdrivers, half a hundred washers, and a pair of pliers. I never fixed a bathroom faucet before, but as soon as I found the right wrench—the word TOYOTA was printed up both sides of the handle—the job almost did itself. As far as I was concerned, it was over way too soon.

I went back to the bedroom and began to talk to myself so I wouldn't think about going crazy. The things I said, though, were all crazy.

And then I would look over at the clock, and it would be twenty minutes after four, and I would get a picture of myself in bed at 4:20, talking crazy, and it would start all over. "Don't let this bother you," I said. "You've been under a lot of pressure."

Right after that I decided to clean up the living room. "Mrs. Dexter," I said, "I'm sorry to bother you . . . no, no, I'm fine now, I was just wondering, do we have a vacuum cleaner?"

It turns out we do, but Mrs. Dexter wouldn't tell me where it was, so I changed a few lightbulbs and put the Sunday *New York Times* back together in the order it came in, and put an extra leaf in the dining room table, just in case we had company.

The next time I got in bed it occurred to me that I was probably breaking new ground. I know something about hypochondria—I once developed all the symptoms of lockjaw, including a slight fever, one by one as I read what they were in a medical dictionary—but I'd never heard of anybody going crazy by thinking that they were going crazy.

By daylight, though, it had happened.

I called my doctor and made an appointment for four o'clock in the afternoon. I went outside and mowed the lawn. I washed and waxed the Jeep. I changed the washers on the kitchen sink. Something inside me kept saying, "*Keep moving, keep moving. If you stop to rest, you'll freeze.*"

Before I went to the doctor I came to the office. I sat down with one of the people who run the paper and explained the problem. "I am going bananas in a serious way," I said.

The person I was speaking to looked at me as if that was not breaking news. "What's different?" he said.

I said I wasn't sure, but I couldn't make any promises about not throwing somebody through a window. We are on the seventh floor.

The person I was speaking to looked out over his staff. "Do you know *who* you might throw?"

I shook my head no. "I'm sorry." All I knew was that I'd probably want to put the new window in if I did it.

"Well," he said, "take the week off, then, get some rest, don't worry about anything. It can happen . . ."

Hearing that, I swear to you I felt better. All the way over to the doctor's office I kept saying it, "It can happen . . . it can happen."

Then I'd say, "What does that mean?"

Then I'd say, "Do you realize you're still talking to yourself?"

Then I'd say, "Yeah, but it's not about going crazy anymore." But, of course, it was.

I wondered what they'd put in those little black letters at the bottom of page 2 on Wednesday. Something not too specific, I figure:

Pete Dexter's gone crazier than a snake caught in a lawn mower and will resume his column when he recovers.

The doctor and I talked it over and decided I wasn't crazy. Not even close, he said.

And he should know. Twice a year I come in with an incurable disease being advertised during the commercial breaks in the two-a.m. movie on Channel 10, and he looks me over and tells me I don't have it.

I like him for that, of course, but the thing I like best is that he always seems to understand.

He gave me a prescription and we shook hands. As I walked out, he went into another examination room to look at a seventy-year-old union man I'd waited with outside. There were two things the union man had never done in his life: crossed a picket line and voted Republican.

Before I'd turned the corner, I saw my doctor put his earplugs in, hold his stethoscope up in the air, and begin a conversation with Hubert Humphrey.

"What's that, Hubert?" he said. "Old Al here's been smoking cigars again? I don't know, Hubert, I've told him over and over . . ."

I walked out almost cured. If a man like that says you're not crazy, what can there be to worry about?

34

The man this story is about died last week. He was sixty years old. His sister didn't want me to write about it, so I won't use his name.

They still talk in the bars about the day he jumped off the Delaware River Bridge. One hundred and thirty-five feet into the river, on a $5 bet with a neighborhood character named Doggie Gardier—tore the ligaments out of both knees.

He was only a kid then—fifteen or sixteen—but nobody ever forgot. His picture was in the *Daily News*.

"I remember he come by the day after he did it," an old man said. "He come by smilin' and laughin' afterwards, even on those broke-up legs. He knew what he'd done, all right . . ."

The old man spit, watched a lazy line of it blow into his pants leg. He was leaning into the shade of a doorway leading to a bar. He wiped at his chin, spit again, this time cleaner. "Hell," he said, "he was always jumpin' off somethin' . . . or into somethin', if you know what I mean."

I thought I ought to buy a drink. I asked the old man if he was going into the bar or coming out of it.

He said yes.

In her house three blocks away, the sister remembers too.

"I was there the day he jumped off the bridge," she said. "I was twelve or thirteen years old, and even then I knew he wasn't brave. If you're from a broken home, by the time you're thirteen you're as smart as you'll ever be.

"I followed him all the way up there, crying and begging with him not to jump. But you know, he and those boys had drink in them, and they were all talking to him too, and finally I saw that he was going to do it no matter what I did and I said, 'Go ahead. I hope you don't make it. You're a damn fool.'

"And then he did jump. Oh, God.

"They still sit and talk about it down at the bar, but most of them weren't there. They weren't there that night, either, when he came home from the hospital.

"They weren't there to hear him crying."

In the bars they say he was fearless. "He never took nothin' off of nobody," said a man who knew him.

"We'd drink, and sometimes, you know, trouble would start. Trouble was always startin' in those days. Two guys'd get liquored up a little, start arguin', and the next thing you know they're out in the street.

"They'd fight a while, then they'd be back inside buyin' each other drinks. He wasn't very tall, but he was put together good, he was a rough guy.

"He was funny too. What was that he was always sayin'? Oh, yeah. He said, 'I can mash potatoes, but I can't pee soup.' He learned that in the circus."

"All my life," said the sister, "I tried to get him to stay out of places like that bar. When we were little children—he was five or six and I was three or four—Mother would take us into bars looking for our dad. My brother inherited a lot of things from him.

"His friends down at the bar, they loved him when he had money. If he had four hundred dollars, he'd spend it all right there. When he was broke they ran from him.

"When he got into all the different scrapes, those people down in the bar would always say, 'Boy, he did this, he did that.' They led him on, encouraged him. Then they sat back, nice and smug, in their little houses, drank beer every night and raised families.

"They never did anything, they just encouraged him. I'm not saying he didn't decide how to live his own life, and I'm not saying he wasn't street smart. But he was so . . . insecure. You know?"

In the bars they talk about some of the trouble he got into with the police, and some of the trouble the police got into with him. They say he was a hard man to keep locked up.

"Mostly, though, before he got all crippled up, he'd drink and talk about the old times," said another man at the bar.

"He'd talk about football or basketball, things like that. After he jumped off the bridge, he got a job for a while in the circus, he'd set himself on fire and jump into a bucket of water.

"He never talked too much himself about going off the bridge, but he didn't mind if anybody else did. Mostly we'd just drink and talk about old times and sports, that's until the stroke.

"After that, you'd only see him sittin' out in front of his sister's house on a chair with a blanket over his legs."

"He came to live with us after the first stroke," the sister said. "That only paralyzed one arm. He'd stopped drinking, and for the six months before the second stroke we were so close . . .

"The second stroke came, and he went blind. He came home from the hospital and that night, he said, 'Mary, I'm afraid.'

"I said, 'Of what? You've never been afraid of anything.' I said that, but I knew it wasn't true.

"He said, 'I don't know. I don't know.'

"And then in the end, he couldn't talk either. He liked to listen to the radio, he'd sit there in his chair, crippled and blind, listen to the news all day long. I saw that and wondered sometimes why I got him to give up drinking.

"When he died, nobody from the bar came to the funeral. The few fellows he'd known forty-five years ago, they were all already dead. Cirrhosis, heart trouble.

"I loved my brother deeply, but he was never anything but a fool. And no matter what kind of stories they tell down at the bar, when my brother died, he didn't have any friends."

35

The rent is $95 a week, and Joline still owes the manager fifty. None of the regulars have called, so it's time to go to work.

She turns off the television and gets into some clothes. It is four o'clock in the afternoon.

Joline checks herself in the mirror on the way out, not especially liking what she sees. "I have one of those faces," she will say later, "you wouldn't find it on a magazine cover. Makeup makes me break out, so I don't wear much. I just don't have that model look.

"I tried to get into the houses outside Reno once, but there's hundreds of girls want those jobs. They took my application but, you know, they didn't encourage me. They want girls that look like models . . ."

Her room is toward the back of the motel. The motel sits along West Capitol Avenue in West Sacramento—one of maybe thirty other motels just like it. She steps outside, wearing jeans and high heels, and makes her way out to the street.

When she gets there, she begins to walk. Gravel, driveways, dirt. Looking into cars as they come past. That is as much solicitation as she does, as much as she needs to do.

"A lot of the girls jump in the car with anybody that stops, but mostly all I date are elderly guys. You don't have to worry about them. I mean, I been out there a while and I know what a good date looks like.

"I won't date young dudes unless they're dressed in a suit and got a responsible car. Or unless they're a salesman or other professional. You can tell the difference between when somebody's a salesman and when they're not. They even talk different . . ."

On this day, however, she walks up and down Capitol Avenue for close to an hour and nobody stops. Finally a car pulls over, an old Chevy, and she looks in and sees a kid, maybe nineteen or twenty years old. He is dressed in a T-shirt.

"That is normally the last guy I am going anyplace with, but I'm having a bad day, you know, so I take a chance and get in."

The kid drives across the bridge into Sacramento. She tries to give him directions to a place she knows. The kid nods and smiles, but he doesn't go where she tells him to.

"About halfway over, I notice he's loaded, some kind of drugs, it's hard to say what. I used to have a pimp in L.A., he kept a briefcase full of heroin. I was his number-one lady. He had five other girls, but he liked me best. I left him and stole a thousand dollars. Sometimes he'd set up a party. It cost the dates a hundred to go into the back with me. He'd make that much in a night. So I left him and stole from him, and when he caught up he got me addicted so bad. I don't ever use that now, and I hate it. I only use crank. I won't date anybody if they're on anything . . ."

The kid drives across town and pulls into a parking lot of a factory near Thirtieth and C streets. He grabs her around the neck with one hand and goes into his pocket with the other.

"Three times in the last year, somebody's pulled a knife when I got in the car. It doesn't happen a lot, but when it does, you give them what they want. Once you do that, they leave you alone."

There is something about this kid, though, that makes her think that he may hurt her no matter what she does, and she hits him as hard as she can between the legs, then scratches at his eyes and pulls free. She opens the car door, rolls out, and begins to run—stumbling in her high heels— through some high grass.

The kid comes out of the car behind her, and begins to close the distance. She sees a broken bottle on the ground and picks it up. She turns around to face him.

The glass stops him cold.

"I saw then that he was scareder of me than I was of him. I told him to leave me alone while he could still walk out of it, and he turned around, calling me something I couldn't understand, and went back to his car and left."

She walks south until she finds a taxi, and takes that back to her place in West Sacramento. It is getting dark, she is dirty and scared. She thinks of her pimp, and wishes there were someone now to protect her. She thinks of her child—eighteen months old, living in a foster home—she thinks of a court appearance she has coming up for shoplifting.

She calls a stranger and tells him her stories. She says she wants to get off the street, maybe go into computers.

They talk a long time, and then she has to go. The rent is $95 a week, and she still owes the manager fifty. She says that is two dates, maybe three.

Joline is twenty-three years old.

She says she'll have it in two hours.

36

I met a man last week in Nevada who'd bought his girlfriend a horse. The man and his dog live alone in a ghost town forty miles south of Reno, and female company is a serious matter.

"It's one of those things," he said, referring to the sudden decision to buy a horse. "You just surprise yourself."

And so, surprising himself, he drove to his friend Dave's ranch to pick one out. "I had six hundred dollars," he said, "but when I got out there the first thing I saw was this beautiful Appaloosa. Perfect conformation, with a big, muscular rump, and she was full of spirit, the kind of horse I've always wanted for myself. Dave isn't stupid, though, and wasn't going to let go of her for any six hundred dollars. We aren't that good of friends.

"I told him it was for my girlfriend and asked him what we could work out, and finally got him to let go of her for twelve hundred. And so I called up my girlfriend and said, 'Can you get six hundred dollars and meet me right now?' And she did, no questions asked, which is the kind of person you want to buy a horse for in the first place.

"So I took her money and bought the Appaloosa. She didn't quite understand why it cost her six hundred dollars for me to buy her a present, but she believed me when I said it was the opportunity of a lifetime."

The man took the horse back to his place in the ghost town, and presented her to his girlfriend during one of their conjugal visits. "She loved that animal," he said, "right up until the moment she got on. You could see it then, that it was too much horse for her. The horse sensed it too—they can feel it when somebody's timid or scared, and they take advantage."

The girlfriend rode the horse several times over the next few weeks, but the man saw it wasn't going to work. The horse and the man's dog, on the other hand, were inseparable.

"Seeing how the dog and I both liked the horse," the man said, "and my girlfriend didn't, at least not close up, I decided the only honorable thing to do was buy it from her. I said, 'Honey, I don't have the whole six hundred right now, but I'll buy her, pay you twenty a week or so until we're even, or until I don't like you anymore.'

"That was on a Friday. Saturday morning, I was coming out the road that leads to my place when I happened to look over into the pasture, and there was the Appaloosa, lying stiff-legged on the ground—rigor mortis—and my dog was right there beside her. I got out of the truck and climbed over the fence, and that's when I noticed the dog was chewing on one of her legs.

"Wow! On one hand, my girlfriend didn't like the horse, at least not to get on it and ride. On the other hand, she was attached to it in a sentimental way—attached enough, at least, that I did not want her driving up to my place that afternoon and seeing the dog eating it.

"And so I came back to the house and called Dave and asked him to come get the horse. He's got a flat bed and a winch, and I've got no way to move her. He said, 'What happened?' I told him I didn't know. The horse seemed fine the last time I saw her, that maybe she twisted a gut or had a heart attack. He apologized for what had happened. He said, 'I swear, that horse was sound. I never would of sold her to your girlfriend if there was anything wrong.' Then he considered the situation a different way and said, 'Holy Rolly, I'll bet she's upset . . .'

"I told him that she hadn't seen it yet, which was what I was trying to prevent. I asked how soon he could make it over.

"He said, 'There's a real problem, on account my winch is broke.'

"I said, 'I got a dead horse in the field and my dog's eating it, and my girlfriend's on the way over this afternoon. Can you borrow somebody else's?'

"He said he didn't know, that he would try. Then he apologized again for the horse. 'I swear,' he said, 'there was nothing wrong with that animal, or I would never of sold her to your girlfriend.'

"I said, 'The truth is, Dave, it isn't hers anymore. She was scared of it, so I took it off her hands.'

"He said, 'You bought the horse?'

"I said, 'I didn't give her the cash yet because I didn't have it on hand, but yeah, I'm paying her twenty dollars a week until we're even.'

"He thought about it a minute, and then he said, 'Don't pay her, man. The bitch sold you a bad horse.'"

37

We have arrived at a time of great sensitivity in this country, and nowhere is this sensitivity more clearly at work than in the popular press.

The word *wop*, for instance, has disappeared completely from the *New York Times*. Likewise, all the various slang words for Asians, blacks, Latins, Poles, Jews, the chronic unemployed, the handicapped, and any other group whose members are voting age and numerous enough to represent an economic or political force have been excised—except in the case of direct quotes from Jesse Jackson or Earl Butz—from the pages of all of our newspapers. You do not ever call women "girls," and you are very careful about whom you call a boy.

But as heartening as this progress has been, I wonder about the spirit behind it.

What brings this to mind is a commentary this newspaper reprinted Sunday from the *Washington Post* dealing with the upcoming heavyweight title fight between Mike Tyson and the former champion, Larry Holmes.

Now, the *Washington Post*, of course, is every bit as enlightened as the *New York Times*, and probably even more sensitive. After all, it didn't take the *Post* fifteen years to change Miss to Ms.

But reading the fifth paragraph of this commentary, I find the following reference to Tyson's opponents: "as carefully chosen an array of stiffs as was ever arranged."

Now, this particular piece was written by a man named Shirley Povich, who apparently has been watching heavyweight boxing since the days of Gene Tunney without learning anything about it.

And while that doesn't bother me much—at least not once I found out that Shirley Povich wasn't some twenty-three-year-old woman that Ben Bradlee had hired as a token boxing expert—what did bother me was the worn-out, insulting reference to fighters as "stiffs."

Meaning that somehow professional fighters have been excluded from the age of sensitivity. It is not just the *Washington Post*, of course, and it is not just the word *stiff*. Ordinary fighters are routinely called "bums." It is nothing unusual to hear a fighter's courage or intelligence questioned on national television.

Now, some of that comes from the sport itself, where the words *bum* and *stiff* are part of the regular vocabulary of the gym, and a fighter's heart is in issue because so much depends on it. But as innocuous as that is in the gym, where it is understood, it becomes something else in a newspaper or a magazine or on television. Especially in contrast to the sensitive way we treat everybody else.

We have come to the place now where people sitting on street corners sucking on wine bottles cannot be called bums, but some poor guy who has run three miles every morning for the last eight weeks, boxed every afternoon in the gym, skipped rope, done his sit-ups, hit the bags, and gone without sexual intercourse—all to help him do his job better—can.

Not to mention having enough sand to climb into a boxing ring.

We have come to a place where fighters can be "stiffs," but dead people can't. I'd love to see that in the *Washington Post*, by the way: "A police spokesman said the stiff had not been identified."

And it's fair to say, I think, that it is a harder and riskier thing to climb into a boxing ring than it is to write the story about what happens there. It is harder than editing that story, or laying it out, or selling the newspaper or magazine it runs in.

And maybe we ought to keep that in mind. Even if fighters aren't an official minority, that doesn't mean it's all right to insult them when they get in over their head.

The people doing the insulting are mostly waders, after all, and do not know what the deep water is like.

38

In the sixteen or seventeen years it has been since my mother allowed me out of the house alone, I have stayed in five memorable hotels. That is out of maybe 300.

First there was a motel just outside Oklahoma City, attached to a bar. My friend Fred and I walked into the room they gave us, and there was a body lying on one of the beds. The eyes and mouth were open, and there was dried blood on the teeth. We were younger and harder then, and Fred went over to the other bed and lay down. "I think I'll take this one," he said.

We were in another hotel someplace in Missouri, an old place with big, clean rooms and high ceilings and we looked around and couldn't figure out why they only wanted three dollars a night. This was back in 1968, but even at the prices then, something was wrong.

It was two o'clock before the train came by. It seemed to come out of a dream, a whistle from a long time ago, a far-off rumbling that got louder and closer until suddenly it was shaking the bed and sucking the curtains out the window.

We got out of bed and looked, and Popeye's girlfriend could have stood where we were and left nipple marks on the caboose.

Locally, there was a hotel on Nineteenth Street where the only shower was on the ground floor, and the residents spit on the stairs with a kind of spit that never seemed to dry. If you stopped on the way down for more than a couple of seconds, your feet stuck.

I was there my first Christmas in Philadelphia, and that morning on the way to the shower I found a half-naked man drinking wine and urinating on the stairs. I said, "What the hell, Norman. It's Christmas."

He said, "I know that. I was jus' cleanin' up the steps."

And then there is the jailhouse in Winner, South Dakota, which counts as a hotel because they let Fred use one of the cells for a night, and one of the police even went to the liquor store to get him a pint of blackberry brandy. If you ever decide to give yourself up, the Winner, South Dakota, police station isn't a bad place to do it.

Of course, you have to get there first. On that same night I tried to turn myself in, and the same guy said, "Oh no you don't. We got one like you in here already and we ain't takin' no more." So they will never be able to handle the volume that a big-city facility can, say the one Chuck runs here at the office.

What brings all these accommodations back to mind is a hotel I stayed at last week, the Hyde Park Hilton in Chicago.

It is a new hotel, built across the highway from Lake Michigan, and some of the hired help seemed a little green. I noticed that for the first time, I guess, when I checked into the room. The towels were folded in their places on bathroom racks, but they were still damp from the last person who had used them. The washcloths were all stiff.

I went looking for the pool to take a quick swim, and on the way I ran into a man who said he worked there. I told him about the towels. He said, "Were they real dirty?"

I asked him about the pool. "Of course we have one," he said, and pointed me around the corner. "This is the Hilton." But the Hilton hadn't put any water in it yet.

So I didn't go swimming. I went to the bar and had a drink instead. The waitress wore plastic flowers in her hair, and when she brought the drink over she said, "I tol' the bartender this was the wrong thing, but she says to give it to you anyway."

"What is it?" I said. I'd ordered bourbon and water.

"I don't know," she said, "but it might be scotch and somethin'."

Scotch and Pepsi-Cola. I smelled it and went back to the room. Forgetting about the towels, I took a shower. The water alternated hot and cold. I danced dances that haven't been invented yet.

I called the front desk and asked about reserving the room for Saturday and Sunday. It was Friday, and I hadn't been able to book it through the weekend, and because of the business I was doing I needed to be in that part of town.

There were no rooms available, but the woman said to keep trying because there was a 25 percent rate of no-shows. I asked if they could notify me when a no-show occurred; the front desk said that was strictly against policy.

"Then everybody would want to be on the list," she pointed out.

The next morning I called again. No vacancies yet, so I packed two suitcases and moved out. I don't like to pack suitcases, and I didn't like it an hour later when I called and a different woman said, "Of course we have rooms. Would you like the same one?"

I suppose I would have ignored all of this if I had not been hungover and desperate for something to eat when I woke up Sunday morning. That was when I called room service. I wanted two greasy cheeseburgers and four Pepsi-Colas without scotch as fast as they could bring them.

"We can't do that right now," the woman said.

I said, "Why not? This is room service, isn't it?"

The woman said, "This is room service, but you have to come get it yourself."

I cradled my head between the phone and my hand, realizing what she had just said. She said, "Sir?"

I said, "You know, I think what you've got here is a memorable hotel."

She said, "Thank you very much, I'm sure," and hung up.

39

Hell's Angels in the Holiday Inn.

There are Harleys all over the Black Hills this week—newspapers put the number at 300,000—but nobody knows how many showers there are. The place is perfect for the uncouth, but somehow it still surprises me to find the Hell's Angels, the real thing, parked in the driveway outside the room.

I don't know where I thought they slept—maybe caves—but you don't expect to see them sitting poolside at the Holidome.

This is the week, however, to see things in the Black Hills that you don't expect. If you believe the T-shirts, this is the fiftieth anniversary of the annual motorcycle rally here, and the occasion seems to have made philosophers of everyone who owns a Harley-Davidson motorcycle.

Which is to say everybody's an easy rider this week, and next week it's back to work at Sears or the phone company.

The philosophers give interviews on the local television stations and say that riding a motorcycle is the only tie we have left to the days when America was really free.

And once started on the subject of a free America, some of them turn out to have strong opinions on Vietnam. For instance, they think it was a mistake for America to enter a war it did not intend to win. They think that America did not do enough for the veterans of that war when they got home.

These startling thoughts are expressed not only on television, but on the T-shirts the riders wear. I'm picturing a sullen-looking, hugely over-weight woman I saw sitting outside a rest stop on Interstate 90, wearing a petulant expression and a shirt that said WIFE OF A VIETNAM VETERAN, and glaring contemptuously at the civilians who got out of cars.

One of the most curious things about the assembled Harley owners, by the way, is the physical appearance of the women who ride with them. Most of them, putting this as nicely as I can, look like they would flatten the tires they sit on, and a surprising number are hairier than the springer spaniel riding in the backseat of my car. It seems there are appearance problems here that even black boots and tattoos of snakes cannot correct, which I hope does not sound chauvinistic.

Many of the men are every bit as ugly and hairy as the women, who are referred to, among the riders themselves, as old ladies.

This is not to say that all the motorcycle women are ugly or fat. My brother Tom, who is traveling the same highway, reported seeing a woman on the back of a motorcycle so stunning he almost ran off the road.

"Delicate features, small, feminine, jet-black hair," he said. "And there was something about her mustache, a full perfect black mustache, that made it so I just couldn't take my eyes off her face."

Tom is the family romantic.

Anyway, the highway is an endless line of Harleys, and the bikers are in every rest stop, every restaurant, every roadside attraction along the way. And the spaniel watches the bikers from the safety of the backseat, making growling noises deep in her throat that have the potential, I think, to cause her trouble later on.

But when we stop for food or gas or to stretch, she is suddenly quiet. I think perhaps it is the smell of leather—did I mention these people are riding through the heart of a South Dakota summer in leather pants?—that calms her down.

At any rate, we quit for the night at Rapid City, just east of the Hills, and I take the dog for a walk. The parking lot is full of Harleys and cars and trucks from both coasts towing Harleys. The easy riders stand pro-tectively near the bikes, drinking beers, talking, waiting, I suppose, for someone from Eyewitness News to interview them about being free.

Soft bodies, hard T-shirts.

BAD TO THE BONE, one of them says.

And then I see the Angels' bikes, and then I see the Angels. The dog sees them too. She stops dead in her tracks, staring, as two of them walk past us on the sidewalk. A moment later there are two more. "Good dog," I tell her as they approach. "Be a very good dog."

And it works. She doesn't growl, she doesn't sniff; she just leaves them alone. This is, by the way, the happiest I've ever been with this animal since I bought her from a man in Sacramento who promised me that the breed was exceptionally lovable and smart.

We walked through clusters of motorcycle people on the way back to the room, some of them pretending to look bad, some of them not having to pretend—ax murderers who didn't wash their hands—and the dog, who will growl at a cricket in the night, doesn't even seem to notice they are there.

Not the bikers, not their bikes. They pull in and out of the parking lot, engines without mufflers, she doesn't flinch.

And then we get almost to the door, and I'm watching her, trying to understand this change in personality, when suddenly a frail old woman comes slowly up the sidewalk, pushing her husband in a wheelchair. The dog studies them a long minute, and then I hear it.

A long, low growl climbing slowly out of her throat.

Lovable is still up in the air, but it turns out the dog's as smart as the man said.

40

All right. I didn't mind when the dog came home with a rabbit. In fact, I kind of liked the screaming when he walked into the kitchen.

It didn't make me real happy to look out the window last week and see him lying in front of a bulldozer, chewing on something half as big as he was, but I figured when you move into a new neighborhood, your dog develops new interests.

I can't say what he was chewing on, by the way, because he dropped it when I screamed at him, and the bulldozer ran over it. I looked later, but all I can tell you is that it was brown and hairy and made a spot on the ground about the size of a throw rug.

I try to talk it over with my family. I say, "You know, McGuire's developing a real macabre side to his personality."

"I don't think this is dinner-table talk," Mrs. Dexter says.

"What do we talk about at dinner?" I say. "Chopin?"

Mrs. Dexter gives me a look and continues cutting a slice of roast beef into bite-sized pieces for my daughter. My daughter likes her meat cut into small pieces, she likes to dip it in Wish-Bone Italian Dressing. She is seven years old—which I think is too old for that. I think she's old enough to have her mother cut her meat into bigger pieces, like she does with mine.

She also puts Wish-Bone Italian Dressing on her mashed potatoes, so I don't see where pointing out that I have noticed a little streak of

the bizarre in the family dog is anything that can be reasonably sin-
gled out as inappropriate behavior at the table.

Anyway, it's America, and the Constitution says I can say anything
I want, as long as it's not *Fire!* If you say *Fire!* in Mrs. Dexter's kitchen,
even in America, she's going to think you're still telling the famous
turkey-that-turned-into-a-shrunken-head story, and you tell that around
her again, you might as well forget about the press of warm flesh forever,
unless, of course, you want to go lie under the bulldozer.

And so, ignoring objections and invoking the Constitution of the
United States of America, I discuss McGuire.

"He had something over in front of the heavy machinery last week," I
say. "They're paying seventy-five dollars an hour for that bulldozer, and
I look out the window and McGuire's lying in front of it with a dead
animal in his mouth."

I happen to know how much a bulldozer costs because the guy who
did my driveway recently had his lawyer send me an itemized bill, along
with a summons. And so, on one hand, I find myself criticizing McGuire's
sudden interest in the dead, on the other hand I am thinking, *If only it
could have been the driveway guy in McGuire's mouth.*

And my daughter puts her fork beside her plate and covers her stomach with her hands. "I'm sick," she says.

"No dessert unless you eat something," Mrs. Dexter says.

"I want to be a vegetarian," she says.

"You can't be a vegetarian, you don't like any vegetables," Mrs. Dexter says.

"I'm not going to eat any animals," my daughter says. "All I'm
going to eat is lettuce with Italian dressing and Kentucky Fried Chicken
Nuggets."

Mrs. Dexter says, "Where do you think Kentucky Fried Chicken
Nuggets come from?"

She says, "Kentucky."

And then she says, "Dad isn't eating either."

Which is true. I ever want to lose weight, all I've got to do is think
about the guy who graded my driveway. Or his lawyer. Have I mentioned lawyers lately? You may remember I began compiling a list of all

the good ones in the Delaware Valley last year, and already we have two. Who could have guessed the list would grow this fast?

Anyway, we compromise. I quit talking about McGuire, my daughter agrees to eat eight bites of meat, and Mrs. Dexter unnarrows her eyes and says it is nice to have everybody home for Sunday dinner.

After dinner we all head into the living room and sit down. Mrs. Dexter reads the annual *New York Times* special magazine section on spending $80,000 on living-room furniture, my daughter turns on the television set and watches a show called *Punky Brewster*, and I start to build a fire.

And then I look outside on the porch, and there is McGuire. He is standing at the window, covered with dirt, holding a bone in his mouth.

It isn't an ordinary bone.

"What's he got now?" Mrs. Dexter says.

I am not going to say it was a human leg, but I have seen more than my share of them in X-rays, and I am not going to say it wasn't. There are little cemeteries everywhere in the area, and my thought is that dead animals are one thing, but if he's turned into a grave robber, we're going to have to seek professional counseling.

"What's wrong?" Mrs. Dexter is saying. "Has that rascal got another rabbit?"

41

Back in October, the Sacramento Association of Realtors had a golf tournament at Northridge Country Club, and it was followed, as these things often are, by a banquet.

A young woman who works for a local title company was sitting at one table, a young real estate agent was sitting at the next. "I know him from the last office where I worked," she said. "He used to do a lot of business there. He'd come in, tall and clean-cut, the All-American boy."

Toward the end of the banquet, this All-American boy leaned across his chair and offered the young woman a glass of his wine. "He asked me if I could get him World Series tickets," she said. "It's part of the business. People give clients tickets to the World Series. This guy wanted them for a glass of wine. I told him he could keep his wine.

"He said he was only joking, and said maybe we could go out for a drink later and talk about doing some business. I was really tired, but then he asked again and I figured I'd have one quick drink, talk to him a little, and then go home and get in bed."

She followed the real estate agent in her car to the Peppermill—a great place to talk if you can read lips—and they went inside and had one drink. "He put his arm around me and I told him to get away," she said. "He's married and I didn't want anything to do with him in that way. I didn't feel particularly threatened and he moved away."

The woman does not like the Peppermill and said she wanted to leave. "He asked if we could go outside and chat in his car. I was tired and wanted to go home, but he kept asking . . ."

And so she got into his expensive, successful real estate agent car, and he started the engine.

"He asked if I wanted to go drive down by the river," she said, "and I told him no. I told him I was really tired. He pulled into a church parking lot and stopped. I still wasn't afraid. I'm thirty, I'm single, people have come on to me before when I didn't want them to. He looked at me and said, 'You seem nervous.'

"I said, 'I feel awkward,' and then he came across the seat and tried to kiss me. I said no.

"He said, 'Why not?'

"I said, 'Because I said no.' I'm not about to argue with somebody about that. Then he grabbed my wrists and held them both with one hand, over my head, and got on top of me. I said, 'Look, stop it.' But he just seemed to be somewhere else.

"He said, 'I really want you.'

"He was pulling at my clothes by then. I began yelling at him, shaking him, butting him when I could get loose, but it was like he didn't notice."

The All-American boy real estate agent had sexual intercourse with the woman from the title company.

"He finished and I was crying," she said. "He got off me and went back to his side of the car, and I put my hands over my head and my eyes and couldn't stop crying. Nothing like this ever happened to me before."

The All-American boy started his car and drove back to the Peppermill, neither of them speaking.

"When we got to the parking lot, he said, 'We both have a lot at stake,' and I jumped out of the car before it even stopped rolling."

The woman called a friend, went home, and then called the Sheriff's Department.

The All-American boy was arrested at home and released that same night.

The woman went to Mercy San Juan Hospital, where she underwent an unpleasant examination to gather evidence of rape, and then she went home and took a long, hot shower. She was afraid to sleep in her own house that night and stayed with the friend she'd called.

The case went from the Sheriff's Department to the district attorney and was turned over to a prosecutor named Jeff Rose. "I talked to him Monday [a week after the incident]," the woman said. "I was an emotional wreck, but I tried not to show it. I told him the story, and he told me he'd have to talk with his supervisor. He thought there might be a problem convincing a jury, that there might not be enough physical evidence."

A week later, she spoke with him on the telephone.

The district attorney's office had decided not to prosecute. "I couldn't really talk," she said. "I was crying and didn't want him to hear it. I just said yes and no when he asked questions, and then we hung up."

For his part, Rose said it was a hard decision.

"She's a very nice, presentable witness," he said. "But he's presentable too. That wouldn't stop me if the case was there, but you look at him the way a jury would—he's got no record, a very clean-looking guy. Her story is similar to his, except at the end, he says it was more consensual. There is no evidence that real force was used or real fear was displayed, and those are requirements for forcible rape under the law.

"I believed what she told me, but I'm left with a question about if she let him know she didn't want to . . ."

And that was that.

The law, of course, is imperfect.

It favors the rich over the poor, the strong over the weak. And sometimes—in the front seat of a parked car, for instance—it isn't there at all.

And so in a few moments a young woman's life is changed, and then she is dropped off in a parking lot and left. She goes to the sheriff, she goes to the hospital, she sleeps at a friend's home, she ends up in counseling.

She moves through her days holding it all inside, and falls apart when she is alone.

The All-American boy goes home in his expensive car, and a day or two later he's back at the office, shaking hands, talking to home buyers about safe neighborhoods.

And there's not a thing that can be done about it now.

42

In an editorial delivered even before the last of the serious charges against one of the defendants was decided, *USA Today*, the nation's largest general-circulation newspaper, urged its readers last week to put the matter of the beating of Reginald Denny behind them.

I single out *USA Today*, but the sentiments expressed in its lead editorial Oct. 20 were echoed wherever right-minded, socially progressive people gathered.

The paper applauded the jury for bringing to the trial "that community's sense of right and wrong."

The newspaper also seemed pleased that the jury had not been able to decipher what was in the minds of Damian Williams and Henry Watson eighteen months ago as they tried to crush Denny's skull.

Their state of mind, the newspaper said, was hard to judge in the aftermath of another jury's having found officers of the Los Angeles Police Department not guilty of the videotaped beating of Rodney King. That verdict, after all, sent "thousands of otherwise law-abiding people to loot and burn."

You may remember those otherwise law-abiding citizens grinning as they came through the broken windows of stores carrying television sets. You may remember they set fire to the Korean community. How, one wonders, has *USA Today* determined that those were "law-abiding citizens" before the riot.

And what does that say about the people of South Central Los Angeles who refused to steal and burn and maim? Are those law-abiding citizens indistinguishable from the ones who rioted?

It seems likely to me that a riot is one of those times when people are most themselves. When the choices are presented—when it is possible to loot and burn without consequences—some people choose to loot and burn and some don't.

But more to the point, what *USA Today* is saying, what the defense attorneys in the case were saying, is that blood lust is an excuse for murderous behavior. That not knowing specifically what was in the mind of Damian Williams as he hurled the brick at the dazed and bleeding Denny and then danced off in victory precludes a jury from finding that act as having "malicious intent."

But be clear about this: what you saw happen to Reginald Denny was the closest thing to a lynching that has ever appeared on mass-market television. Through no fault of his attackers, Denny failed to die, but that is the single distinction between what happened to him from the lynchings that have stained the country's history for hundreds of years.

There is nothing with less conscience than a lynch mob. That is as true in Los Angeles as it was in the rural South fifty years ago. The notion that aggrieved minorities are not accountable, after all, boils down finally to the assumption that they somehow lack the ability to act otherwise.

Beyond that, the idea that being part of a mob in some way mitigates responsibility for a person's actions flies in the face of every good impulse we have. And the idea that we now decide matters of innocence and guilt out of fear of violent consequences makes a joke of criminal justice.

No criminal justice system is perfect, of course (quoting *USA Today* again, "If at times some see [juries] as too lenient, that's better than the alternative: Railroading people for crimes they either didn't commit or for which there were extenuating circumstances"). But if the system we have simply reflects the popular politics of the day or the region of the country, then we head right back to the days when white men murdered black men without worrying about going to jail.

There has been no battle in the history of this country as important as the one for civil rights. Thousands of human beings have died to make us accountable for what we are and what we have done, to give us our conscience.

They did not die to make it safe for a thug like Damian Williams to throw a brick at the head of a helpless man he did not know and then walk away free because of the color of anyone's skin.

43

The kid has been in the Navy four years, but he must have been standing on his toes when they measured him to see if he met the height requirement. He sounds big enough, though. That voice is nine miles of bad road.

In four years, he'd become a second-class petty officer, and if he'd stayed out of trouble he would have made first-class on his reenlistment. He had a wife and a daughter, and a plan to retire when he was forty-one. He wanted to be a commercial diver. He was twenty-five years old.

He'd been stationed at Mayport Naval Base in Jacksonville, Florida, but he was on the way home to Philadelphia. His transfer had been approved, his wife and daughter had already moved up to Delaware County. He was living on board the aircraft carrier *Forrestal*, which was scheduled to make a six-month cruise to the Mediterranean, and then come here for overhaul.

The kid decided to spend his last two days in Florida scuba diving, and took a tent and his diving equipment to Hannah Park, near the naval base.

He'd set up his tent and had a fire going when the two men walked into his camp. He thought they were campers too. "The first thing I knew," he said, "one of them had hit me over the head with a bottle and the other one punched me in the stomach. I thought he'd punched me."

The men tied the kid's arms to small trees, and his legs to the pegs he had used to set up his tent. They took his scuba gear, his wedding band, and six dollars in cash. They also slit his throat from one ear to the other, and the medical examiner would say he had been "disemboweled." That was the punch in the stomach.

"They didn't have to use the knife," he said. "I'm little. They could have just kicked the hell out of me and taken what they wanted."

He thinks it took about an hour to get loose.

Detective Buddy Terry of the Jacksonville Sheriff's Department said it took another six or seven hours to crawl a hundred yards to the road. "He had to hold his stomach with both hands to keep his intestines from falling out," he said. "He was also smart enough to keep his head down, or he'd have bled to death."

Someone in a car found him in the morning, and a helicopter took him to the hospital.

"They ran three pints of cleaning fluid through him just to get the leaves and dirt out of his abdominal cavity," Terry said. "I been on the force thirteen years, and it's the worst I ever saw. I wouldn't have given you a dime for his chances."

The kid remembers a nurse getting ready to shave his stomach and the surgeon telling her there wasn't time. The sheriff's report says the knife cut through his "voice box" and an interior vein. The doctors sewed up what they could and inserted a tube into his stomach so he could eat without strangling.

The Navy called the kid's wife, and after she'd finished talking to them, she got ready to make funeral arrangements.

But three weeks later he was still alive. "I walked in there to see how he was doing," Terry said, "and he was sitting up in bed drinking beer through the tube into his stomach. I won't ever forget that."

He also won't forget that as soon as the kid got out of the hospital, the first place he went was Hannah Park. "I don't know why I went back there," the kid said.

"I know why," the cop said. "He was lookin' for them. And the first thing he sees when he gets there, I swear, is the two guys who almost killed him."

The two men are on trial in Florida now.

The kid doesn't want his name in the paper, he doesn't want people to know where he lives. He babysits the daughter while his wife goes to school, trying to become a registered nurse. He is waiting now, with his scars and shortness of breath, for a medical discharge from the Navy.

He doesn't know what he'll do after that. You can't be a commercial diver if you have trouble breathing.

"You don't think about it," he says, "but there's people in this world who don't give a damn about your plans. You don't think about it, but they could be waiting for you just around the next corner."

44

I got a collect call last week from Big John's Bar on Armitage Street in Chicago. I said to the operator, "Who?"

She said, "What was your name, sir?"

The man in Chicago said, "This is Big John's Bar."

The operator said, "Big John's Bar is calling collect for Mr. Dexter."

"Well, good," I said. I never got a phone call from a bar before, at least not one in Chicago.

The operator said, "Are you Mr. Dexter?"

"Yes, I am."

"Go ahead, please," she said. "And thank you for using AT&T."

The call was from a man who used to live in Yardley. He said he missed the *Daily News* and Mort Crim and Vince Leonard.

"But that's not what I'm calling about," he said. "I'm calling about Villanova. Somebody ought to write this."

I said, "I know we'll have a special section, I'll send you one . . ."

"No, I don't need a special section," he said. "I got a story for you, okay? All right, Big John's is kind of a sports bar. A lot of different kinds of guys hang out, some of them connected guys from River Forest, some of them are just regular nice guys, some of them are just regular assholes. So you know people from seeing them there, but you don't know who they are, okay?

"Anyway, before the [NCAA basketball] tournament starts, the bar has a drawing. You put ten bucks in the pool and pick a team out of a hat. Whoever gets the winner gets all the money. Six hundred and forty dollars, there ain't no second place. And there's a lot of interest here, enough so all the chances sell out the first day.

"Now, there's this guy who drinks here that graduated Villanova. Real nice, regular kind of guy. He minds his own business, says something, it isn't always bullshit, buys his share of the drinks without making it a production, like some of the guys with River Forest addresses.

"So everybody likes this guy, even if he did graduate Villanova, and nobody minds much when he reaches into the hat and pulls out Georgetown. It's a *'Well, if I couldn't have got it I'm glad he did'* kind of thing.

"Guys that don't know him that well, they could say, *'At least Rodney didn't get it.'*

"Rodney is the biggest pain in the ass in Chicago. Everybody hates him, even in here. He's loud all the time, he's always thinkin' somebody is trying to rob him, take advantage of him. The nicest thing I ever heard anybody say about him was he went on vacation.

"So anyway, the guy from Villanova picks Georgetown, Rodney gets Villanova and immediately begins to bitch. Says he's got the worst team in the tournament. And every game Villanova wins, it's the same thing. He's always got the worst team left.

"He keeps saying he'll trade with anybody still in it. Especially whoever's got Georgetown.

"Okay, now the guy who's got Georgetown is getting a bad conscience. I mean he's from the Philly area, he keeps track of everything Villanova does. He took it hard when Jumbo Elliott died, that's the way he is. And the thing is, he can use the six hundred bucks like anybody else, but what he really cares about is that Villanova don't embarrass itself.

"And the farther along the tournament goes, the more it bothers him that he has to worry about somebody upsetting Georgetown when all he wants to worry about is Villanova.

"So the tournament goes to the Final Four, and Georgetown kills St. John's and Villanova beats Memphis State, which figured to be the last team with even an outside shot at giving Georgetown a game, right?

"And the guy from Villanova can't stand the thought of watching the last game knowing he's got six hundred dollars on Georgetown. I mean, it's the NCAA finals, right? And he just doesn't want to have to sit and watch it with mixed emotions.

"So he comes into the bar on Monday night to see the game, and the guy that's got Villanova, he's over on one side abusing a bartender about what kind of a world it is that he's in the finals of the NCAAs and he's got the worst team that ever got there.

"And then the guy from Villanova does something that nobody can believe. He walks over to the guy right before the game starts and says, 'You want Georgetown?'

"The guy, of course, thinks the guy from Villanova is trying to rob him. That, or it's a cruel joke. He says, 'All right, what do you want?'

"The guy from Villanova says he wants Villanova.

"The guy says, 'For how much?'

"The guy from Villanova doesn't know what he's talking about. The guy everybody hates says, 'I'll tell you what I'll do. I'll give you fifty dollars to trade teams, take it or leave it.'

"And the guy from Villanova, he takes it.

"I just thought you'd want to know."

45

ast Friday was my sixth anniversary.

The way I remember it, six years ago on a hot, miserable, sticky Friday afternoon I walked into a bank in New Jersey with a date, and a man I didn't know or like, who had gravy stains on his clothes, asked us if we would love, honor, and obey each other forever. The man was the president of the bank and the mayor of the town, and according to the laws of New Jersey he was entitled to marry us.

And I went along with it. Look, a lot of people had driven into New Jersey that afternoon to see us get married, and my first obligation is always to the fans.

The way my wife remembers it, we walked into a bank in New Jersey on a warm, romantic summer afternoon. Inside, I promised to love, honor, and obey her forever, and then disappeared until six o'clock the next morning.

She remembers it that way and mentions it every August, possibly because I haven't done anything to complain about since. She says it means I am not romantic. "You know," she said this year, "a lot of wives wouldn't have understood that."

"That's why I married you," I said. "From the minute I saw you, I knew you were understanding. The day you threw that ashtray past my head and through the window, I said to myself, 'There is somebody who understands.'" Then I said, "But look at it from my point of view. We'd only been married two hours and you were already trying to take my Friday nights away." And then I said, "Why dwell in petty details when you've got it all now?" It was ten o'clock in the morning, and I was taking her to one of the best diners in the Williamstown, New Jersey, area for breakfast. Just the two of us, and a couple of the dogs.

"All what?" she said.

"All of me," I said. "I've changed. I'm twice as romantic as I used to be."

It was, in fact, another one of those warm, romantic Aug. 19ths, and one of the dogs was drooling on my wife's shoulder. The other one was riding with her head out the window. I leaned over at a stoplight and gave Mrs. Dexter a bite of a sexual nature on the eye.

Considering the heat and the time of day, there is no question that it was a romantic thing to do. Six years can change a woman, though. She stuck her fingers into my throat and said she hated it when I bit her eyes. I smiled and looked into her eyes and said, "I know better."

I found a place to park under some picturesque trees, and, taking her by the hand, I led her into the diner. I gave the lady in white shoes a dollar and said, "A private booth, you know what I mean."

She led us to a booth with a view of the Black Horse Pike, and I slid in next to Mrs. Dexter and began whispering in her ear. First I read her the menu, then all the selections on the jukebox. People were all around us, but nobody realized what we were doing.

"Peter," she said, "please get on the other side of the table now."

"I love it when you play hard to get," I said. Looking deep into her eyes, I moved around the table and slid in across from her. Looking deep into her eyes, I picked up our water glasses and put one in her hands, and entwined our arms and drank.

"What's it going to be," the waitress said.

"Tongue," I said. "A tongue sandwich." Mrs. Dexter looked at the ceiling.

"What number is that?" the waitress said. She looked over my shoulder at the menu.

"I don't know," I said.

"Well, we don't have it if it's not on the menu," the waitress said.

My wife said she would like scrambled eggs.

"Number three?" the waitress said. "French fries with that?"

"No," my wife said. "Hash browns."

The waitress was gone fifteen minutes. I held Mrs. Dexter's hand and whispered to her of some of the evenings we'd had together. Then, looking deep into her eyes, I opened up the ketchup bottle and ran one of my fingers around the rim. "The French are not the only men in the world who know what a woman wants," I said.

And then the waitress came back with egg-salad sandwiches, and that ruined the whole mood. It must have, because as soon as she left, Mrs. Dexter said, "Look, it's our anniversary. For old times' sake, why don't you go out till six o'clock in the morning?"

46

The year I turned five my family moved to Milledgeville, a little town in central Georgia, where my father taught physics at the military college.

Our house was on a red clay road, next to a pine woods and a sawmill. The plums came off the trees hot from the sun, and I had a cocker spaniel puppy that followed me everywhere I went. Nobody wore shoes all summer long, except to Sunday school.

The puppy was almost grown when he was killed. A city garbage truck hit him and left him where he stopped rolling, beside the road on a hill half a mile from the house. I heard about it from a kid named Kenny Durkin, who was the kind of kid who would spend half the afternoon looking for you to be the one to tell you your dog was dead.

He is probably working for a newspaper now.

Anyway, Kenny found me down at the sawmill, walking around the inside edge of a round cement building where they burned scrap wood. The building had a clay floor, dug out into a pit, and if you fell off the edge, that's where you ended up, in there burning with the wood.

I went there once or twice a week and waited for the watchman to chase me out. I wanted to see it when he fell off the edge.

Kenny Durkin stuck his head into the open door and yelled at me. "Peedah," he said, "the city truck done run over your dog and he's dead."

We ran from the sawmill to the hill where the city truck had left my dog, stopping every now and then for Kenny Durkin to get his breath.

By the time we got to the place on the hill, the sun had baked one side of the dog's coat so hot you could hardly touch him. The flies were all over his ears and eyes, and I brushed them away and picked him up. He had never seemed so heavy before.

I carried the puppy up the hill, stumbling under the weight. I fell in some stones, and he rolled into the ditch. I pulled him out by a leg, and there was a trail of blood and bubbles where his mouth had slid along the ground.

It was cool in the ditch and I thought about leaving him there, but there was something worse in that than in what had already happened.

I picked him up and started for home again. I moved him from one side to the other, trying to get rid of the ache in my muscles. But the ache got worse and worse and the next time I fell I couldn't pick him up again, so I dragged him home by the leg.

And I was crying as much from the ache as for the dog.

A neighbor woman came out from behind her screen door and told me to leave the puppy out in the street. "Come on in and have some ice tea," she said. "Your daddy'll be by directly."

But I was dizzy from the heat, watching my feet move, one in front of the other against the red Georgia dirt, and I didn't answer.

And a long time went by before I got the puppy home.

I remembered all that last week. I was driving some back roads near Elmer, New Jersey, when I came on a kid carrying a dead dog.

He was older than I had been—he might have been nine or ten—but you don't pick the times you grow up, they pick you. The dog was a mongrel, maybe thirty-five pounds, and the kid was trying to balance it in front of him on the frame of his bicycle.

He'd pedal a few yards, then the handle bars would get away from him. He'd reach up to steady himself and the dog would fall off onto the road. I stopped the car behind him and asked what had happened.

"She got run over," he said. The dog was lying at his feet and the boy couldn't control his voice any more than the handle bars. Everything was falling apart all at once.

I said, "I can help you get her home."

He said, "I can do it." He picked up the dog and lay her across the bicycle. The eyes swung in the air. The boy got back on the bicycle and tried again, the dog fell off again. "Oh, Goldie," he said.

Then the kid laid his dog across the bicycle, held her there with one hand and began to walk toward a red and white farmhouse a long ways down the road. From the back you could see him crying. Maybe if I'd asked him again he would have let me drive him home.

But, then, maybe after the dog was buried, getting her home by himself would be all he would have to take her place.

47

have a story today about a tooth. A cap, actually. The cap sat in my mouth on the lower right side, fastened there by a post that was cemented into the root. I'd had it six years, long enough so I'd forgotten all the trouble I went through getting it put there.

That is the truest kind of love—of teeth or wives or friends—when you finally get to the point that you don't remember the trouble they gave you before they straightened out.

As the story begins, the tooth is six years old and I am eating a little something Mrs. Dexter put together in the kitchen, when I bite a piece of wire and feel the tooth come loose. You might wonder what wire is doing in a little something Mrs. Dexter had put together. In fact, I myself wondered the same thing out loud, and the answer is—and I believe this is an accurate quote—"You think you hold a roast together with Elmer's glue?"

Strange as this is going to sound, I didn't know you had to hold a roast together at all. I said, "Shit, cows hold together, don't they?"

And she says, "Cows have bones."

So, you lose a cap, you gain a little insight into nature's plan. I'd have to be pretty ungrateful to complain, so instead I just reached into my mouth and pressed the cap back into place.

"Remind me to get this fixed," I said.

Two days passed, and on the morning of the third she said, "Did you remember to get your tooth fixed yet?"

I was eating scrambled eggs at the time, carefully watching out for wire. After all, chickens have bones too. I put down my fork and stared at her. "Will you get off my back?" I said. "I'll get it fixed when I get it fixed, and after I do that, that's when it'll be done."

"Aren't we touchy?" she said.

Touchy. Now there is one of my favorite, all-time words. And I love *we* in that particular context. In fact, "Aren't we touchy?" may be my favorite question in this world. I got up without answering and fixed myself a piece of chocolate cake and a Coke. When I get angry I let my actions speak for themselves.

"My, that looks nutritious," she said.

"Well," I said, "it beats fence."

I left the house and drove to the dentist's office. It was Wednesday, though, and he was closed. He is always closed on Wednesdays. I think he plays golf.

So I forgot about the cap and went on to work, and then to the gym.

And that's where I was when I swallowed it.

I'd been fooling around in the ring and got bumped on the chin with another person's shoulder. I stepped back and opened my mouth—I had a sore jaw and wanted to make sure it would still bite. A sore jaw, by the way, makes you appreciate less-fortunate people in this world who have no jaws at all. After all, how do they eat wire?

Anway, the jaw seemed all right, and I closed my teeth down on my mouthpiece again and fooled around a while longer, and when we finished I took out my mouthpiece and the tooth was gone. I opened my mouth and looked in the mirror. I poked everywhere with my finger, but the truth is there isn't anyplace to hide a tooth in there. And then I remembered swallowing something in the third or fourth round, and I knew the tooth was history.

I went back to the office and called home. I told my wife what had happened. She said—and I believe this is an accurate quote—"Well, it'll come out, you know."

I hung up and walked into the city room and told my friend from Texas what had happened. Only the insensitivity of her remark keeps me from mentioning her name. She said—and I believe this is an accurate quote—"Well, you'll just have to get you a pail and a shovel, won't you?"

I went from her desk to the other desks, then I called people in Tennessee, California, New York, Montana, and Chicago and told them all what had happened, looking for somebody to say, "Damn, that's strange." That's all I wanted out of this, just somebody to say he'd never heard of it before.

It didn't happen. Everybody said the same thing.

It turns out that I have friends and relatives all over the country—people who never got beyond cutting up frogs in high school biology, some of whom believe warts are caused by handling toads, some of whom believe in bleeding the sick—and every one of those people knows what happens to a swallowed tooth.

And cannot wait to tell you.

48

One of the earliest things I can remember is sitting on the railroad tracks down the hill from my grandmother's house in Vermillion, South Dakota, waving at airplanes because I thought my Uncle Buck might be inside.

I was four or five years old, and Uncle Buck was always going somewhere. Usually, I guess, it was in a Cadillac. He traveled with his partner, Jack Lowe. They rode in the Cadillac, and they hired a couple of guys to follow them in the truck.

The truck carried two Baldwin pianos. They rolled out of the back as heavy and black as the train to Sioux City, and you could see your face in the shine. I never cared for the music, but I loved to watch those pianos unload.

The music itself was classical. Uncle Buck and Jack Lowe dressed in bow ties and tails, and played duo pianos all over the world. *Whittemore and Lowe*. Jack was short and had beautiful manners. Uncle Buck had manners until he drank too much scotch, at which time he became colorful.

Even colorful, he was never mean.

I don't know enough about it one way or another to have an opinion, but I have been told they were as good at what they did as anybody there was.

Uncle Buck was the fourth of five children, the only boy. He was named after his father, who was an early surveyor in South Dakota, an all-America football player, and later the coach of the team at the University of Vermillion.

I do not know what my grandfather thought of his namesake, five years old, sitting at the piano in the living room playing Brahms and Mendelssohn. My grandfather was dead before I was born, and nowhere in the house full of pictures were there any of the two of them together.

He took his talent from his mother, and his sisters never begrudged him that, or the attention it brought him. At least not that I saw. He sent money for Christmas and made them feel special at parties after his concerts. They would drive halfway across big states, towing husbands and children, to hear him play.

They never forgot his birthday, because Uncle Buck was never married and didn't have a family of his own. And even in the days when there was a new Cadillac every year and a yacht off Long Island and his picture was in *Time* magazine, there was always an unspoken agreement, I think, that in some way he was secretly sad.

I never saw much of that myself. When I was eight years old, the man got me and a dog drunk at my cousin's wedding. He went on the *Today Show* in the early fifties, and when Dave Garroway asked him to play a little something, Uncle Buck sat down underneath the piano, reached up over his head as if he were going to chin himself on the keyboard, and gave him "Mary Had a Little Lamb."

I was in my grandmother's living room, along with half of the town, when he did that. Buck had bought her the first television set in Vermillion. Grandmother went into her bedroom for a long time, and when she came out her guests all complimented her on how smart Bucky looked in his new jacket.

"He's a smarty, all right," she said.

The last time I saw him was in Traverse City, Michigan, where my brother Tom and my cousin Bill and I drove a truck more or less into his motel room, about fourteen hours before he was scheduled to play. We had been heading north that afternoon into the Upper Peninsula when we saw the signs for the concert. It took eight hours on bar phones to locate the right motel.

He got out of bed naked and white-haired, looking into high beams, until he made out who it was. Then he said, "Holy shit, it's happened," like it had been out there waiting for him for twenty years. He wouldn't come drinking with us, though; he wanted to look good at the concert.

He was always thinking about his looks. He would finish a Canadian tour in the winter with a tan. I never knew how he did that.

I never knew anything, really. It's one thing to love somebody, something else to understand what's going on in his life.

The last time I ever talked to him he was in a hospital on Long Island, forty pounds too light, his voice as weak as his body. The nurse was holding the phone. He said he'd fallen in the night and put a lump on his head the size of an egg. "It better go down tomorrow," he said. "I look awful."

Then his voice faded, and wandered away, like the sound of an airplane from a long time ago. It was quiet, and then I said, "Take care of yourself," but I knew he wasn't there. The truth is, I always knew he wasn't in the airplanes, either.

49

I was sitting at the window Friday afternoon, watching the blizzard freeze the livestock in the backyard, when it suddenly hit me that I had to have a package of pinwheel cookies.

"Everything is closing," Mrs. Dexter said, "and the roads are getting worse by the minute." She was just coming out of the shower.

"I know, I know," I said. They listen to KYW radio fifteen minutes, they think they understand everything. I put on my coat and my boots and walked outside to the car. There was a coat of snow around it a foot thick, and inside it was dark and quiet. The engine turned over and started and I turned on the radio.

It said the roads were getting worse by the minute.

But when I need a package of pinwheel cookies, I need a package of pinwheel cookies.

There are, of course, two schools of thought on driving in a blizzard. One school holds that you ought to scrape the foot of snow off the windows so you can see what's coming, and the other school holds that it doesn't matter if you can see it or not—when it's your turn, it's your turn.

I put the car in reverse and backed out of the driveway. Mrs. Dexter was watching from the front door, and as soon as I was in the street, she came running out of the house in boots and a blanket, flashing a little leg as the snow blew up under the blanket. She pounded on my window.

I couldn't see much of her face, but I could tell she wanted to talk to me. It's uncanny sometimes, the way that woman and I communicate. I rolled down the window a couple of inches and she shouted to me over the wind. "You backed over the mailbox," she said.

I shouted back, "Were you expecting something important?"

And then she was running back through the snow toward the house, and the wind was blowing up the blanket, and covering her footprints in the snow as soon as she got through making them. Her legs were already a little blue.

If I am ever lonely and stuck in the trenches over in France, fighting another world war against Germany, that is what I will remember. Blue legs against the snow. I dropped the car into a forward gear and started up the road, looking for pinwheel cookies.

I don't know if you've ever had a pinwheel cookie. They're chocolate with marshmallow inside, but the thing that separates them from regular cookies is the feel. They have a solid, precise quality that is only found on these particular cookies and on the dials to combination safes.

You can *control* a pinwheel cookie.

I drove out to the highway, thinking of blue legs. "If you do not *have* to be out on the roads," the radio said, "then for goodness' sake stay off them. It's serious out there now."

The nearest store to my house is six miles away, unless you count the hardware store, which I don't. I got there just as the manager was locking the door. I recognized him from the pictures they hang inside on the wall. There must be a dozen of them. Produce manager, business manager, meat manager, assistant produce manager. They go down the list of jobs until there is nothing left to manage.

"I know this is going to sound funny," I said, "but I need some pinwheel cookies."

The manager finished locking the door. "That doesn't sound funny at all," he said.

I got back in the car and headed farther up the road. There were accidents every two miles, the most impressive of which involved a truck and two cars on the north-south freeway, coming into Philly. By that time I had tried three more stores, and all of them were closed or closing. I had that feeling like not being able to find a motel.

Then the truck jackknifed, the car in back of it stopped, the next car didn't. Everybody got out and looked at their back ends and front ends and shook their heads, blaming the weather. The woman driving the car that caused the accident said, "It's their own fault, they can't keep the snow off the highway."

She had been grocery shopping. I could see the packages in the front seat. I said, "You wouldn't happen to have any pinwheel cookies in there . . ."

The next accident I have to report occurred on Vine Street, in the city. A car was coming out of a gas station, another car wasn't going to let it in. They came together at maybe two miles an hour, looking right at each other, and then they bumped fenders.

I didn't stop for it—nobody had any groceries—but I figured out something then that I've wondered about since the day I showed up in this city. Thirty inches of snow can fall on Vermillion, South Dakota, and people get around. Six inches stops everything in Philadelphia or New York. The reason isn't that Vermillion has more snowplows or less cars.

The reason is that in Vermillion, South Dakota, people give each other a little room.

That doesn't make South Dakota a better place than Philadelphia, of course.

What makes South Dakota better than Philadelphia is that, hell or high water at five o'clock Friday afternoon, you can find pinwheel cookies.

50

It's a Sunday in Milwaukee, and the buffet is $4. Chicken, ribs, four different kinds of pizza. It is driving Garcia crazy.

Garcia is the day manager. He stands behind the ribs, mothering them, keeping track of each one that's taken. He has posted homemade signs everywhere. "Take as Much as You Want. But Eat What You Take," and "Clean Your Plate If You Want More," and "You May Not Take Buffet Food Outside the Restaurant."

When he's not mothering the ribs, Garcia is inspecting the food left on dirty plates. He picks up half-eaten pieces of chicken and makes a noise that's full of anguish, and although he does not speak directly to the customers, the chicken leg he is holding is meant to be a lesson to us all.

Uneaten pieces, by the way, go back into the kitchen. If you watch Garcia much, you don't eat the chicken.

The kid comes in about two in the afternoon. He is six feet tall, his body is a giant accident of the sort that happens in the kitchen, spilled and settled all over the floor. His two friends are smaller, and they make him fifteen or sixteen years old.

He stands in front of the buffet signs a long time, reading the rules. Garcia pretends he isn't there. "Hey, mister," one of the friends says, "is this all you can eat for four dollars?"

Garcia looks up and points to the signs. "That's what it says."

The friend says, "No time limit?" Garcia says, "Time limit? Does it say time limit?" The friend smiles and nods his head at the kid. "The drinks are extra," Garcia says. "The drinks are not included in the price of the meal."

The kid hands him a five-dollar bill and smiles. The friends smile too. "It's four dollars each," Garcia says.

One of the friends says, "We're not eatin', we just came to watch." The kid picks up a plate and walks over to the ribs. When he walks away, the plate is a half-foot tall. He puts them down on the table and goes back for a Pepsi-Cola.

"The drinks are extra," Garcia says. It is the last thing he has to hold on to.

The kid orders two twenty-ounce Pepsi-Colas and goes back to his friends and the ribs.

The kid is a vacuum cleaner. The whole rib goes into his mouth, you hear something wet happening and the bone comes out clean. He lines the bones up on the table. There are fourteen of them when the first plate is gone. When he goes back for more, Garcia smiles. "You're not still hungry," he says.

One of the friends hears him. "Mister," he says, "that was the appetizer." The kid loads up the plate, his fingers and face are covered with barbecue sauce, and everything he touches he marks.

About three ribs from the bottom of the second plate, the kid begins to slow down.

The first sign is that he starts looking at the ribs before he puts them in his mouth. He finishes the plate and heads back for more. There are twenty-nine bones on the table.

Garcia watches him load up. "You going to eat all that?" he says. "You can't take it out with you." He points to the sign that says that. The kid buys another Pepsi. Some of the other people in the restaurant notice what is going on and are moving in their chairs for a better look.

The kid eats two more ribs and belches. Then he breaks out into a sweat. One of the friends says, "Come on, Rocco, you said a hundred."

The kid blows, juggles his stomach, and picks up one last rib. He looks at it a long time and then runs into the bathroom.

The whole restaurant watches him all the way to the door, everybody hears the noises he makes inside, losing the ribs. Everybody but Garcia.

He has disappeared into the kitchen. When he comes back out he has a new sign, a great sign. The kid and his friends have gone, along with most everybody else. Appetites fell off after the kid hit the bathroom. Garcia uses a stapler to put it up. Perhaps the greatest sign in any restaurant anywhere in the world: NO THROWING UP.

51

One day my daughter asks me about chickens and eggs. She wants to know how a chicken does that. I begin to tell her about chickens, that for them it's as easy as blowing soap bubbles, but just then Mrs. Dexter comes through the front door, carrying two sacks of groceries. "What luck!" I say. All my theories of education include use of audiovisual aids.

Mrs. Dexter sets the groceries on the counter and heads back out to the car for more. I take an egg out of the refrigerator and when she comes back in I begin to follow her around the house.

As I close the distance, she begins to walk faster. "What are you trying to do now?" she says. She pulls a chair out behind her into my path, and begins to run for the bathroom. I am closer, though, and cut her off.

She turns and runs for the bedroom, beginning to squawk now. "Notice the panic," I tell my daughter. "That is why chickens are called chickens."

She gets to the door and turns around in time to see what I am carrying. Suddenly she becomes very serious and confrontational. "Peter," she says, "put that egg back in the refrigerator. We don't play with eggs in the house." She says that like it's store policy, like there is a sign over the door that says WE DON'T PLAY WITH EGGS IN THIS HOUSE.

As soon as she says it, though, Mrs. Dexter sees that she made a mistake. She sees a man with no respect for law and order. She tries to run, but I'm too close now. I grab her around the waist and lift her a few inches off the ground, and carry her back into the middle of the living room. She is kicking and biting and flapping her arms.

"The most important thing about getting chickens to lay eggs," I tell my daughter, "is to keep them calm. So what you should do is rub her on the beak and tell her we're all part of the same team."

"This is sick beyond words," Mrs. Dexter says, and so—gently, to keep her calm—I put her back down on the floor, pull out the waist of her jeans in back, and drop the egg into her pants.

"What we've got now," I explain to my daughter, "is a loaded chicken."

"And what we've got to do is keep her from getting away and hiding her egg. She'll try to lay it where no one can find it, and we want her to lay it here, so we can eat it."

My daughter says she doesn't want to eat any egg that's been where that one's been. And she no sooner says that than Mrs. Dexter runs off toward the bathroom, reaching behind her into her pants.

She steps into the bathtub and turns around, out of breath, her arms still in back trying to get the egg out. "Look at those eyes," I tell my daughter. "She's protecting her young now, and you don't ever want to get careless around a mother hen."

For half a second after I say that, Mrs. Dexter relaxes, and in that half-second I make my move and grab her again. She begins pulling my hair out with her teeth. Gently, to keep her calm, I carry her out of the bathtub and put her down on the floor.

Then I give her a little pat on the back and say, "Easy now."

And then my daughter gives her a little pat, a little lower, and says, "Easy now," too. And in that moment, Mrs. Dexter quits biting my hair and jerks away. She loses her balance and sits down on the closed toilet seat with a sound that I fear will haunt the marriage for a long time.

She stands up slowly, all the panic gone from her face. I pull back the waist of her jeans in back and look down there. It's hard to believe one egg could cause that kind of a mess. My daughter looks down there too, and begins a hysterical kind of laughing that will leave her with the hiccups the rest of the day.

Mrs. Dexter's face seems to settle on a look somewhere between controlled anger and profound regret, although what the woman could have to regret is beyond me.

"Get out of here," she says—not the voice you get when you call Eastern Airlines, but not unfriendly either, just sort of cool—and after my daughter and I leave the bathroom, she opens the door once and tosses out her jeans, and again to toss out her *Leave It to Beaver* undershorts.

She takes a shower, wraps herself in a towel, and comes out of the bathroom. I look at her face and think all is forgotten. It might be forgotten, too, except she looks down and sees one of the dogs licking the egg off her underwear.

She sees that and turns crazy. And when I tell her, "Hey, it's supposed to give him a shiny coat," she turns even crazier. And I think for a moment she's going Lizzy Borden on me. She doesn't, but the damage is done. This is, after all, my kid's role model. I mean, I understand that women have their moods, but right there in front of the child? Whatever happened to old-fashioned dignity, anyway?

52

This is a story about a man named Dally Aubin who got pushed too far by a pig, and I might as well break this to you now: its name was Dolly.

I love pig stories. They are my favorite kind of oral history.

Anyway, Dally lives in a remote part of central Florida with his wife, Nancy, and their two small daughters. The pig lived next door, and belonged to a neighbor that Dally did not trust.

"She's the kind," he said, speaking of the neighbor, not the pig, "that a cow wandered onto her property a couple of years ago, and the owner came to claim it back and she said it had torn up her fence and she wasn't returning it until she had a new fence. So the man said, 'Keep the cow,' and a month later it had a calf, and she kept that too."

All right, last year the woman's pig began showing up in Dally's yard, eating corn and scraps that Dally's wife left on the lawn for the squirrels.

"What we had was a rogue hog," he said. "Every morning I'd look out the window and there she was. I'd run it on home and a day or two later, there she was again. My little girls were two and four, and the sight of a seven-hundred-pound sow in the front yard scared them till they were afraid to go out the house."

So Dally visited the neighbor to explain the problem. "She said that hog was more trouble than it was worth and I ought to just go ahead and shoot it. I mentioned, though, that this woman is kind of funny about things like that, and I thought if I did it, I was probably going to end up paying for the hog, and I didn't want to do that."

The next morning, though, there it was again. "I'd just laid sod in the front yard," he said. "It looked like a bulldozer been in there, done the first day's work to put in a swimming pool.

"So I called a friend of mine who lives about fifteen minutes from here, and he agreed to come over and shoot the pig the next time I saw her in the yard. I told him I didn't ever want to see her again, except wrapped in white paper in the freezer."

Now, one of the reasons Dally called his friend instead of shooting the pig himself was that the friend had a .22 automatic, and that makes less noise than a 12-gauge shotgun, which is the only gun Dally owns.

"I didn't see any reason not to do this discreetly," he said.

And so a few days later, Dally's wife opened the front door at seven-thirty in the morning, and the pig was back.

"I called my friend," he said, "and then I went to the bathroom. Nancy stood in the bedroom, looking out the window. I was reading *Field and Stream*, and pretty soon Nancy says, 'Bob's here.' Then she said, 'He's got a gun.'

"Then I heard a shot. Blam. And I thought, 'Well, it's over.' Then I heard another shot. Blam. And then another one, and another. I said, 'My word, it sounds like a war.' "

Dally ran from the bathroom to the front yard and found Bob standing on the edge of the yard, looking in the direction of the neighbor that Dally did not trust.

"I asked him did he shoot the sow, and he said he did, but it hadn't done any good. He'd shot her behind the ear, and she'd just shook her head and walked off. He'd shot her twice more and she hadn't paid any attention.

"Then he says, 'What do we do now?' Have you ever noticed that nobody asks you that when you know what to do? Anyway, it looked to me like we had a situation here, where the hog was going to die, and the neighbor was going to have the Sheriff's Department in my front yard by afternoon.

"On the other hand, I couldn't see going on her property and hauling the pig back over here and shooting it some more. And so we ended up doing nothing, figuring we ought to let the rest of the day take care of itself, because we wasn't doing any good trying to steer it.

"And I went to work and Bob went to work, and when I came home, what's in my front yard? Dolly. I walked right past her, into the front door, and called Bob. And, unable to kill it, we decided we really ought to give the hog a chance to live. So Bob and I called more friends, and the next time Dolly came into the yard we called them in to help trap her.

"They arrived in two trucks, an unmarked police car, some kind of Jeep. There were six of us in all, every one a hundred ninety pounds or better, and we all went out to the back—she'd changed yards after Bob shot her—and tried to figure out a way to wrestle her into this little trailer Bob brought.

"Now, there is a principle in all this," he said. "The farther you are from a seven-hundred-pound pig, the easier it is to imagine wrestling her into a trailer. The closer you get, the less ways there are to do it. Then you start thinking, This animal's been shot three times that you know of, and didn't mind.

"And so we're out there an hour, an hour and a half, arguing, jumping at her, seeing if there's anything she's scared of. My two little girls come out on the porch to watch, and then Nancy. They're eating Twinkies. Finally, Nancy says, 'Well?'

"I said, 'We're thinkin'.'

"She said, 'About what?'

"I said, 'About how to move this pig into the trailer.'

"And she picks up a can of corn and comes off the porch, drops a little of it in front of the hog's nose, and then backs into the trailer, saying, 'Here, piggy, piggy, piggy,' and it followed her right in."

I said, "That must have been something to see."

And he said, "It was, until it followed her."

53

Friday night in the Northeast, about two blocks from Liberty Bell Race Track, three kids kicked an unarmed, off-duty Philadelphia policeman unconscious in front of his own house.

The kids were somewhere around twenty years old, and they had been sitting on top of a car across the street, drinking vodka, when the cop came home from visiting his mother.

He had his wife with him, and a seventeen-month-old baby.

The wife had seen these three before. They were not regulars on the corner, but they showed up sometimes to drink on weekends. The regulars drink there all the time. They break glass and yell and urinate in the front lawns of people who live on the street.

It is a fact that there are places in this city where the streets belong to the kids who drink on them, and sniff their paint thinner on them, and take their drugs. And it is a fact that once in a while they kick somebody senseless.

The cop is thirty-eight years old. His jaw was broken, he was cut.

His wife is thirty-two. They married late, two years ago, and had the baby ten months later.

"My husband, he doesn't like to carry his gun off duty," she said. "I don't know exactly why. He says he never wants to go through what cops go through when they have to use it off duty . . ."

Or doesn't want to use it at all. Sometimes when you get married a little later than other people, or have a baby when you're old enough to glimpse what that's about, it mellows you. You reach out a little farther to be fair, and if you forget what you're dealing with, it can get you hurt.

Because, I promise you, fairness does not exist on the streets run by drunk children.

The cop and his wife moved into the house in April. They were both brought up in tough sections of this city and wanted someplace safer for the baby. They thought it was the Northeast.

From the beginning, though, there were kids on the corner outside their windows, drinking late into the night, screaming, breaking glass. In the morning the cop and his wife would smell the urine as soon as they opened the front door.

"I wasn't so surprised that it went on," the wife said. "But what did get me was that nobody in the neighborhood cared. The attitude is like, 'These are my children, and if you don't like what they do, move. We've been here twenty years, you just got here.'"

And so the cop would call the cops.

And the cops would come, and the kids would leave the corner until the cops left the street, and then the kids would come back onto the corner and pick up where they'd left off.

And they began to insult the cop and his wife, and threaten them, building courage over the months.

And then, Friday, the cop and his wife and the baby came home, and the wife and baby went inside while the cop put a ladder away along the side of the house. The three kids were sitting on a car across the street, drinking vodka. They called the cop and his wife "motherfuckers," and the cop walked toward them.

He said, "How about taking that someplace else?" He showed them his badge, and one of them threw the vodka bottle at him, and he does not remember what happened next.

The wife said, "When I heard them, I went back outside. He was unconscious on the sidewalk and they were kicking him in the head. I yelled at them and turned the hose on them to get them off—just like animals. When I got to him, he came to enough to tell me to call for an 'assist officer' and get their license plate."

And she did, enough of it anyway.

The police are going to find these kids, and some of the residents of the Great Northeast—who believe living in one place twenty years entitles their children to turn the streets into a sewer—some of them are going to have to hire lawyers and attend hearings and make up lies about their sons' previous good behavior.

And maybe something will happen to a couple of these kids along the way, bad enough to scare the others. I hope so, because there is another side to all the mellowing I was talking about before.

You come to understand that you are half your baby's life.

And no eighteen- or twenty-year-old kid is going to take that away because he's drunk or dumb or mean.

Once you know the stakes, you will kill him first.

54

The woman is in her bedroom writing a letter when the banging starts at the front door. It is a little before ten o'clock at night, November 1; all three of her children are in bed and asleep.

Sue gets up and walks into the living room and hears his voice, yelling over the banging. "I got to talk to you . . ."

"Go away," she says.

The man is an old boyfriend, someone she hasn't seen in four months. He yells again that they have to talk, and beats on the door until it shakes the walls. She picks up the telephone and calls 911, reports that the man is trying to break into her house.

The dispatcher says someone will be right out, and then, while the woman still has the phone against her ear, the glass screen door shatters and the front door is kicked in.

The man walks a few steps into the room and stops. "He's in the house," she says into the phone.

The dispatcher tells her help is on the way.

The man stands still another moment while the woman's youngest daughter—she is eight—comes out of her bedroom, sleepy-eyed, to see what is causing all the noise.

"You want me to wait for the cops?" the man says.

She looks at her door frame, which is broken, and the hundreds of little pieces of broken glass spread across the floor.

"Yeah, I want you to wait," she says. "You're going to jail."

He had done something like this once before, choked her with the phone cord, and she let it go then.

Something in his face changes. "Then this is what I'm going to do while I wait," he says, and hits her in the face with his fist. The punch knocks her backward, almost into the youngest daughter, who begins to scream.

The other daughter, who is twelve, comes out of her bedroom, sees what is happening, and runs for the door in her bare feet, heading next door to her grandmother's house for help. The woman stops her before she runs into the glass.

The man turns and goes back through the door.

The woman thinks then that he is gone, and then hears the noise as he kicks in the headlights and the grille of her car. The woman picks up the phone and calls a friend, and is just asking for help when the man comes back inside and tears the receiver out of her hand.

The man takes a fistful of her hair in his hand and pulls her outside, dragging her through the glass to the car. She hears her daughters screaming then, but from a long way off, in a dream. He throws her onto the ground, punching her, kicking her in the face. He breaks her nose, cuts her lip in a way that will require twelve stitches, bruises her back and arms and head.

The screaming wakes up the woman's mother, who comes out of her house and stands with her grandchildren, begging him to stop.

And for a moment he does. He looks up at the older woman and asks if she wants him to come back later and do this again. Then he begins hitting the woman again, perhaps half a dozen more punches, and then he runs away.

A few neighbors begin to come out of their houses as he leaves, then an ambulance arrives, and finally the police. The woman thinks it is about half an hour since she called 911.

The woman tells the police what happened.

She tells them who the man is and where he works and two days later—after prodding from a lawyer—the police arrest the man and charge him with assault with a deadly weapon (kicking her in the face).

By this time the man has already called the woman twice, leaving messages on her answering machine saying he is sorry, that he was drunk, and that if she wants to press charges he'll turn himself in.

The man is held seven days after his arrest, until bail is dropped from $100,000 to $25,000, and he has been out now for over a week.

"I called the police," the woman said, "to ask if they wanted the tape recordings, but I haven't heard back. One of the police did tell me [the man] was saying I'd invited him in and hit him with the phone, and that there wasn't a mark on me when he left."

This kind of thing, of course, happens all the time, I guess because the world is full of real men.

Most likely, this one will plead to reduced charges and walk.

The woman had surgery on November 15 to correct her broken nose, and seems tough enough to handle the feelings that follow an assault like this.

The kids—who can say what seeing something like this does to kids?

"They seem all right," she says, "except [the younger daughter] is still having trouble sleeping . . ."

The woman has trouble sleeping too.

"The door won't lock now, the way he kicked it in," she said. "I sleep on the couch with a gun on the floor where I can reach it, and listen in the night for someone to break in."

55

was at Dr. Stan's office last week to talk about my throat. For the last couple of weeks, there's been a feeling in there that's hard to describe. "If you were a snake," I said, "and swallowed something that wasn't dead yet, this is what it would feel like when it tried to climb back out."

Dr. Stan was taking notes for my file when I said that. I saw the pencil stop moving, then start, then stop again. He looked up, measuring me, squinty eyes and a worried forehead.

"Dakota," he said, "have you been under any abnormal stress lately?"

By "abnormal stress" he means have I bitten anybody on the street. I thought over the last couple of weeks, and there wasn't anything out of the ordinary. I've got an old, blind, crippled, deaf, senile dog that is taking longer to die than a redwood, and a book coming out, and a bunch of bankers in Maryland who tell me that the way to borrow money to build a house is to wait until after it's built. I said to the bankers, "That is the dumbest thing I ever heard of."

They said, "Look at it from our point of view."

And, of course, every day when I come into work the office has more people in it. It's about like the airport in here now, except you can't buy insurance. And it scares me to say this, but no, none of this represents any kind of abnormal stress at all.

"Look," I said, "don't get me wrong. I don't actually think there's something alive in there trying to get out. I'm just trying to describe the feeling. I mean, what could be in there?"

Dr. Stan had me take off my shirt. He put his stethoscope against my chest and told me to take deep breaths. While I did that he moved the stethoscope from one place to another, nodding, making me feel like I was doing it right, and finally he centered it on the spot where I felt the movement. "Can you hear it?" I said.

He shook his head. "Completely clear, Dakota," he said.

He wrote down "completely clear" in my file, and then told me to turn around. I did. He climbed on the footstool and put his hands around my neck and began to explore my thyroid gland. Which is medical talk for strangulation. "That's a little tender," I said. "But it feels like the right spot."

Dr. Stan shook his head. "No," he said, "it's not your thyroid." He sat down in his chair and rested his chin in the cup of his hand. "Does physical activity bring it on?" he said. "Eating? Does it wake you up in the night?"

I said, "Sometimes, sometimes, and no." He wrote that down and waited for me to explain. "What wakes me up in the night is when the cat turns on the television."

I could see Dr. Stan didn't want to write that down in my file. "It's the cable people, they fixed it so the cat could turn on the television," I said.

I got a picture of him at home that night, sitting across from his wife over supper and saying, "One of my patients thinks he has swallowed something that is trying to get out and the cable television people have taught his cat to turn on his television at night."

For now, he made a few more notes in my file and invited me into his office. I followed him in, noticing the license to practice and graduate degrees on the wall. I don't know why, but the only places you see licenses anymore are places you are likely to die. Doctors' offices, bars, elevators, and taxis.

"Have a seat," he said. When I was comfortable, we talked a little about tennis and boxing—he asked if I'd been sparring without headgear—and then he told me what he thought was wrong with my throat, and began to write a prescription to fix it.

While he was doing that his phone rang. It was another doctor and they talked for four or five minutes. Dr. Stan had put a mutual patient in the hospital.

"The thing is," Dr. Stan said, "if he doesn't get off his feet I feel it could lead to real problems . . ."

The other doctor said something and Dr. Stan said, "Well, his feet were swollen and warm all over . . . yes, well, I think eventually he'll lose that toe . . ."

The longer they talked about the patient's feet, the more graphic it got. By the time it was over, I could have picked the feet out of a lineup. By the time it was over, I was trying to remember if my own feet were pink and warm.

I took the prescription, shook hands with Dr. Stan, and walked out of his office. In the car outside I took off my boots and socks and sat there, in zero-degree weather, staring at my feet. I couldn't tell if they were swollen or not, but they were pink.

I thought it over and decided to watch them for a couple of weeks, measure them, touch them now and then to see if they felt warm and check the ends of my socks after I took them off at night for toes.

I almost went back inside to have Dr. Stan look at them too, but it didn't seem fair. The truth is, it takes Dr. Stan and me a little while to get ready for each other.

56

Looking back on it now, it seems almost as if the bullet that took Martin Luther King's life as he stood on the balcony of the Lorraine Motel in Memphis, Tennessee, twenty-two years ago took Ralph Abernathy too.

That he reeled from that shot as surely as if it had hit him; and never quite found his footing again.

The reason for saying something like that is simply that the civil rights movement changed on the day Martin Luther King was murdered, and Abernathy, of all the men who followed him, was least equipped to change with it.

He was the least political of King's disciples, the least charismatic, the least eloquent.

Perhaps that was why King trusted him most.

Or perhaps it was because he had followed King when it was hardest to do, because Abernathy had gone to jail with him seventeen times, had stood with him in the face of violence—before the law was any help, when what they stood on was faith—and hadn't blinked.

And it's probably fair to say that as much as Martin Luther King depended on Abernathy, Abernathy depended even more on King. That while he shared King's faith and conviction and courage, he did not share his stature. He could not move a whole people with his presence, and could not move their hearts.

And, with King gone, he could not move them at all.

King's death left a hole that Abernathy couldn't begin to fill, and in the long political struggle that followed inside the civil rights movement—as well as the larger struggle going on outside—Ralph Abernathy was somehow left behind.

He took over King's presidency of the Southern Christian Leadership Conference but resigned in 1977, unable to generate money or enthusiasm. He stood to the side and watched men like Jesse Jackson and Andrew Young and Benjamin Hooks stake their claims, watched them inherit what King had left, and in some way ignore the fact that it was what Abernathy himself had left too.

And so, ten years after Martin Luther King's death, Abernathy would find himself in an undignified public fight with Coretta Scott King over a six-hour television docudrama on her husband's life. He called the series a "distortion of history," which, of course, a "docudrama" is by definition.

He objected to being ignored.

Mrs. King endorsed the series as faithful to her husband and the early civil rights movement.

By 1980, Abernathy had strayed far enough from the civil rights movement to endorse Ronald Reagan for president.

By then, of course, he had simply become part of the movement's past, and as he fell further from grace, his earlier contributions—as it seemed to Abernathy, at least—were being diminished or ignored.

His health faltered, he had a couple of strokes.

And perhaps, wanting to preserve what he had done, to reclaim it from the politicians, he wrote his autobiography, *And the Walls Came Tumbling Down*, and overnight became a pariah.

The reason, of course, were two pages of the book that dealt with Martin Luther King's infidelity.

He wrote that the night before King died, he enjoyed the company of two different women—neither of whom was his wife—and then argued with and struck a third woman who showed up furious at the motel in the morning.

The fact that the infidelities were common knowledge did not matter. Neither did the fact that the book was overwhelmingly admiring of and loving toward King.

"He had a particularly difficult time with that temptation," Abernathy said. "We all fall short of the mark . . . sexual sins are by no means the worst."

Immediately, Jesse Jackson, Andrew Young, Benjamin Hooks, and Joseph Lowery sent off a cable, calling on Abernathy to "repudiate" what he'd written. They said the words must have been put into his mouth "by others who needed a sensational story to sell books and slander the name of your martyred brother."

This from Jackson, who had appeared on television the day after the assassination, wearing a bloody shirt, claiming he had held King as he died. It was Abernathy, for the record, who held King. Jackson was on another floor.

The columnist William Raspberry wrote: "The question that crackles like wildfire through the civil rights community is: why?

"Why did Abernathy betray his friend?"

Raspberry mentioned possible reasons—jealousy, money, mental weakness—but rejected them all; in the end, he said, what Abernathy had done diminished himself more than it diminished King.

It apparently didn't occur to Raspberry that it isn't a disservice to Martin Luther King to present him as he was. That what he was is enough.

The "community," as Raspberry calls it, shut the door on Abernathy after the book was published; and at the same time on an era when, for a little while, the truth did in fact set us free.

And Ralph Abernathy died Tuesday, still waiting at the door.

57

Jimmy Breslin went back to work last week, but I don't really know if he's seen the error of his ways.

The newspaper he writes for, *Newsday*, had suspended him for two weeks without pay for remarks he made on a New York radio show, remarks which indicated to the people who decide these things at *Newsday* that Breslin wasn't sincerely contrite for an earlier outburst in the newsroom. What Breslin is doing at a paper as sterile as *Newsday* in the first place, by the way, is a mystery to me except that it's connected to money.

Anyway, Breslin's newsroom remarks have now been widely reported, and without going back over it all word for word, let me acknowledge that they showed racial insensitivity toward people of Asian ancestry.

Breslin made these remarks in a fit of anger after a young Korean-American reporter at his newspaper lodged a complaint about a humorous column he'd written concerning the problems of living with a professional woman. Breslin's wife, as it happens, is a New York City councilwoman.

The young woman, perhaps believing that holding a job at *Newsday* in itself makes you a professional, did not find the living-with-a-professional-woman column humorous, and fired off a letter calling Breslin a sexist.

And Breslin, obviously operating under the impression that he understands the underpinnings of his marriage as well as some twenty-six-year-old yuppie, reacted with his customary restraint. He threw the best fit he could, given the short notice.

And in doing that, broke the rules.

The very first rule, in fact, says Breslin is not allowed to call anyone a "yellow cur." And Breslin knows that as well as anyone, as he would tacitly acknowledge during the tirade—"let's make it racial," he said at one point—and later in a written apology to the woman and the entire *Newsday* staff.

But despite that, I doubt if the argument was racial.

Instead, it recalls Roberto Duran waving Ray Leonard off in their second fight, doing the most contemptuous thing he could think of at the time, which in Duran's case was simply quitting the fight.

And just as that moment did not change the fact that Roberto Duran had fought some of the great fights of his time, nothing Jimmy Breslin said in a few moments of anger is going to change the hundreds of columns he has written over his life demanding a fair shake for ordinary people of every color.

And while I won't presume to say what is in Jimmy Breslin's heart, I do know that his work speaks to his sense of fairness, to his sense of humor and to his sense of himself. You can't write columns and hide who you are, and Breslin, more than most, is there in his words.

It isn't always fashionable, but it's real.

And while it's more fashionable to call someone a sexist than a "yellow cur," maybe this is a good time to point out that it is every bit as disrespectful.

We have arrived, however, at a point in history where it's okay to label people any way we want except by sex, sexual preference, religion, or race.

An exception is made, of course, in the case of white, male, heterosexual Protestants or Catholics.

And because—right off the top of my head—Breslin is at least two or three of those things himself, he ought to know better than to get into a name-calling contest in the first place, especially with somebody who has so many more names to use.

But he did what he did.

And because it happened in a newsroom, Breslin's behavior was soon being reported in newspapers and television broadcasts all over the country.

Following the outburst, Breslin wrote his apology to the woman and the staff. I haven't seen the apology, but I've been told it was a beauty.

And so for a little while things were all right in the world, although the offended reporter was miffed that Breslin hadn't been suspended or fired.

Not long afterwards, however, Breslin went back to being Breslin.

Informed that a New York radio personality named Howard Stern was discussing him on the air, Breslin called the station and in the conversation that followed indicated the yellow-cur situation was something less serious than, say, the amputation of a major limb.

Which did it for the people who decide these things at *Newsday*, and Breslin was suspended for two weeks without pay—not for what he said in the newsroom, but for what he said on the air.

Leaving only the question of when Breslin is going to suspend *Newsday*, for good.

On that signal, I will know beyond doubt that Jimmy Breslin has seen the error of his ways.

58

And so the district attorney's office, having spent a month "looking at the law and the facts," has decided to charge Gerry Gilmore with manslaughter.

Gilmore is the man who killed a burglar about two o'clock in the morning on July 5th. He had caught the burglar trying to break into his apartment, and the man was running away when he was shot. "Our decision is that Mr. Gilmore had no equities going for him in this thing," said Deputy District Attorney Dick Gilmour. "It was a judgment call. The law says you cannot use deadly force unless it is a serious felony being committed where there is forcible danger threatened to yourself and your loved ones."

This judgment was based, at least in part, on a Sheriff's Department report saying Gilmore was not in personal danger because the man—Ronald James Schmidt—was running away when he was shot, and wasn't armed. The report also made the point that Gilmore had not called the Sheriff's Department for help before he went outside after the burglar.

And that, according to the district attorney's office, amounts to no equities.

So it might be useful now, I think, before this goes any farther, to take a moment to look at the equities in the case of Gerry Gilmore and Ronald James Schmidt, and see what kind of imbalance it is that the district attorney is trying to correct.

Gerry Gilmore, for openers, is fifty-one years old. He has no wife or kids, and lives in an apartment over the small construction company he owns. He has been in Sacramento all his life, working in construction since he was twenty-three years old.

Twenty years ago he got a traffic citation, paid that, and hasn't had any trouble with the law since.

Ronald James Schmidt, who was born about the same time Gilmore got his traffic citation, hasn't done much work yet. He had three prior arrests for burglary, however, and was on probation at the time things caught up with him at Gilmore's building in South Sacramento.

Which is not to say that a twenty-year-old kid ought to get his ticket punched because he cannot keep himself out of other people's houses. But there is a certain risk you assume when you go into the burglary business, and that risk is part of the equities of this thing too.

At any rate, before Ronald James Schmidt tried to climb into Gerry Gilmore's apartment on July 5th, he had broken into a camera store in the same building. He had stolen some camera stuff and a stereo and a ladder, which he was using to climb to the apartment.

Gilmore was asleep. "I heard some noise. It may have been a scrape, something out of the ordinary," he said. "I got out of bed, opened the screen, and poked my head out the window, half asleep, my eyes out of focus. I thought I saw a ladder in the Dumpster, and figured it was somebody after beer cans or something.

"So I lay back down, ready to go back to sleep, when it occurred to me that it might be a character from down the street who has been told to stay away from the property. And I thought, if it is, I'm going to call the police."

And so Gilmore got out of bed again, walked into his living room and put his nose against the screen, and saw a man on a ladder, a foot and a half away.

"At that moment," he said, "I was suddenly wide awake. It's something like if you opened a cabinet for a glass and found a rattlesnake. It gets your attention.

"He was looking down at the time, and I got into my boots, grabbed my revolver and ran downstairs. I deliberately set off the burglar alarm, which hooks up to the Sheriff's Department, but there weren't seven minutes to wait around for them. The alarm goes off at the building too, and it's loud.

"Anyway, I ran toward the ladder, grabbed it and kept running until it fell. It fell on top of him, but it didn't faze him. He jumped up and started to run. If I'd wanted to kill him, I could have done it then, or I could have just slipped outside and waited for him to come down. Or I could have shot him in the face through the screen. Instead, I fired to one side, trying to frighten him. I never took aim . . ."

Ronald James Schmidt was about 150 feet away when the .357-caliber Magnum slug hit him square in the neck. You have to go back to the night Dave Winfield threw a baseball from a hundred feet away and killed a pigeon in center field in Toronto to find anything remotely as unlikely. Gilmore's gun has a two-inch barrel, and there is nobody in the world who, under the same conditions, could make that shot on purpose.

"Right after [Schmidt] went down, a car pulled up," Gilmore said. "I thought it was an accomplice. I was empty, so I ran back up into my apartment, spilled cartridges all over the floor and finally got three of them into the cylinder, and went back downstairs.

"But it was my neighbor, the man who owns the photography store. He said he'd been hit [burglarized], and we stood there a minute, the alarm bell ringing so loud, and I looked over at the man on the ground and I asked the neighbor to call the sheriff.

"Within a few minutes, there were seven or eight deputies, they all came at once. One of them went over to the man on the ground, and when he came back he said the man was dead. That's when I found out. I didn't say anything to the sheriff, I was speechless."

For about a week, the thought that he had killed Ronald James Schmidt bothered Gilmore at night. "I thought about it all the time," he said, "and then one day the phone rang, somebody said, 'Eat a good dinner tonight, you don't have long to live.' My neighbors were threatened too. One of them was threatened this morning.

"After that, I quit thinking about [Schmidt]. After that, I began thinking about being killed myself. You don't know what kind of person is threatening you."

Gerry Gilmore paused for a moment. Then he sighed. "It happened so fast," he said. "One minute you're sound asleep at two o'clock in the morning, the next minute—literally, the next minute—you've killed somebody. In sixty seconds, your whole life has changed . . ."

And that is something to remember when you consider the equities in the case of Gerry Gilmore and Ronald James Schmidt. Gerry Gilmore had one minute. He did not have the thirty days the deputy district attorney has taken to make a "judgment call."

He did not shoot Schmidt point-blank. And he could have.

"I was trying to arrest him," he said. "I never in my life meant to kill him."

That, of course, is the chance you take when you shoot a gun.

It is also the chance you take when you break into somebody's house on business.

What happened is bad enough, there is no reason to make it worse.

The deputy district attorney may not believe that, but he will play hell putting twelve people in a jury box that agree with him.

59

Burglars, of course, are people too.

They've got problems on the job. They've got bills to pay, habits to support. And they've got mothers who want them to do well, just like you and me. Ronald James Schmidt, for instance, had a mother. Schmidt was the twenty-year-old kid who was killed early in July, running from a burglary he'd screwed up in South Sacramento. He had three prior arrests and was on probation at the time.

His mother's name is Alice Schmidt, and last week she told this newspaper that Ronald was a "good kid" who believed in God. "He had that thought, at least," she said.

"He did do some burglaries, some petty stuff. But he's always been caught, and he was punished for what he did, the hard way. The hardest way."

I do not know how Mrs. Schmidt knows that Ronald was always caught. If that is true, however, we are looking at a kind of dedication you don't see much in the workplace anymore. Most people who were 0 for 3 at burglary, anyway, would try something else. Banks, automobiles, purse-snatching, going to law school. I mean, there are other things to do.

But whatever his successes were, Ronald kept at it, and early on the morning of July 5th, a fifty-one-year-old man named Gerry Gilmore put a round from a .357 Magnum into the back of his neck from about 150 feet. And Gilmore—who has said all along that he was firing warning shots, trying to arrest Ronald James Schmidt—has now been charged with manslaughter by the district attorney.

Monday, Gilmore showed up in front of Sacramento Municipal Court Judge William Ridgeway and said he wanted to represent himself against the charges. Gilmore told me last week he would act as his own attorney because he believes what he did was right and does not want to turn his life's savings over to some lawyer to defend him.

Monday, he indicated the attorney's fees would total $100,000.

Judge Ridgeway, however, cautioning that a conviction could result in as much as four years in prison, gave him a couple of weeks to think it over.

And Gilmore took the two weeks to weigh the situation, and as he walked out of the courtroom, Mrs. Schmidt slapped him across the face and screamed, "You murderer! You murderer!"

Gilmore stood quietly while Mrs. Schmidt was pulled away, and later he declined to press charges, saying, "She's just upset."

Which I don't think you can argue with. Last week, Mrs. Schmidt was quoted as saying, "As far as I'm concerned, [Gilmore] can rot in hell, because that's where he is going." And Monday, after she had slapped Gilmore, she said, "I want justice done, and I intend to get it."

You wonder, though, where Mrs. Schmidt's sense of justice was all the years young Ronald was out doing business in other people's buildings. Did she slap him in the face as he was coming out of courtrooms? Did she care about the people he was stealing from, did she think about the emotional crisis burglary—"petty stuff" or not—generates in the person it happens to?

The price here is not the question. A kid breaks into your house and steals a $300 television set, and you jump at every noise in the night for two years. How much is that worth?

I'll tell you what it is worth on the street. It's worth the life of the next guy who tries to come in the window. And as I said the first time I wrote about this, the district attorney is going to have more than a little trouble finding a jury with nobody on it who understands that.

On the other hand, you have to understand Mrs. Schmidt a little too. Her child is dead and, burglar or not, it is her child. You cannot feel good about that. She may be trying to cleanse him now, or cleanse herself. I don't know.

I do know that what Mrs. Schmidt did outside the courtroom Monday has a staged feel to it, and that it was cheap. And that it was misdirected.

Ronald James Schmidt is dead in a work-related accident. If his mother needs someone else to blame, she ought to take another look at the way it happened. A 150-foot shot, in the dead of night, fired by a frightened and excited man holding a revolver with a two-inch barrel.

Mrs. Schmidt has offered repeated suggestions of her faith, and her son's. I do not see how anyone could hold those beliefs and not recognize what happened as an act of God.

60

A little before five-thirty in the afternoon, the lights dim over the audience gathered in the theater of the Macklowe Hotel on Forty-fourth Street to watch game seven of the world chess championship. A man comes on stage and says he would like to remind us of the absolute necessity for absolute quiet.

Having said that, he exits the stage, returning attention to the elevated black table on which this game will be played, and the two empty black chairs sitting on either side. A board divides the area beneath the table in half, I suppose to keep the contestants from kicking.

I am sitting in the balcony, perhaps thirty yards from the stage, in the company of a foreign correspondent who tells me that the match so far has belonged to the brash young champion, Garry Kasparov.

Those are the words the foreign correspondent uses, brash young champion. He is the kind of correspondent, I think, who borrows the prose he uses in his stories for his conversations.

For perhaps three minutes the stage remains empty of chess players. The balcony fills with spectators, almost all of whom are men in dark suits. I'm not sure when the necessity for absolute silence begins, but seeing how nobody is on stage now I lean over and ask the foreign correspondent if he knows what happened to the women.

He smiles at me over the top of his glasses. "Well, it's a man's game, isn't it?" he says. "Appeals to the warrior's instinct, and all that."

Oh.

I am looking around the room at the collected warriors just as Anatoly Karpov, the challenger and former champion, makes his entrance onto the stage. There is some polite applause while he walks quickly to his chair— he's got one with arm rests—and sits down. He looks at the board a moment, then moves a pawn into the center of the board and hits the clock that keeps track of each player's time.

Then he gets up and walks off the stage, which strikes me as a little rude.

"These are the warriors?" I whisper, not wanting to break the abso-lute need for absolute silence.

The foreign correspondent looks around the balcony, and then back at me. "It's why they're here," he says.

Down on the stage, Garry Kasparov appears, wearing a brown suit, and sits down at the table. He touches his pieces, centering them in their assigned squares, then studies Karpov's pawn a moment and moves his knight. He hits his side of the clock, stands up and walks out of view.

"Karpov's too old for this," the foreign correspondent whispers, sounding sad. "Physically, he can't take it."

I look at Karpov carefully when he comes back, trying to figure out how old he is. Maybe forty. He moves another pawn, but somehow man-ages to hide the physical exertion. I suppose all the great ones make it look easy.

I have been told, of course, that Karpov is the bad Russian—that is, Russia's Russian—and Kasparov is our Russian, but this is the first I've heard that he's too old.

"Too old for what?"

The foreign correspondent gestures toward the stage. Kasparov re-appears, walks to the table and the two men shake hands in a perfunctory sort of way before Kasparov moves again.

"Too old for what?" I ask again. Some of the men in dark suits look sideways at me, a reminder of the absolute necessity for absolute quiet.

"He does not have the endurance anymore," the correspondent says. "Kasparov tears away at his flesh until he is too weak to fight."

"Are these guys doing something to each other behind the curtains?" In which case, that is where I'd like to go to watch.

The correspondent points to the stage, and I watch it, absolutely quiet. The men move seven or eight times each, and then my friend the correspondent leans over and whispers, "The King's Indian defense."

I nod, as if this is something I agree with, but the correspondent holds up a sly finger to caution me that this is not an ordinary King's Indian defense after all. "The knights," he says, and I notice Kasparov's knights are at the sides of the board and not controlling the middle squares.

Karpov seems to notice it at the same time. He drops his head into his hands, hovering over the board for perhaps twenty minutes. "He is completely intimidated," the correspondent says. "Kasparov is quite the bully-boy, isn't he?"

I nod, looking at the two men sitting at the board. Time passes. "How long do you think this might go on?" I ask.

The foreign correspondent looks at me in a satisfied way. "They're just beginning," he whispers.

I shake my head, thinking of the relative shortness of life, and how much of mine I want to devote to two Russians playing chess. A few minutes later, with Karpov still holding his head and studying the board, I gather my notes and stand up to leave.

"Are you ill?" the correspondent says.

I look down at him and shake my head. "I can't handle violence."

He says, "It is hard to watch sometimes, isn't it?"

61

The police have closed off the street, and one of them stands at the barrier, leaning into the windows of cars that drive up and stop, explaining that they can't come any farther.

"Can't allow you in," he says. "They're making a picture show in the Wards' old place."

Beyond the policeman, four long trucks are parked against the curb, the last one stopped right in front of the old wooden house where we are shooting. A dozen people are sitting in chairs on the lawn, sweating in the wet Georgia heat, and a dozen more are walking in and out of the house, everybody hurrying.

It is the second day of filming, and worries about finishing on time have already eclipsed problems with the script or location or actors. An extra day costs $70,000, and a bitter argument has broken out this morning between an assistant director and a woman representing the executive producers, and more arguments are coming.

Watching this particular woman work, in fact, I come to understand that the bitter arguments are what she is after. She has tasted blood and wants more.

I am sitting in one of the chairs on the front lawn, reading the accounts of the Mideast in the local paper, and at the same time watching the situation here build into a war.

I have been on movie sets before, but the scenes being filmed inside a gentleman named A. C. Ward's old house come out of my novel *Paris Trout* and—more to the point—they come out of my life.

In some ways, I come from a place sixty miles south of here, a town called Milledgeville. My family moved there when I was four—my father had died and my mother remarried—and left when I was ten, and in the years in between certain things settled in me that never changed.

And I know the smells and colors and feel of this place as if I had never left. A black bumblebee floats in the flowers, as round as a grape, the ants crawl up the leg of a chair I'm sitting on—I suddenly remember digging up an anthill in the yard, the ants crawling up the handle of the shovel, and then up my hands and arms. I remember the way the house looked to me as my stepfather ran, carrying me in his arms, onto the porch. I remember lying in the bathtub, my arms and legs covered with red welts, a hundred ants floating around me on the surface of the water.

The heat is wet and familiar and smells exactly the way it did in the early 1950s.

"Quiet please," a man yells, and everyone in the yard stops talking and moving to wait for the scene inside to be shot.

I remember other things too.

A kid up the road whose father took him fishing one Sunday morning, locked him in the trunk of the car, and then shot himself in the mouth. The man next door who would invite me in once in a while and show me the guns he kept under the cushion of his davenport. The last time I was ever in his house, he said he'd shot "a nigger"; I don't know if that was true. "Your daddy don't let you say that word, does he?" he said.

The woman who represents the executive producers passes by now, her expression at least as terrifying as the one on the man with the guns in his davenport. She is stalking the director, but he is inside making the movie and she can't get to him until lunch.

A production-company car pulls up and a woman climbs out of the backseat, towing a three- or four-year-old black child. The child is supposed to audition for a one-minute part which calls for her to scream. The woman locates the casting supervisor and presents her daughter.

"You want to scream for the man, honey?" she says.

The child shakes her head.

"Come on now, just like you did for the other man . . ."

The child pulls free of her mother and drops into a ditch, refusing to move.

"Please, honey, get up out of there and scream for this man before you get your dress all dirty."

The child looks up, her eyes wet and round, and silently shakes her head.

And that is familiar too, and I know how it feels to be in that ditch. Her mother pulls her back into the car and she presses her face against the glass as the driver takes them back to Atlanta.

It is one of those mornings, everything is familiar, everything is strange. And four hours later, I am in a car going back to Atlanta myself when we pass a bridge over the highway and see two old men standing there holding an American flag—it is so big that it takes both of them to hold it in the wind—over the traffic passing underneath.

"What are they doing?" I ask the driver.

She is just a kid, eighteen or nineteen years old. She looks out the window a long minute. "It's for the soldiers," she says. "They're taking them from here over to the Mideast. There's been convoys on the highway all day."

And I stare at the old men on the bridge until they are out of sight, and I am lost in bittersweet moments. Moments that shape us and then, in repose, become the heart of who we are.

62

By nature, I am not a public person.

Writing a column like this one, however, there are times when it becomes necessary to discuss matters of a personal nature. You walk into the office once in a while and can't come up with a single reason to pick on the district attorney, you've got to write something.

There are limits, though, to how personal I will get—it's a matter of good taste, really—and I do not violate them. I never talk about how much money I make, I never discuss my medical history except in the broadest terms, and I never discuss my skinny legs. All these things are too distasteful to talk about with strangers.

On the other hand, I do feel that as regular readers you are entitled to know what Mrs. Dexter is like in bed.

Which is what I am going to tell you about today.

The first thing you ought to know about Mrs. Dexter, I guess, is that she is of Greek extraction. These are the people, you may remember, who climbed into an artificial horse, waited until the poor Trojans pulled it inside their gates, and then, after the lights went out in town, crawled out and reopened the gates for the entire Greek army, which conquered Troy.

Obviously, a people capable of this sort of thing—I mean, who would even think of something like that?—are light sleepers themselves, and are not easily surprised in their tents.

It is also fair to say, I think, that thousands of years after that one night squashed inside the horse, sitting on each other's heads, they are still fanatically defensive of their sleeping space. There is an old Greek saying, in fact, which pretty well spells this out: Do not touch a sleeping Greek.

Which means if you have any thought at all of getting lucky, do it before they go to sleep.

Now, my own heritage is not nearly as steeped in violence. I come from a peace-loving, straightforward, practical people who, as a rule, sleep very well. In fact, we are not unlike the poor people of Troy, now that I think about it, except, as I mentioned before, we have a certain innate sense of good taste and would never bring the horse inside the city gates. At least not the one I saw in the movie.

We are also an affectionate people who, on awakening in the night, like to reach for our loved ones and hold them closer to our bosoms.

And so when one of us marries a Greek, and then wakes in the night, perhaps frightened, and reaches out in the dark for our loved one, what happens is that we are handed our lunch.

Here she is in the morning, staring horrified at my cut lip: "My God, what happened?"

The fact that this lip was cut by her own elbow or shoulder or—this is the one to watch out for—her head, is a source of a secret ethnic pride, although she will swear she has no memory of the assault.

But coming, as I do, from a peace-loving, straightforward, practical people, I do not try to change her. Instead, I adapt. When I awake in the night and feel the need for something to hold close to my bosom, I reach for my second-string pillow. It is soft and cool, does not jump up unexpectedly into my chin at small noises, and, no matter how close you get to it, you never hear that faint whistle of air passing through a nostril.

And the truth is, it fits better.

All in all, a hell of a pillow.

But life is complicated, right? Greek women, it turns out, always know when their men are in bed with their arms around another, and at three o'clock in the morning she is suddenly staring at me in the dark.

"What are you doing with that pillow?" she says.

"What pillow?" I ask. As a people, we are not great liars.

"You're hugging a pillow," she says softly. "Why don't you just hug me?"

Very competitive, the Greeks.

"I didn't want to wake you up," I said.

I toss the pillow back onto the floor, and she slides half a foot across the bed, and takes its place. Warm, soft, lithe; smelling like strawberry shampoo.

I whisper, "Good night, I love you."

She whispers, "I love you too."

I whisper, "Mrs. Dexter?"

"Yes?"

"I was talking to the pillow."

There is a long, satisfying pause, but the Greeks are very tricky.

"So was I," she says.

63

On the same day the twenty-two-year-old millionaire basketball player Len Bias died in Maryland of an overdoes of cocaine, a kid named Yolanda Johnson, who was the same age, was found in a closet in the 3400 block of Fourth Avenue here, and she was dead too.

She was missing enough clothes so that the police and the coroner's office believe she may have been raped. There was enough blood spattered around the room so that they believe she may have been murdered.

No one is saying either of those things for sure, however, because the test results aren't in yet. It has been a big year for homicides and deaths of suspicious nature in Sacramento, and the coroner's office is backed up with cases.

On Monday, for instance, besides one official homicide, there was a twenty-three-year-old woman named Tammy Peterson who was found shot in the head on Fourteenth Avenue near Oak Park, possibly a suicide, and a thirty-eight-year-old man who was found dead in a flea-bag hotel on Twelfth Street, downtown. Possibly the victim of muggers.

"The young lady [Tammy Peterson] had previously been raped and threatened," a woman at the coroner's office said. "That may have led to this, and that's what we're looking at. The man [whose name has not been released pending notification of relatives] had been mugged or beaten up before. We've had so many of these things this year, we're just way behind . . ."

I couldn't get anybody at the Police Department Tuesday to tell me how far behind they are, but I think it's fair to say, just from the few weeks I've been looking at the local news, that they've got their hands full too.

Even before last Friday.

Friday, of course, another big-time athlete was dead, another overdose. Don Rogers, a local kid who became a defensive back for the Cleveland Browns, was fatally stricken in his mother's house in South Natomas the day before he was supposed to get married.

And the coroner's office, responding to the crush of attention the death got, moved quickly on Rogers' case and came back in a couple of days with a toxicologist's report indicating Rogers had enough cocaine in his body to kill himself maybe five times.

And the police waited until Monday, when many of the witnesses who had been around Rogers in the hours before he died were out of town, before they began their investigation into where the drugs came from. A police spokesman said initially that the family had requested that the department wait until after the funeral.

And that, of course, isn't much of a reason to put off an investigation into a death, and the police took some pointed questions about it over the weekend. A much better reason to put off the investigation was announced at a press conference Monday—that there isn't much to investigate. The police didn't put it exactly that way. They said that investigations into the source of drugs used in overdose cases were seldom fruitful, and that Don Rogers' death would be handled like any other drug overdose.

The truth, though, is that the police have better things to do. The truth is, it doesn't matter who brought the drugs—nobody killed Don Rogers but Don Rogers.

This was not an eleven- or twelve-year-old kid, getting talked into something on a playground. This was a professional athlete, who had been warned and threatened and lectured and counseled and educated on drugs, every four minutes or so since the day he could fit into a football helmet, and who—if you believe the interviews with friends and fans— had absorbed these warnings, and passed them along to others.

And as comfortable as it might be to find somebody else to blame in this, it doesn't work.

As comfortable as it might be to call for mandatory drug testing for professional athletes, that doesn't work either. If you want to test somebody, test lawyers, or doctors, or pilots. An athlete on drugs can't do much damage, except to himself. And in this country there is always a way to do that; it's guaranteed in the Constitution.

But let me tell you what works least of all. It is the talk now that Don Rogers was not a regular user, or that this was his first time. The man does not need to be graded on some kind of curve for drug abusers, he needs to be buried.

Listen, nobody could have paid attention to this story and not felt it. But Yolanda Johnson has a story too, and Tammy Peterson, and the man who was found in the fleabag on Twelfth Street. None of them climbed as high as Don Rogers, so their falls were not as spectacular.

But they all lost the same thing—everything they had—and the police are right to concentrate on the others first. Someone might have taken what they had: Don Rogers gave his away.

64

The woman was sitting in a corner of the emergency room at Parkland Hospital in Dallas—the same place they had taken John Kennedy. It had been too late for him; it was too late for her.

It was early afternoon now, she had been there for a couple of hours at least. The blood on her skirt and shoes had dried black, her wrist and hand were bandaged, and she was sitting alone, waiting for the doctor to come out and tell her what she already knew about her husband. They had offered to bring her inside, but she'd shaken her head. "I've got to wait for my momma," she'd said. "She's old, and this will confuse her."

There were eighteen or twenty people in the room with her, most of them were on the other side, watching the television. Some of them were nurses and orderlies, some of them were customers, supporting damaged parts of their bodies, waiting to get them fixed. Anwar Sadat had been shot in Egypt.

The woman's mother came in a few minutes later, holding on to a man's arm. He was uncomfortable with her there and smiled when he saw the woman. He said, "I brought her as soon as I could get off. I had a bail hearing . . ." He was dressed in a suit and cowboy boots, a family lawyer.

The woman stood up to meet him. "How's Billy?" he said. He handed the old woman over the way you would move a parrot from one arm to another.

The woman looked into his face, and you could see then that she had been given something to calm her down. "There's nothing they can do," she said. He shook his head.

"How did it happen?" he said.

Up on the television screen, Dan Rather was trying to put together what CBS knew. There were sources saying Sadat was dead. There were sources denying it. There had been a parade.

The woman said, "I don't know. We were driving . . . It happened before I knew anything was wrong."

The woman's mother squinted up at the television. A CBS reporter in Cairo was saying that Sadat's wife had left the hospital, a sign that he was dead. The woman's mother said, "I never liked hospitals."

The family lawyer asked what he could do. He looked at his watch, he said he had some business he had to look after. "I'm gonna send over Lucy," he said. "You want me to send Lucy?" He waited a few seconds, then gave her a shallow hug. "You call me as soon as you know something."

The woman nodded. The lawyer squeezed her hand, smiled at the woman's mother. "Miz Roberts," he said, then he was gone. You knew then the family didn't have much money.

The woman led her mother over to the corner of the room away from the television. The mother looked at her dress and arm and said, "Lord, child, what's happened to you?"

The woman said, "There's been an accident, Momma. We were in a wreck." Her mother looked back up at the television set. "Billy's hurt bad."

Hearing herself say that out loud, her face broke and she began to cry. One of the nurses heard her and left the others by the television set. She knelt beside the woman and asked if she wanted something.

The woman's mother said, "It's all right, thank you," and she put her arm around her daughter and rocked back and forth in the chair.

The woman let herself be held. She cried quietly into her mother's neck and tried to tell her what had happened. "There was a truck, Momma," she said. "Billy's head went up against the windshield."

The mother rocked her and watched the television set. CBS news made the announcement: Sadat was dead. "There's nobody can protect you from the world, honey," the mother said. "Not even your momma."

The woman said, "Momma, you don't understand . . ."

The old woman pulled her daughter closer. "Hush now," she said. She smoothed her daughter's hair and held her like that, rocking in a straight-back chair, until they came out to tell her that Billy was dead.

65

The dog came with papers. It was $200 to take him home and another quick $800 in furniture when he got there. He could eat industrial carpeting.

The man who bought him planned to teach the dog to retrieve ducks, and so the animal wouldn't grow up afraid of guns, he took him along whenever he drove into Philadelphia.

To teach him to live with hardship—as you must occasionally do when you go duck hunting—he sometimes fed him Kentucky Fried Chicken.

The dog ate even that, as much of it as the man would give him. Once, as a test, the man bought a thrift box—nine pieces, no fries—and set it on the front seat next to a Gino's cheesesteak. The dog ate all the chicken first, then the cheesesteak wrapper, and then the cheesesteak.

He spit the onions on the floor.

Naturally enough, that touched the man. Would anybody else eat a thrift box and a cheesesteak for him? Would his own wife? As a test, he bought a thrift box and set it on the front seat next to a Gino's cheesesteak. The wife said, "You've gone completely fucking through the other side of the mirror, haven't you, Peter?"

In this way the man found out who his true friends were.

The dog grew a pound heavier each hour for six months. When the man worked, the dog lay beneath his desk, resting his head on the man's feet until they numbed from a lack of blood. Once, he found the dog asleep with his nose and as much of his head as would fit buried in the man's boot.

Was his wife that devoted? Ha! And, being less devoted, she came to resent the retriever's fidelity. "The dog ate the baby's braids today," she would say as soon as the man came home. Or, "The dog ate all the cotton out of our mattress."

But the man loved his dog and didn't care, and if you have ever loved a dog, you may understand how he felt when McGuire was stolen. It happened last week, at the liquor store. The man had stopped there to get a six-pack of beer on the way home from the supermarket.

He'd left the keys in the car, a window rolled halfway down, and three sacks of groceries in the backseat. Sticking out of one of the sacks was a twelve-pound piece of uninterrupted filet mignon wrapped in clear plastic that showed pools of blood at the bottom. It had cost a shade over $50 and the man would tell the police later that night that the thief probably saw the meat and took the retriever as an afterthought.

He stood in the parking lot of the liquor store a long time calling the dog, but there was no answer. The liquor store is eight-tenths of a mile from the man's house, down two narrow roads, and the man spent most of the night driving up and back, hoping that somehow the dog would be there.

Finally, he went to bed. He woke up depressed and lonely. "I hope whoever got him feeds him enough," he said.

His wife said maybe the dog would be back. "He might have just jumped out when the thief opened the door," she said. "Maybe he just got scared and ran away." But the man had watched strangers get too close to McGuire before; he'd seen the dog lick their faces.

But don't worry. Here comes the part where the dog crosses 1,500 miles of wilderness to find its way home again. Yes, he found his way back. No one will ever know exactly how, but about five o'clock in the afternoon the man heard a strange gagging noise in the backyard.

He hurried to the door, and there, standing beside a porch step that he had gnawed half off the week before, was the dog.

Throwing up.

His stomach was so swollen that the man thought he had been hit by a car. He called his wife, then hurried out the door to see how badly the dog was hurt.

The man ran his hand along the stomach, then the ribs. There were no broken bones he could feel. The dog choked and threw up huge chunks of dark red meat.

"That looks like steak," the wife said.

"It's something he found on the road," the man said. "That's what's making him sick." He checked the dog's legs. "I wonder how he got away." The dog choked again, more hunks of red meat came up. There was no blood.

"That's steak," said the wife.

The man threw her a look, but before he could say anything else, the dog emptied himself one more time. More dark-red meat, and in the middle of it something that caught the sun. Something shiny.

The man pulled it out of the pile of wet meat. A piece of plastic, something stuck to it. A price tag, intact: $4.59 a pound.

66

The news caught us all in the jewels, but it hurt my friend Spencer, who runs this place, worst of all. In fact, it was Spencer who called me into his office to break it to me. It was better that way than hearing it on the radio. "Zerna Sharp is dead," he said. Zerna Sharp, of course, is the woman who invented Dick and Jane and Spot and Puff the cat.

There was a long silence.

"Did you ever read *Dick Goes to School*?" he asked.

"I'm not sure," I said. "What was that one about?"

"It was fantastic," he said. "Wait a minute, let me read you just one part . . ." He went to his bookshelf and pulled out an old, clothbound book. There was a picture on the front of Dick going to school, carrying his lunch. Spot was a step behind him. Spencer sat back down in his chair and lit a cigarette. He leaned back, the ashes dropped onto his shirt, and the book opened almost by itself to the passage. He began to read.

Dick said, "Oh. Oh! Go home, Spot. School is for boys and girls."

Spot ran into the schoolyard. "See?" Jane said. "See Spot run?"

I closed my eyes as Spencer read the story. It was all fresh to him again. I could hear it in his voice. He was involved with the characters, excited as he sounded out the words, picking up nuances in the plot even after all the years.

And I remembered Dick and Jane and Mother and Father and baby sister Sally. Spot and Puff. And Miss Binion.

Miss Binion taught third grade, and that was about the time people began to notice that I couldn't read. Miss Binion kept me inside during recess to correct that. She also sent a letter home and, not being able to read, I delivered it to my folks, who kept me inside after school too.

That is how I came to know Dick and his family. Sitting inside, looking outside, holding a book in my lap about a kid who was enough of a candy-ass to name his cat Puff.

Miss Binion would say, "You aren't being punished, Peter. When you learn to read, you'll be able to find out what all these stories are about yourself."

I already knew what the stories were about. They read them out loud in class. Some of them were about birthdays, some of them were about other children reading books. They talked about it every time Spot ran. None of the people in the stories was anybody I wanted to meet.

And Miss Binion not only kept me in during recess; every day after I'd proved I still couldn't read, she would ask me to try later in front of the class. "Sound out the words," she'd say.

Then I got a break. Miss Binion became engaged—I would like to think knocked up, but I don't know—and that got her mind off my reading problem. Some days she would forget to keep me in during recess, some days she wouldn't pay any attention to me when she did keep me in.

And it was during that period that I came across the fundamental rule of academia. If you don't know it, fake it. When I didn't recognize a word, I threw one in. And Miss Binion never corrected me.

In fact, she sent a letter home saying I had begun to improve. It never got there—I still couldn't read and wasn't about to put anything Miss Binion had written into my mother's hands again, but eventually my folks called her and heard how well I was doing and I got to go back outside after school.

Gradually I went from throwing in a word to throwing in a sentence. Then I started to look at the pictures and tell stories about them.

And then I got tired of stories about Puff and the ball, and when Miss Binion called on me to read that afternoon I made up my own.

What I remember about that day is a picture of Dick sitting in front of a birthday cake and the fact that I'd wanted a knife for a long time.

And I remember the beginning of the story. "One day, Father gave Dick a knife for his birthday. Then he cut the cat's head off . . ."

Spencer finished reading and closed the book. His shirt was on fire. "We owe Zerna Sharp," he said.

And you couldn't argue with that. If it weren't for Zerna Sharp, I would never have seen the look on Miss Binion's face that day. If Zerna Sharp had written a story I wanted to read, I might not have written any of my own.

67

The kid was driving a seventeen-year-old Chrysler that must have weighed four tons.

I was stopped at a red light and it was two o'clock in the morning. I had more things on my mind than it can hold, but none of them was that a kid driving a four-ton Chrysler wouldn't notice a red light, or the car sitting in front of it waiting for it to change.

Actually, he did notice it. He was about eleven feet away at the time, though, so the tire screech didn't last more than half a second before he landed, nose first, in the middle of the back bumper of—yes, I'm afraid it's a company car again.

I was eating a box of Oreo cookies at the time and had a wide-open, forty-eight-ounce cup of Coke between my legs. The 7-Eleven sells them with lids, but the lids never fit over the lip.

Anyway, I stuck one Oreo halfway up my nose and the Coke spilled over my lap. In the confusion of those first moments—before you know what has happened, only that something has—the first clear thought was about the Coke and all the things it was freezing. I thought, *Why couldn't I just buy a medium?*

The car bounced a few feet into the intersection, and when it stopped, I got out and stared at the Chrysler. The kid got out and ran his fingers through his hair. We came together between cars, in the exhaust of the company car, and he laid his wallet on the hood of the Chrysler and looked for his license.

His hands were shaking so bad he couldn't separate the cards. "I didn't need this tonight," he said.

I said, "Have you got insurance?"

He looked at me a second too long, and said yes. Then he found a bill of sale for the car, and his registration. He'd had it two days. "I hope this is what you need," he said.

That was when I looked into the front seat of the Chrysler, and in there was one of the two or three worst-kempt human beings I have ever seen, sitting against the door. He had horrible, stiff hair, and a flat nose and tattoos all down his arms. He was wearing an undershirt without sleeves, and it was stained, and you could see the fat in his chest and stomach under it.

I looked in, and he looked out.

"I've been driving eight hours," the kid said. He was still holding the registration against the hood. "I never did this before. I don't know how it happened."

A car stopped in the next lane and a man asked if I needed a doctor.

I thanked him for asking, but it wasn't blood, it was a Coke. The kid looked at my lap then and saw it was all wet. He said, "That must have been cold." Not smart, just sorry.

"Actually," I said, "it felt more like I'd plugged into a light socket."

"I'm sorry about your car," he said.

"It's not mine," I said, "it belongs to the company."

Which the kid took all wrong. He thought that made it worse. And we stood there in his one headlight, and he looked through his wallet for his driver's license and I tried to figure out if I could give him a break. The bumper was going to need replacing, the trunk might need to be realigned. It didn't look like $300.

It also didn't look like the kid had insurance, and if he'd had any money to pay for an accident he would have been driving something better than the Chrysler. I was nineteen once, and I know how these things work.

On the other hand, it seemed like the kid ought to have insurance and that he ought to be able to see a car stopped at a red light in time not to run into it.

And while I was trying to figure out what I was going to do, the passenger door opened and the passenger climbed out. He was cleaner-looking outside the car than he'd been sitting in the front seat—there were bugs all over the windshield—but not enough to keep him from being one of the two or three worst-kempt human beings I have ever seen.

There was something annoyed in his posture that I didn't like, and he walked to the back end of the company car, frowned, and then ran his hand over the damage. He grunted.

The gesture irritated me, the grunt irritated me, and I said, "What's that?"

The kid said, "That's my girlfriend."

And I looked closer and, yes, it was a girl. And I looked at this kid and his seventeen-year-old Chrysler, and his shaking hands, and his girlfriend, and I said, "Why don't you get in your car, I'll get in mine, and if you don't run into me again tonight I'm going to forget it happened."

He followed me back to the company car, thanking me. He kept calling me "sir."

I said it was all right, maybe eleven times, before he let me go. I told him I knew what it was like to be in trouble.

He said thank you again, and I closed my door so we wouldn't have to shake hands any more. He leaned over so his face was even with the window and called me sir. And he didn't believe I knew what it was like at all.

68

Jimmy French came to the *Daily News* as a weekly columnist in 1971, when he was twelve years old and in sixth grade. He stayed one year. Rolfe Neill—who was editor then—hired him sometime after spotting the phrase "even a dumb kid . . ." in one of the many letters signed "Jim French" that were published in the *Daily News* in 1970 and 1971.

Jimmy French called himself a dumb kid a lot.

His columns began in April and appeared Monday mornings on the page opposite Neill's signed column, "The Editor Speaks to You." People would open the paper and find Rolfe's picture on one side, Jimmy's on the other.

He wrote his columns the same way Neill wrote his. They were full of enthusiasm, humility, positive thinking. Philadelphia was a wonderful place, super terrific, in fact. The people were congenial, cordial, charming, sweet, impressive, exciting, and beautiful.

Shortly after Neill hired Jimmy, he held a small ceremony in the newsroom. He gave him a new typewriter and later his own personalized stationary with his picture on the letterhead, sitting behind his desk.

Jimmy, in turn, brought Rolfe cookies and candy from time to time, referred to him as "my big, strong, understanding editor" in print. He brought him an Easter basket. He called the *Daily News* "my serious love."

And Rolfe made the kid a star . . .

Jimmy French's mother was killed on Christmas Eve 1959, when he was ten months old. She was electrocuted in the bathtub, listening to Christmas carols. The police said the radio fell into the tub with her.

When he was three, he was put in the Forrest Child Care Center in the Northeast. Some years later he was taken out and went back to live with his father.

Neill made sure the *Daily News* audience knew that about Jimmy French.

After that, Jimmy's neighbors remember he was almost always alone. He didn't like sports, he didn't seem to like other kids. He hung around a neighborhood newspaper, he wrote letters to the editor to the *Daily News*, the *Inquirer*, the *Bulletin*.

His father didn't think that was unusual. Other fathers would ask him why Jimmy didn't play ball, he'd ask why they didn't take their sons to the library.

And then one night Rolfe Neill called and everything changed.

He gave an insecure twelve-year-old kid a free hand. He let him write about old age, taxes, capital punishment.

"To burn or not to burn? That is the question. Do we plug in the electric chair and light a man up like a Christmas tree? Or do we study him to find where society went wrong?"

When Jimmy got a D in spelling, the paper allowed him to chastise the teacher who gave it to him. He endorsed candidates for mayor.

He went to Washington to meet President Nixon—*"October found this dumb kid unpacking his bags in Washington, D.C. . . . I was saddened because the President didn't have time to chat. But I was grateful that I met him."*

He appeared in national magazines. He was on *To Tell the Truth* and *What's My Line?*

America's youngest columnist was doing more for the *Daily News* than Rolfe Neill was. When people questioned if Jimmy actually wrote the columns himself, Neill emphasized what a mature young man he was.

At the office, twenty-year veterans would get notes from a twelve-year-old kid's personalized memo pad congratulating a "Colleague" on a well-written column or story.

And under Neill's wing, twelve-year-old Jimmy French came to believe he was their colleague. He was removed from adolescence—where he'd been uncomfortable anyway—and made to feel he was something beyond that. And a year later—when he didn't have the paper and Rolfe anymore—there was nothing to go back to.

In an editor's note replying to a letter asking what had happened to Jimmy, the *Daily News* said that on leaving, his last words had been, "Thank you for making me king for a year."

Jimmy French resigned, thinking Rolfe Neill wouldn't let it happen. When the editorial-page editor had refused to run two of his columns, he'd gone to the managing editor. And when the managing editor had backed the editorial-page editor, he'd threatened to go to Neill.

And that was the end of it.

Jimmy French began having more trouble in school—it had begun while he was writing the column—he ran away from home for days at a time. Neighbors saw him shoot out windows, they told their kids to stay away from him. Later he got a job with the Redevelopment Authority as a guard.

After that, I didn't know what happened to Jimmy French, until yesterday afternoon at the Roundhouse when he was charged with shooting a nineteen-year-old kid in the chest and forehead in what police said was supposed to have been a "fair fight." It had started in a mall over a cracked car window.

He was sitting on a bench when I saw him, hands cuffed behind his back, wearing soft, expensive-looking clothes. He looked confused more than anything, in some ways younger at twenty than he had looked in the picture that ran with his column.

And he had a silver belt buckle that said "Pontiac." Seven years ago it might have said "Daily News."

"He's got a '77 Trans Am," his father said. "Jimmy loves that car."

I don't want to be misunderstood here. I am not saying that the *Daily News* or Rolfe Neill is responsible for Jimmy French.

What I am saying is that Rolfe Neill and the *Daily News* used him, and that sometimes when you use people, you use them up.

Rolfe Neill knows that better than anybody, and it should have mattered that the kid was only twelve years old.

Neill was somewhere in the mountains last night, on vacation, and not available for comment.

69

There was a small story in the back pages of the paper last week about a man in Rome, Georgia, who was sentenced to eight years for raping his wife. She was in the hospital, in a coma, at the time.

The man's name is Dennis Brown, and he is sitting in Polk County jail as we speak. Mr. Brown was a housepainter and he lived in a house in Cedarville, Georgia, with a thirty-four-year-old woman who was his common-law wife, and her daughter. They had been together eighteen months.

In February, the wife was critically injured in a truck accident. The truck was Brown's business, and the family's only transportation. His wife was taken to the Floyd County Medical Center in a coma, and never recovered. She is in the care of a nursing home now.

Brown came to the hospital shortly after the accident and stayed. He slept in chairs and on the floor and in the halls. He took pills to stay awake. He sat by her bed forty-two days, waiting for her to wake up.

At the trial, half a dozen neighbors and friends testified that Brown and his wife were happy together. That they were affectionate. Some of them used the phrase "loving couple."

The woman's mother even testified that Brown and his wife loved each other. And her interest in the case, and the family's interest, was to see Brown punished. "Her family was furious," said Wade Hoyt, who is Brown's lawyer. "They were so angry after the charges came out, they went to the house when he was in jail and took all the furniture and his clothes. They destroyed his clothes . . ."

On the forty-second night that his wife lay in a coma, Dennis Brown, according to his attorney, "just snapped." A nurse and an orderly came into the room and found him on top of her in bed.

The orderly went for Mary Barbee, a nursing supervisor, who reported the incident to hospital security guards, who reported it to police. Twenty-seven days later, Brown was arrested for rape.

He was refused bond by Superior Court Judge John Frazier, and has been sitting in jail since April.

"The first thing I liked about Dennis," his lawyer said, "he didn't try to give me twenty-five excuses for what he did. He didn't remember all of what happened, or what got into his head. He didn't lie about it, he honestly didn't understand how."

The trial centered on Georgia's rape laws. They say that if a woman is in a coma, she cannot give her consent to sexual intercourse, and that any penetration of her is rape.

Judge Frazier instructed the jury to disregard the relationship between Brown and his wife, and largely prevented that line of testimony.

"Once I wasn't allowed to establish their relationship," Hoyt said, "I'd lost the only case we had. The human side."

For its part, the prosecution dwelled on the wife's deteriorating condition, the tubes keeping her alive, the hopeless prognosis. They put the nurses on the stand, and the one who had found Dennis Brown on top of his wife said that when she saw him in the hallway afterwards, "I just wanted to kill him."

"In the end," Hoyt said, "I told the jury that they could go back and do the right thing. That it didn't matter what the law said, they weren't accountable to anyone but themselves. By then, Dennis had been in jail half a year, and there wasn't much left to punish. I said, 'Dennis Brown has had about all the justice one person can stand.'

"I was scared to death the jury would find him guilty and recommend leniency, because I know Judge Frazier, and he is a wonderful man, but, like anybody else, he has his own feelings about things. And I knew if they convicted Dennis, he was in trouble."

Which is exactly what happened. The jury was out for three hours. They found Dennis Brown guilty of rape, and eleven or twelve asked the judge for leniency. The foreman suggested probation, saying Brown was "the sort of individual who needs psychiatric help."

The judge gave him ten years, two of them to be served as probation.

Hoyt said he has already begun the appeals, but doesn't know what kind of shape Brown will be in by the time they're heard. "He doesn't have a lick left in him," he said.

And even if he gets out, Dennis Brown has still lost his wife, and her child. He has lost his truck, which wasn't insured, and his job. And his furniture and his clothes.

And the hospital is billing him—as his wife's legal guardian—for $42,000.

"I was aware that I had done something terrible," he said on the stand, "but I didn't know why."

I would guess that neither do the people who wrote the law, or the people who enforce it. I would guess that in hindsight, they could look at what happened—forty-three straight nights with her in the hospital room, waiting for her to come back to him—and see that this wasn't what the law had in mind.

70

I came to this city from Florida more than twelve years ago, just before Christmas. I am leaving it now.

It took a long time to get used to Philadelphia. The weather, the traffic, the ground rules. I'd never seen a place where people were as rude to each other for no reason. Of course, I hadn't been to New York.

I'd lost my car and my clothes and my books and my wife before I came here—I think the bank got the good stuff—and there wasn't anybody down there sorry to see me leave except maybe my friend Geringer.

He and I had worked in a gas station together in West Palm Beach. All the gas station stories have been told, of course, except the truest one, which is that it felt like we had used up all the luck we would ever have just getting those jobs. And there wasn't anybody who wanted to give us a chance to be writers again.

Girls? They wouldn't even let us look at their legs while we were cleaning the windshields. They still won't let Geringer look at their legs, by the way, and he spends a lot of time out in front of the paper on Broad Street, offering to do windows.

Anyway, one day at the gas station, I got a phone call from Philadelphia, from an editor I'd heard of but never met, and he asked how I'd like to come north to be a reporter. I arrived three days later with one pair of boots, no coat, running as close to empty as I've ever been.

And I went to work here, but things didn't get any better. I did get a coat, but there wasn't anything warm in me for a long time.

The people who hired me regretted it almost from the beginning. They came after me in strange psychological ways, and with strange people. Their idea of creating anxiety was to have a city editor write a memo and put it in a secret file. My idea of anxiety—well, I remember calling up the editor of this newspaper one weekend and asking his wife out on a date.

I was not somebody then you could reach with subtleties.

And looking back on it now, that editor was probably right to want to fire me—it never occurred to any of them to just ask me to leave, by the way, because I would have—and I was probably right to ask his wife out.

And things went along like that until the large bosses left for jobs in other cities, and the little bosses began to disappear. Which happened shortly after Gil Spencer stumbled in the door and took over.

Spencer did a couple of other things I will always be grateful for. He gave me a chance to write columns, and he gave me room to figure out what they should be about. And then, about a year later, he gave me a shot at this.

The first column I wrote was about going home to South Dakota to hunt pheasants with an old friend named Fred. I liked column writing so much that I went out and got married.

I mean, you can't write about Fred forever, right?

And then my wife had a baby, and I wrote about her for a while, and as if that wasn't enough, I ran into Randall Cobb one afternoon at the Who-Dun-It? bookstore on Chestnut Street, and he took me, among other places, to Mickey Rosati's Gym in South Philadelphia.

Now, a lot of nice things have been said about me in the couple weeks since the announcement was made that I was leaving, but the truth is that anybody who came into this city and got a column—mainly because nobody wants to be his editor anymore—and then was introduced to the cast of characters I was introduced to could not help writing some of the things I have written.

And could not help loving some of the people I have loved.

And in the end, that is what this city gave me. Some people I loved. And what am I giving back? I'm letting you keep Geringer.

There have been things to talk about, of course. Unforgettable sights and unforgettable stories. There was a three-hour siege at Tasker and Twenty-ninth, police with bullhorns trying to talk a piece of local color called "Beatnik" into surrendering himself and a stolen 200-pound meat slicer. Beatnik came out late in the afternoon in a robe, yawning, saying he had been asleep the whole time. And the police took his house apart—right down to the toilet—and never found a trace of the slicer.

I have seen a pope, I have seen Julius Erving at the top of his game. I have seen a city administration burn down a neighborhood. I watched Randall Cobb slowly realize he would never become heavyweight champion of the world. One night I almost watched myself die.

And as moving as those things were at the time, they are not what endures.

What endures are the people I loved.

I came here empty twelve years ago, and I am not empty now.

Somewhere along the line, this city has done me a profound favor. I glimpse it once in a while at night in the street, among the people who live there, or along the road. Hitchhikers. It cuts fresh every time.

I recognize the lost faces because one of them, I think, was supposed to be mine.

71

The first day the fighter came into the gym he went two rounds with a weight lifter from New Jersey who was just learning to keep his hands up—and he tried to hurt him.

I didn't know if it was something between them or if the fighter just had a mean streak. Some of them do. Whatever it was, the fighter went after him, turning his weight into his punches, missing some, but dropping enough right hands in so that at the end of the two rounds the whole left side of the weight lifter—without ever having been hit perfect—was blotted pink. It's an honest gym, and what happened wasn't particularly violent, but it was out of place.

I was sitting by the windows with Mickey Rosati at the time, and his son, little Mick.

The two of them are with each other all day. They work together in their garage downstairs, they run together, they box each other two or three times a week. The kid is a world-class amateur. They know each other inside out—moves and moods—and I've never heard a hard word between them. You get the feeling sometimes that they're the same person, spaced about thirty years apart.

Up in the ring, the weight lifter was getting packed into the corner like one shirt too many in a hamper. "What's that about?" I said.

Mickey shook his head. "They're both from Jersey," he said. "Maybe they got on each other's nerves."

The weight lifter had a brother named Dennis. He was fourteen years older—closing in on forty—and two or three times a week the two of them came over the bridge from New Jersey to work out.

The gym sits on a narrow street in South Philadelphia where people park on the sidewalks and sneakers hang from the telephone wires. Inside, it's honest and clean; at least, for a gym it's clean. We are not speaking here of Nautilus-center clean, but people have been known to hit the bucket when they spit, and when Mickey's hawk—which is another story—used the ring for a bathroom one afternoon, the spot was scoured with Lysol before anybody fought again. That might not sound like much, but in most gyms, hawk shit will petrify before anybody cleans it up.

The weight lifter liked to box when he could; Dennis wasn't as serious. He slapped at the heavy bags or shadow-boxed, and once in a while he mentioned that he ought to be getting paid for his entertainment value, which was probably true. If it came into his head, Dennis said it.

During the month or two Dennis and his brother had been coming up, Mickey had spent some time in the ring with the brother, getting him used to the feel of soft punches, showing him how to relax.

At the start, the brother had gone home depressed. Dennis reported it while Mickey was doing sit-ups on an elevated board, his teeth biting a cold cigar. "My brother's got guys terrified of him in Jersey," Dennis said. "He can't believe somebody as old as you could do that to him. All weekend long he's messed up."

Mickey lay back on the board and closed his eyes. "Suddenly," he said, the cigar moving in his teeth, "I don't feel like doing sit-ups no more."

As a step in the mending, Dennis and his brother decided Mickey probably wasn't human; at least they had no idea he could be beaten or hurt. They called him the Punching Machine.

You could see how they might think that. Mickey Rosati is fifty-one years old and left-handed, and he can still fight. But he is fifty-one years old. His shoulders hurt him after he works out, he gets poison ivy just looking at the woods, and the speed he had when he won twenty-two straight fights back in the fifties isn't there like it was. On brains and shape, he would still beat most of the four- and six-round fighters at his weight in the world, but he pays more to stay that way than anybody who isn't around him could know.

The fighter from Jersey was back two weeks later. He came in with Dennis. Mickey was sitting in a chair, holding a cold cigar in his teeth, trying not to scratch his arms. He was just back from the Pocono Mountains, poison-ivyed half to death. He'd gone there for squirrels. Mickey has been hunting since he was seven years old—ever since he went after stray cats in the alleys of South Philadelphia with a baseball bat. As he gets older, though, he gets gentler, and cares less about the shooting and more about just being outside. This weekend, as a matter of fact, he'd left his gun in the cabin.

"This same path, I must've walked it a hundred times," he said. "But this time, I was just walking along, and you know, there's apples in all those trees. Millions of them. I been through there a hundred times, and I never saw the apples before . . ."

Dennis bent over him then. "Hey, Mick, I told this guy you'd give him two or three rounds," he said.

Mickey looked at Dennis, then at the fighter, putting together what was doing. "All right," he said. Mickey will always give you the benefit of the doubt; he will always give you his time.

The fighter dressed and wrapped his hands and then got laced into a pair of black gloves. He loosened up five or ten minutes, then fit his mouthpiece over his teeth and climbed into the ring.

Mickey slipped his unwrapped hands into an old pair of pull-on gloves and got in with him. He doesn't use a mouthpiece or headgear. He was giving away twenty-five pounds, and twenty-five years. "Three rounds?" he said.

The fighter said, "I don't know if I'm even in shape to finish one." Mickey has been around gyms all his life and knew better than that.

The bell rang and the fighter came straight at him, throwing right hands and hooks, trying to hurt him. Little Mickey sat down a yard from the ropes and watched.

Mickey took the punches on his arms and gloves and shoulders, moving in and out, relaxed. A minute into the round, he threw a long, slow right hook at the fighter's head, which the fighter blocked, and a short left under his ribs. Which he never saw.

The punch stopped the fighter cold. For two or three seconds he couldn't breathe, he couldn't move his hands. In those seconds, Mickey could have ended it and gone back to his chair and let him go. And when the fighter could breathe again, he began to find Mickey with some of the right hands.

The gym was quiet, except for the sounds of the ring itself. Mickey and the fighter seemed even for a round and a half, but somewhere in it the fighter got stronger. He used his elbows and shoulders; Mickey gave ground and landed some hooks to the side, but his punches didn't have much on them.

Between rounds Mickey walked in circles, breathing through his teeth, looking at the floor. I thought about being fifty-one years old, working all day pulling transmissions and engines, and then coming upstairs with bad shoulders and poison ivy and having to fight life and death with some kid who didn't even know who you were.

The third round started, and the fighter, if anything, was throwing harder now. Mickey let the punches hit his arms and sides and glance off his head, moving in the direction they pushed him. One of them scraped some skin off his eyebrow.

The fighter followed him, forgetting what had happened to him in the first round, forgetting that Mickey hadn't hurt him when he was helpless. And then I heard little Mickey say, "He's got him now." I looked down at him to see how he knew that, and by the time I looked back up, Mickey was hitting the fighter with twelve clean punches in a row.

For the last minute and a half of the fight, Mickey hit him with every-thing he threw. When the fighter tried to come back at him, it opened him up for something else.

At the end, he had stopped fighting and was leaning against the ropes covering up. Mickey patted the fighter on the head, climbed out of the ring, and worked two hard rounds on the heavy bag, jumped rope, and then put a cigar between his teeth and did sit-ups, looking happier all the time.

I said to his son, "He shouldn't have to do that."

Little Mickey said, "Yeah, but you know my father. He liked the challenge, having to do it . . ."

I looked around the gym—a clean, honest room with enough windows so you could feel the street—and as nice as it was, that's what it was for. Having to do it. Not every day or every week, but if you're going to box, then once in a while it's going to happen.

And Mickey doesn't own the place by accident. Now and then you've got to let the dog out of the house to run.

Driving home from the gym that night, I told him I wouldn't have patted the fighter on the head, no matter how grateful I was that he tried to kill me.

Mickey said, "Yeah, I should have bit him." His mood was getting better and better. He looked down at his arms, though, touched his neck where the poison ivy was. "Five days," he said, "before it goes away. I lie in bed at night, thinking about scratching it or not."

"That long?"

"The doctor said they got some kind of shot, it gives you the worse case you ever got, and then you don't get it anymore. You can't take the shot when you already got poison ivy, though. You got to be cured, and then they can give it to you, and then they can cure you. Probably."

He shook his head. "There's nothing you can do about poison ivy," he said, "but stay out of the way."

He dabbed at the scrape over his eye. "And what good is that?"

72

The boss's name is Tony Scarduzio, and Tuesday afternoon he goes out on the job with Jose Colon. Just to keep his hand in. "To make sure that things are being done to my specifications," he says.

Jose Colon is a parking-meter repairman. Somebody gets drunk in Camden and runs over a parking meter because he put a dime in and didn't get any bubble gum, Jose fixes that too.

It doesn't matter to Jose, he likes his job. "You don't have to go to school or nothing, and it's very enjoyable," he said.

So Jose and Tony are out on the truck, going up Broadway, when they come to a broken parking meter. It's broken in a way that they can only fix back at the shop, so Jose gets out a wrench to replace the head. While he is doing that, though, he happens to notice a white paper sack leaning against the stem.

"It's a nice paper sack," he said later, "got a label on it from some store on Germantown Avenue in Philly. It looks almost new, you know, a real nice paper sack, and somebody stapled it up. So I pick up the sack and it looks to me like there's a co-co-nut in there. I say, 'Hey, Tony, we better look inside. I think we found a co-co-nut.'"

Tony shrugs, and Jose opens it carefully, not wanting to damage a real nice paper sack, and looks inside. Tony waits, Jose just stares inside the sack. "Hey, Tony," he says after a minute, "there's a head inside this paper sack."

"A what?"

"It's not a coconut, Tony. It's a head." And Jose sees that his boss doesn't believe him, so he reaches in the sack and pulls the head out. A human skull. The jaw bone is missing and so are the teeth, but outside of that it is perfect. "It's not a coconut," Jose says again.

Tony says, "Oh my God!" and as soon as they fix the parking meter, they take the head over to Juvenile Division, where Tony has a friend who is a detective.

Tony and Jose go into the detective's office and put the sack in his hands. "I think I found Jimmy Hoffa," Tony says. The detective smiles and looks inside.

Then he stops smiling.

"I can't do anything about this," he says. "You better take it over to the administration building." And he hands the almost-new white paper sack with the head inside back to Tony, who gives it to Jose, and tells him to carry it over there.

On the way over, Jose stops to see his friend Kevin McKeel, who is also a supervisor for the city, and tells him to look inside the sack. Kevin does. "Surprised, huh?" Jose says.

And then he walks it the rest of the way to the police administration building, and has a short talk with the detectives' receptionist. "I bring in the bag and say, 'I found a head in the street,'" Jose says. "She says, 'This is serious. Do you really want me to go get a detective and tell him you got a head?'

"I tell her I'm not joking. I say, 'You want to look inside?' She don't want to, but another woman comes out of the office and she wants to look inside. I don't know who she was, she didn't say nothing after she looked. She just went back where she come from."

The receptionist, meanwhile, has located Sgt. Albert Handy, who comes out and takes the sack from Jose and checks inside, and then thanks him for bringing it over.

Sgt. Handy puts a tag on the skull and gives it to a detective to take over to the coroner's office in Cherry Hill. "We can't do anything about it here," he would say later.

So the detective drives the skull over to Jerry Healy, who is an investigator, and Jerry Healy puts another tag on it and sends it to Newark. "There was nothing we could do about it here," his wife would say later. Jerry was out collecting a body and couldn't be reached for comment.

And so, as the day ended, Jose was back at work in the street. Tony had gone back to work in his office. The skull was on a bus for Newark, and Sgt. Handy was working on new cases. "A man brings in a skull in a paper sack," Handy said. "It's nothing to stop work for." Sgt. Handy has been with the department fourteen years.

"Hey," he said, "this is Camden."

73

As my old friend Norman used to say, you follow the bear tracks long enough, eventually you see the bear. Norman was a philosopher as well as something of an outdoorsman, and he had seen the bear a lot. One of them had chased him up a tree, in fact, and it was an experience he never forgot. "You cannot understand what a she-rip really looks like," he told me once, "until she's close enough so that you can smell the fish on her breath."

Because Norman was a philosopher, his take on bears, of course, applied to everything else. Meaning, you don't really know what anything looks like until you're close enough to smell the fish.

I was reminded of this again last week, not by an argument with Mrs. Dexter, who has been known, on occasion, to turn into something of a she-rip herself, but the announcement that the old activist lawyer William Kunstler had decided to defend Colin Ferguson, the man accused of walking down the aisle of the Long Island Rail Road's rush-hour train to Hicksville and shooting twenty-five human beings he didn't know, killing six of them.

Ferguson, who is African-American, looked on these shootings as repayment for the years he had been the object of discrimination and insults. As repayment for being expelled from Adelphi University.

And Kunstler, along with co-counsel Ronald Kuby, are pleading him not guilty by reason of "black rage." Which is to say that the history of racism in America spawned a wrath against whites in Colin that relieves him of responsibility for his actions.

As Kuby said in last week's *New York* magazine, "Nobody is saying that Colin Ferguson did a good thing. We're not saying he is justified. We're not saying that people should name their children after him or follow in his footsteps. We're just saying that he was not responsible for his own conduct. We're saying white racism is to blame."

That is not quite true, of course. In the same magazine story, a caller to predominately African-American radio station WLTB was quoted as saying, "These people who enslaved our fathers, enslaved our mothers— they earned it [getting shot]."

And Laura Blackburne, counsel to the NAACP, said that Ferguson "is as much a victim as the rest of us."

At any rate, we have heard Kunstler's argument before. We heard a version of it from Jesse Jackson and U.S. Rep. Maxine Waters (D-California) when rioters were burning and looting Los Angeles, maiming strangers simply for the color of their skin.

Waters and Jackson lectured us then that the rioters should not be called thugs or thieves, that they were frustrated people who felt powerless to vent their anger.

They all but destroyed Koreatown, these frustrated people.

We heard the same rationale explaining away the poisonous anti-Semitism that is currently spewing from the leadership of the Nation of Islam.

We heard it after an African-American mob pulled a white man from his car in Crown Heights and killed him.

We hear it, in fact, all the time, explaining not only the criminal actions of the financially and culturally impoverished, but, in some cases, the actions of African-Americans who are born to privilege.

We have heard it over and over: that wasn't a riot in L.A., it was a social movement. It was rebellion; it was a people rising up together to protest injustice. We followed the bear tracks.

And now, through William Kunstler, we have followed the tracks long enough to finally run into the bear.

A man walks onto a commuter train at 5:30 p.m., waits until he is outside the city limits so as not to embarrass Mayor David Dinkins, and then opens fire on strangers, picking out his victims by the color of their skin. And an American court of law will decide if the man is responsible for these actions, or if the country's history of racism takes the blame.

And that, in a strange way, is the logical place the argument that we all carry the sins and grievances of our forefathers properly leads: to the idea that a whole race of people is infected with diminished capacity.

You wanted to see the bear; there it is.

74

Early on the afternoon of February 4, 1982, a truck driver named Albert Brihn, on the way to a sewage-treatment plant off PGA Boulevard just outside Palm Beach Gardens, Florida, noticed something lying in a clearing of pine trees sixty feet off the road connecting the treatment plant to the street. It looked like a dummy.

Mr. Brihn delivered his load and headed back out. On the way, the thing in the clearing caught his eye again. Then something else—a buzzard, floating over it, banking again and again in those grim buzzard circles. Suddenly the thought broke, and Mr. Brihn knew what the thing was.

He stopped the truck and walked to the body. It was a man dressed in a black bikini bathing suit. There was a gold chain around the neck threaded through an Italian horn of plenty. He studied the body—there was a hole to the right of the nose, another at the right temple, both with muzzle burns, and there was a tear between the nose and the mouth where a bullet fragment had passed, going out. As he stood there, the chest rose and fell twice. It was one-thirty in the afternoon.

Ten minutes later, the paramedics from Old Dixie Fire Station No. 2 arrived in an ambulance. If you believe the signs you see coming into town, Palm Beach Gardens is the golf capital of the world. It is home to a large retirement community—in this case, a financially secure retirement community—so when one of its citizens expires, serious efforts are made toward not leaving the body lying around long enough to attract buzzards.

This particular body, of course, did not belong to someone of retirement age. The paramedics were there in ten minutes anyway, and took it, the chest still rising and falling, to Palm Beach Gardens Community Hospital, where, at 3:36 p.m., the chest was suddenly still. Michael J. Dalfo was twenty-nine years old, and the coroner's report would say he died of two .25-caliber bullets, shot at close range into his head.

There is not much to say here about Michael J. Dalfo. He lived with his brother, Christopher, in a condominium in the Glenwood section of PGA National, a golf resort and residential development. His father had some money, and he and Christopher and his mother once owned a restaurant, Christopher-Michael's Ristorante. A year after they sold it, investigators say, someone torched the place.

Michael Dalfo had a girlfriend, and he apparently spent a lot of time with other girls, ones he had to pay. He also apparently used cocaine.

On the night he was shot, according to police, Dalfo called the Fantasy Island Escort service three different times. A woman named Diane De Lena had come over first, sometime before midnight, and stayed an hour. Dalfo, in the words of an assistant state attorney, "hadn't been able to get things going" and tried to talk his visitor into staying another hour. He wrote her a personal check for $75, but she refused to take it and left.

Dalfo called Fantasy Island again, this time ordering two more girls. When they arrived, he told them that they were "dogs," and they left.

"He was very untactful," one of the escorts would tell police.

Forty-five minutes later he called Fantasy Island again, and ordered a fourth girl. When the service didn't send one, he ordered yet another—this one from a different outfit, Rainbow Escorts—who showed up at about three-thirty in the morning and found the door to Dalfo's condominium open. She told police she walked in and no one was home. She used Dalfo's phone to call Rainbow Escorts and report she had been stood up. Then she left.

And the next person known to have seen Michael Dalfo was a truck driver named Albert Brihn, who wasn't even looking for him.

Almost from the beginning, the investigation into Dalfo's death centered on the woman named Diane De Lena. Sheriff's investigators say they found matchbooks on Dalfo's coffee table with the names and numbers of several escort services printed on the backs, Fantasy Island among them. They found Fantasy Island's phone number written on a check, made out to cash, for $75. They also found a small quantity of cocaine.

Within a week, a detective from the Sheriff's Department got in touch with De Lena, who, in tape-recorded interviews, admitted that she had been with Dalfo on the night he was killed but said she had left him healthy, sometime around midnight, and gone to a West Palm hotel for her next appointment. She said she hadn't seen him again and, according to prosecutors, stuck to that story for almost five years.

It was not just De Lena, though, who caught the investigator's attention. At the time of the murder, Diane De Lena was living with a man who had once been a major league hockey player. His name was Brian Spencer, and he had spent more than eight years in the National Hockey League—with Toronto, the Islanders, Buffalo, and Pittsburgh. He was an aggressive player without exceptional talent, scrambling to stay even, scrambling to stay in the league. A scrappy five-foot-eleven, 185-pound left wing, Spencer did not produce dazzling numbers but was still a favorite of the fans; he was voted the most popular Islander by the team's booster club in 1973. By 1979, however, the popularity and the scrambling weren't enough, and he was sent to the minors, where he stayed a season and a half and then left the game. His marriage dissolved, and he got in his car and drove to Florida.

The assistant state attorney says the Sheriff's Department "knew" Spencer had done the actual shooting all along. Spencer and De Lena had lived in a trailer on Skees Road, at the far western edge of West Palm Beach. The place may not be officially designated as a swamp, but the mosquitoes come in clouds, the ground is wet all the time, and anything you step on that doesn't bite you either goes "squish" or it crumbles.

Spencer must have liked the swamps. Two, maybe three years later, he began to build a house and a shop in Loxahatchee, which *is* officially designated as a swamp, but he ran out of money and ended up building neither. He was good with his hands, he seemed to understand the way things worked, and could fix them when they didn't. He met De Lena, in fact, when he did some repair work on her car.

During the time he and De Lena lived together, he worked as a mechanic for an electrical contracting company, Fischbach and Moore. His Florida friends say the mechanical work was enough, that it had replaced whatever he had in hockey. Spencer had loved the game and the life of a big league professional. "The travel, the people, I loved it all," Spencer said. But when it was over, he wanted to leave it behind. And in the end, leaving was failure—"Even Gordie Howe, at fifty-two, was seen as a failure," Spencer said.

"He used to talk about playing," said a friend named Dan Martinetti, "but he loved working with his hands—fixing equipment—more than hockey. He went from nothing to having everything, and then he went back to chopped bologna. But he didn't care about money, he still doesn't. You could give him a hundred thousand dollars—he'd look at it and then go spend it on tools and equipment."

Diane De Lena, now Diane De Lena Fialco, has a different story. Offered immunity and threatened with jail for contempt if she did not testify, she has told the state attorney that Spencer bragged constantly about his days in the NHL. She has said that he roughed her up. She draws a picture now of a frustrated and violent man and says she was afraid of him.

Diane De Lena Fialco says a lot of things, and the assistant state attorney who until three weeks ago was handling the case—a woman named Lynne Baldwin—thought that a jury would believe her. Baldwin laid the groundwork in the newspaper, referring to Fialco by her working name, Crystal, in order to protect her for as long as possible from the scrutiny of the press. "She's a very beautiful young girl and, even though she worked for an escort service, there's something about her that makes her seem vulnerable, sort of like Marilyn Monroe . . ." the prosecutor told the *Palm Beach Post* in February. "Because of this incident, she got out of that kind of life and is working a good job and has a family."

The state attorney's office needs Diane Fialco, and needs her to be credible. Without her, there is no case. No gun, no blood, no witness.

And on the testimony of this one witness, who reminds the prosecutor of an actress, Spencer was indicted by a Florida grand jury on charges of first-degree murder and kidnapping. And on her testimony, the state of Florida is willing to end Brian Spencer's life.

There is a temptation here to set Brian Spencer's life on the table, the way museums set out antique silverware and plates and glasses in an Early American dining room and pretend that the setting is somehow what pioneer life was like.

The trouble, of course, is that a life isn't one way or another. A lot of things happen, and the reflections of those things are shaded by time and mood, and are lost and invented even if you were there. Even if you happen to be a professional athlete and thousands of people see what you do, and remember.

And the idea of catching up with such a life, halfway through its thirty-eighth year, at the Palm Beach County Jail, and then picking through the newspaper clippings and the reflections of friends and wives (there have been two) and teammates for some thread of cause and effect is ambitious beyond what can honestly be accomplished.

It *can* be said that somewhere along the line, Brian Spencer was not careful enough about his roommates, but beyond that you're on your own.

Spencer was born in Fort St. James, British Columbia, which is a long way north of anywhere you are, in September 1949. He was a twin, although he and his brother, Byron, do not look much alike. The father's name was Roy, the mother's is Irene. She had been a schoolteacher, and then did office work for the Hudson's Bay Company. Roy had a gravel pit, and drove the boys to hockey practice. Twenty miles round-trip, even when he was sick.

The family lived outside town and owned a generator that was the only source of electricity. When Roy's emphysema gave him trouble breathing, they would start it to run the oxygen machine.

The boys fished in the summer and played hockey all winter. They went to the only school in town—it was three or four rooms in the beginning—through grade ten. There was no high school in Fort St. James, so they began grade eleven in Vanderhoof, a forty-mile bus ride.

Like a lot of NHL players from small towns, Spencer did not finish high school. He quit, devoting himself to the sport, and in December 1970 he was called up to the Toronto Maple Leafs from Tulsa.

On Saturday, December 12, the Leafs were at home against Chicago. The Canadian Broadcasting Corporation televised that game to eastern Canada. In the West, however, the CBC was carrying the Vancouver Canucks versus the Oakland Seals.

Angry that his son's game was not being broadcast by CKPG Television in Prince George, Roy Spencer got into his car and drove the 110 miles to the station, where he pulled a 9-mm pistol and, holding the news director and the program director and six other employees against a wall, ordered them to take the station off the air.

The station shut down, and Roy Spencer told the program manager, "If the station comes back on the air again, I will hold you responsible. I am very upset about the CBC coverage."

Then he backed out of the studio and ran for the door. He was crossing the sidewalk outside the station when the police told him to drop his gun. He turned, fifteen feet away, and shot one of the policemen in the foot, another in the holster.

The police returned fire, hitting Roy Spencer in the shoulder, the armpit and the mouth, and he was dead on arrival at Prince George Regional Hospital.

Two of the police officers involved would comment later, at the coroner's inquest, on the exceptional length of time it took Roy Spencer to fall.

On November 27, 1984, a twenty-five-year-old man named Leslie Raymond Fialco was married in a civil ceremony to Diane De Lena. According to prosecutor Baldwin, Fialco had no hint that his new wife had ever worked for an escort service or that she had been involved in a murder case then two years old. The couple settled into Palm Beach Shores and started a family. According to Baldwin, the marriage has produced two children.

Two years passed, and then one day at work Mrs. Fialco looked up from her desk and was handed a subpoena. It had been a long time since the sheriff's deputies had questioned her about the Dalfo murder, and she did not realize at first what the subpoena was for.

When she walked into the state attorney's office on Third Street in West Palm Beach, however, and saw all the old, familiar faces, she broke into tears. According to the assistant state attorney, she said, "I thought this was over."

Now, one of the many things that is still hazy about this case is exactly what leverage the sheriff's investigators and the state attorney's office used on Diane Fialco to get her to hand them Spencer. She was given "use" immunity, meaning she could not be prosecuted for the murder based on her own statement and would go to jail if she failed to testify, and perhaps that was leverage enough.

Lynne Baldwin has said, "The police knew they [De Lena and Spencer] did it all along, but they just couldn't prove it," and she has acknowledged that part of the deal to get Diane De Lena Fialco to testify was her promise to do what she could to shield Diane from publicity.

There is no question that the Palm Beach County Sheriff's Department wanted Spencer for the Dalfo murder. Here is Lieut. Pat McCutcheon of the sheriff's detective division: "From the outset of the investigation, we looked at him as a suspect. But because of the lack of cooperation [from De Lena] we couldn't implicate him. A couple of times we thought she would testify, but she changed her mind. Maybe out of affection, maybe out of fear."

Fear, of course, can come from a lot of different directions, and in the end Diane Fialco, apparently afraid of something, gave the prosecutors what they wanted. The story she has told, in a sworn statement, goes like this:

On the night Dalfo is killed, she drives to his condominium sometime before midnight, leaving the keys in the car, and stays about an hour. She always leaves the keys in the ignition except when Spencer drives her to a job and waits—a precaution against having to leave without her purse.

While she is there, Dalfo is snorting cocaine and, according to Baldwin, finds himself impotent. He asks her to stay an extra hour and offers to write her a check.

Staying beyond the agreed time and accepting checks, however, are both against Fantasy Island rules, and she starts to leave. Dalfo stops her, writes the check anyway, payable to cash, and puts it in her hand. She gives it back. He drops the check on the coffee table, angry now, and she walks out the door. She is afraid.

She drives from Palm Beach Gardens back to the trailer on Skees Road, but Spencer isn't home. She goes over to the Banana Boat—a bar where Spencer likes to drink—and tells him what has happened at Dalfo's. She also tells him that she is afraid that Dalfo may have followed her home. Then she drives to the hotel in West Palm and sees another customer.

An hour or so later she meets Spencer at home, and he gets upset and wants to go to Dalfo's place. Diane De Lena wants to forget the whole thing, but Spencer won't. She is afraid of Spencer—"Spencer had hit his women," Lynne Baldwin says. "Another woman he knew showed up for work with her face bruised. She said she had been in a car accident. Her boss was suspicious." De Lena thinks he only wants to talk, or at the outside, to rough Dalfo up. She does not think Spencer wants to kill him.

So they head over to Dalfo's. De Lena's plan now is to tell Spencer she can't remember which condominium Dalfo lives in. As all the condominiums at PGA National look the same, this is not a bad plan. There is, however, a built-in flaw: because the condominiums do look alike, it is Dalfo's habit to wait outside his place for visitors from the escort service, and so when Spencer and De Lena arrive, Dalfo is standing out front in his black bikini swimsuit and his gold chain, waiting for his fourth "escort" of the evening. Spencer asks Dalfo to get into the car. (When Diane De Lena told this version of the story to the police, she did not remember Spencer's using a gun. In a more recent version, Baldwin says, that detail came back to her.) At any rate, Dalfo, Spencer, and De Lena drive out of PGA National to PGA Boulevard, turn west and travel six-tenths of a mile and then come to a white sand road. There is a sign at the junction: PGA WASTEWATER TREATMENT PLANT, SEACOAST UTILITIES.

Four hundred feet up the road, Spencer stops at a spot where the trees recede from the road, creating a weedy clearing. A sign says NO DUMPING.

Spencer tells De Lena to get out of the car. Spencer and Dalfo begin to argue and Dalfo says, "If you touch me, I'll call my lawyer." This in-furiates Spencer, and the arguing gets louder. Diane De Lena, who is afraid, begins to run up the road, in the direction of PGA Boulevard. Dalfo is alive when she leaves. She runs, but she never hears any shots. And so when Spencer picks her up in the car a few minutes later, she as-sumes he has beaten Dalfo up and left him.

They drive back to the trailer. According to Baldwin, Spencer then tells De Lena to take off all her clothes. She does that, gives them to Spen-cer, and never sees them again. She believes they were burned or buried.

A week later, the Sheriff's Department is asking her questions about Michael Dalfo's murder. This, of course, scares Diane De Lena. More than Michael Dalfo scared her, more than Spencer used to scare her be-fore Dalfo was killed. She tells the sheriff's investigators nothing except that she was with Dalfo the night he was killed.

And while she will not turn Brian Spencer in, says Baldwin, De Lena now makes plans to leave him. She does not want him to think it is be-cause of the Dalfo murder, however, so she distances herself from him gradually over the next several months, and then she moves out.

Four and a half years later, about eight-thirty on a Sunday night— January 18 of this year—Spencer is sitting in the El Cid bar, drinking a gin and tonic with one of his friends. The El Cid, since closed, was one of the few bars left in South Florida attached to a beauty parlor. Anyway, halfway through Spencer's first drink, his friend stands up, goes to a pay phone, and calls a cab for Spencer. A few minutes later, the driver, a thick-chested man named William Springer, walks in and calls, "Taxi."

Springer is an undercover sheriff's detective. His picture, in fact, hangs in the lobby of police headquarters as 1986's Officer of the Year.

Spencer takes the cab around the corner, to the Mt. Vernon Motor Lodge, and tells the driver to wait. He speaks to someone inside, then heads back to the cab.

Waiting for him are a helicopter with search lights, the undercover detective, a K-9 cop, a K-9 dog, and as much backup as the Palm Beach County Sheriff and the West Palm Beach police have available. In the lights and the noise Spencer struggles with police, but there are too many of them in too many places, and in a few moments he is in handcuffs.

And, for the next three months, Spencer sits in the Palm Beach County Jail.

And that is it, the case against Brian Spencer.

The case was kept in a folder a couple of inches thick, which was balanced across the lap of Assistant State Attorney Lynne Baldwin. She was going through the papers inside, one by one, reading bits and pieces out loud.

Interviews with other girls from escort services, interviews with Spencer's friends.

A report of a possum that Spencer was supposed to have killed with a .25-caliber automatic—the same caliber that killed Dalfo—which initiated a number of searches of his backyard. No possum, no bullets, no gun.

A woman's shoe prints heading away from the scene of the killing.

Lie-detector tests of numerous subjects, none of them Diane De Lena or Brian Spencer.

Dalfo's bank statements, which indicate he spent what Baldwin called "a lot of money."

More searches for the dead possum.

The prosecutor's office is beautiful, and in a comfortable way. Plants, good furniture, a huge antique globe in the corner. And there are signs, one over the light switch in particular: ATTITUDES ARE MORE IMPORTANT THAN FACTS.

"Is what you have," she was asked when she has finished with the file, "anything more than an ex-prostitute who has lied through this whole thing?"

"I don't think it's fair to say she's lied all along," Baldwin said. "She's tried to tell the truth, she's turned her life around. A couple of weeks ago, the *Miami Herald* ran a story about this and called her a 'former call girl,' and she called me up, just bananas . . .

"I'll tell you something," she said. "They [the Fialcos] came into this office together and sat right in those chairs, and we went through it all. And for a while, it was pretty tough going. He is a very Germanic sort of guy, very stiff and proper, and you could see he didn't like it at all.

"But once it was all out in the open, he accepted it. He supports her now, and I think that someone like that, sitting there supporting you, lends credibility. Do you remember John Dean's wife sitting behind him at those hearings? It gave him a kind of credibility . . ."

So, lined up against Spencer we now have exactly one witness and her Germanic husband, who has forgiven her. And we have a question. Couldn't the "untactful" Dalfo have had acquaintances even more untactful than himself? And couldn't a taste for paid escorts and cocaine, and a habit of spending surprising amounts of money, have gotten him into enough trouble with one of these untactful acquaintances that he ended up dead? If, let us say, De Lena knew about an execution committed by such an untactful acquaintance—who we can assume would not look kindly on her cooperating with the police—who is she going to give the state attorney's office when Lynne Baldwin comes around four years later, threatening to put her in jail?

That is what we have.

What we do not have are two tapes of the statements made by Diane De Lena when she was originally questioned by the sheriff's investigators five years ago. "Deputies," Baldwin said, "they're always running out of tapes. So when they need one, they sometimes borrow it from another file, something they aren't working, and tape over whatever was on it."

"A murder case. They taped over evidence in a murder case?"

She nodded her head.

What we also do not have is any proof that Dalfo was ever in the car that was supposed to have taken him to the clearing where he died. "The detectives, for the most part, did a very thorough job," Baldwin said. "They interviewed all these prostitutes, administered all these lie tests, conducted searches for the possum. One thing they forgot to do was search the car."

Lynne Baldwin sat dead still for a moment in her beautiful office. Beautiful office, beautiful clothes, beautiful globe. It is always surprising, the places where things are decided. Baldwin listened to a hard assessment of her case against Brian Spencer. Her expression never changed. "We may lose," she said, "but my job is different from a private attorney's. I don't always have to win." She thought for a moment, and then she said, "I get a lot of cases that aren't as clear-cut as you would like them to be, and I win my share."

That much was evident. Lynne Baldwin is the last person you want to see talking about you to a jury. Or the newspapers.

And then she said, "I'll tell you this, he'll know he's been in a fight."

Perhaps. Two weeks later, Baldwin would pull out of the case when she was promoted—"I got rid of that mess," she says—and turned it over to Fred Susaneck, another assistant state attorney. After a bond hearing on April 24, Spencer was released from jail out on Gun Club Road on $50,000 bail, posted by some old Islander teammates and friends. Still, as he waits for a murder and kidnapping trial scheduled to begin in the fall, you can't help thinking of Brian Spencer and of the time he has already spent in jail, and of the things that happened to him on the way there.

And it is hard to imagine that he needs this murder trial to know he has been in a fight.

75

It has been my belief ever since the issue first came up that there was no need for special laws to protect the rights of homosexuals. That they are protected by the same laws that protect the rest of us.

It has also been my belief that homosexuals—particularly men, who, taken as a group, do significantly better financially than the rest of society—are not suffering the kind of economic discrimination that certain vocal members of the homosexual community insist is the case.

Which left me biased, I suppose, when I came across the story in *The New Yorker* magazine last week of Daniel Miller of Harrisburg, Pennsylvania, who was fired after five exemplary years from the firm of Donald L. DeMuth Management Consultants when Mr. DeMuth found out he was gay.

He was given no severance pay and ordered out of his office by the end of the day.

Miller, a certified public accountant with an M.B.A. from Penn State, thought DeMuth had called him into the office to offer him a partnership. (I can't tell you how many times that's happened to me.)

Anyway, a month and a half after he was fired, Miller opened his own management firm in Harrisburg—across the river from DeMuth's firm, which is in Camp Hill—and in no time at all had taken about one-third of DeMuth's business away.

This in spite of a letter DeMuth sent to his clients saying, in part,

"Right now Dan is on his own. If he ever wants to grow, I question who he will be able to attract as an associate. While there may be other homosexual practice management consultants and CPAs, to the best of my knowledge I've never met one. . . . It's well known that homosexuals are significantly at risk for AIDS. While I have no knowledge of Dan's medical condition, consider getting the results of a blood test from him if you are considering using his services on a long-term basis."

Still, a number of DeMuth's clients—mostly doctors and dentists—were happy enough with Miller's work to change firms. He understood computers, for one thing, and DeMuth did not.

So time passed, and DeMuth discovered Miller's business was costing him about $100,000 a year in billings. DeMuth went to his lawyer and invoked a clause in Miller's employment agreement that, in the event he quit or was fired "for cause," called for penalties if he started a competing practice.

Specifically, 125 percent of whatever money he made from DeMuth's old clients.

Now, at this point it is worth remembering that Miller had signed the agreement when he went to work for DeMuth. He signed, he said later, thinking he had no choice.

Among the reasons DeMuth included as "just cause" for termination were moral turpitude, being charged with a felony, use of illicit drugs, intoxication while working, insulting DeMuth's family or clients, engaging in sexual activities in the office, and homosexuality.

It is also worth pointing out that at the time he signed the agreement, Miller says he had never had sexual activity with another man, and was in fact dating and thinking of marrying a woman. Only later did he admit to himself that he was gay.

All right, so Miller signed the agreement, put in five good years at the office and then came out of the closet.

DeMuth fired him and then sued when he opened his own office. Miller countersued, but his suit was thrown out of court because the state of Pennsylvania has no law on the books prohibiting discrimination against homosexuals.

The case went to court in June of last year, and there was no real argument from either side about what had happened.

In his instructions to the jury, Judge Kevin Hess of the Cumberland County Court of Common Pleas said that the jury was not to consider the fairness of the contract Miller had been made to sign.

"Mr. Miller cannot avoid the consequences of a contract between himself and Mr. DeMuth simply by claiming that he did not intend to be bound by it," the judge said. "An agreement need not be reduced to writing to be enforceable. Oral or verbal agreements between the parties are valid. And the law will enforce them."

Given those instructions, the jury deliberated a day and a half and came back—all members but one (a unanimous finding is not necessary in a civil trial)—with a finding that Miller, who, in spite of the fact he was only trying to save himself professionally and financially after having been fired for his sexual orientation, owed DeMuth $126,648.

As mentioned earlier, I have argued that there is no need for special legislation protecting the civil rights of homosexuals. I have argued they didn't need it.

And as the case of *Donald DeMuth vs. Daniel Miller* illustrates, a lot of the time I don't know what the hell I'm talking about.

76

A pparently, I have been misunderstood.

Having just received the latest dozen or so letters generated by my columns on the subject of diversity in the newsroom, I see that many readers have inferred from what I said—that the business of journalism is no longer guilty of institutional racism—that I do not believe it is important or appropriate to continue to hire people with different perspectives than what now passes for mainstream journalism.

Nothing could be further from the truth.

It seems to me, in fact, that the business is crying for fresh perspective, and it doesn't matter to me if the people who can offer it have light skin or dark skin or wear their skinnies to work. This thought comes to mind after looking over last week's issue of *Newsweek* magazine, which featured a cover picture of O. J. Simpson and the promise of a special report on the double life that Simpson led.

Like a lot of people, I have an unhealthy fascination with Simpson's situation, and I bought the magazine and turned to the piece, which was entitled "Day & Night."

The article filled eight pages, although a fourth of the space was devoted to pictures: O.J. sitting behind a stripper, O.J. with Nicole at a trendy New York nightclub, O.J. with his first wife, Marguerite, and their two children, O.J. with a bunch of white beauty contestants, O.J. with some anonymous white corporate executive, O.J. at the fifth annual Frank Sinatra golf tournament.

The text that went with these pictures made the case that O. J. Simpson's problems stemmed from the inner conflicts produced when a rich, famous black guy from the ghetto tries to live like a rich, famous white guy from Beverly Hills. Evidence offered to support this view: O.J. indulged in sex and drugs and still served as a corporate spokesman for Hertz and a number of other companies, O.J. took speech lessons in order to sound "more white," O.J. wanted to become a great actor, O.J. preferred white women to black.

"At some point," the article says, "a double life can become too much to bear. It is amazing, given the story, how long Simpson kept up the façade."

Now, at the risk of offending *Newsweek* magazine, let me point out that the real façade here was passing this paste-up job off as some sort of revelation.

Back in the first week following the murders, after all, O.J.'s rise from the projects of San Francisco was chronicled again and again. We knew early that he divorced his first wife, and married a younger woman, who was white. We knew that he took speech lessons to make himself more marketable, we knew that he hung out at country clubs and nightclubs.

In fact, there is nothing in the *Newsweek* article that I can find that I hadn't heard before, particularly the idea that Simpson lived a double life. As if the rest of us behave the same way at home as we do in public. As if the easy pop psychology really is, as *Newsweek* says, "an inside look at O. J. Simpson's world."

Which brings us back to diversity, my idea of which is someone— black or white—standing up at the news meeting and saying that it's dishonest to start with the hard fact that two murders have been committed and then pretend to trace those crimes back to a black man's hidden desire to be white.

It's not only dishonest, it's insulting.

If you want to make that case, then apply it to somebody else; show that it is inevitable. Explain why Clarence Thomas hasn't killed anybody, or go find some white guy making it in the National Basketball Association and tell me how long he's got before he goes off.

As a human being, O. J. Simpson is not reducible simply to his race and his ambition. You can always make the case afterwards—if you shoot up the office tomorrow, I promise you that the worst reporter in Oklahoma can talk to six of your fellow workers for two minutes each and explain your entire motivation in ten column inches.

The truth, however, doesn't look in that direction. It isn't found in stereotypes—economic or racial—or pop psychology, or in the observations of unnamed sources.

It does not fit into a box of a convenient size.

And in the interests of diversity, it would be nice once in a while if somebody would stand up and acknowledge the awful truth about the news business: Most of the time, we don't have a clue.

77

The child in the child is somehow faded. She is eight years old but there is nothing in her manner to say she isn't nineteen, with a house full of screaming babies and a high school sweetheart who doesn't always come home at night anymore.

She walks the front yard like walking is already a chore, collecting the mongrel puppies. There are nine of them and her fingers disappear into the long coats as she picks them up, then puts them in a cardboard box next to the front door.

The house is a shack, about a block from the abandoned half-mile dirt track where LeeRoy Yarbrough, the most famous man ever to come out of west Jacksonville, Florida, got his start racing automobiles. About three blocks from the place where, a month before, cold sober, he tried to strangle his own mother.

"He live right up that road there," she says, pointing a puppy. "Him and Miz Yarbrough, but they ain't there now. Everybody knows LeeRoy, sometime he come by and sit on the steps, but now he wrung Miz Yarbrough's neck, he ain't home no more."

The screen door opens and a woman in white socks steps halfway out the door. Missing teeth and a face as narrow as the phone book. "You git them puppies up yet? You know what your daddy tol' you."

The door slams shut, but the woman stays there, behind it in the shadows. In west Jacksonville it always feels like there's somebody watching behind the screen door.

"We got to take the puppies down to the lake," the girl says. "Daddy got back from the county [farm] and says so. He goin' take them out to the lake with him tonight."

I ask her why she just didn't give the puppies away. She shakes her head. "I *tol'* you," she says. "Daddy got back from the county."

I'm going to tell you right here that I don't know what picked LeeRoy Yarbrough off the top of his world in 1969 and delivered him, eleven years later, to the night when he would get up off a living room chair and tell his mother, "I hate to do this to you," and then try to kill her. I can tell you some of how it happened, I can tell you what the doctors said, what his people said. But I don't know why.

It has business with that little girl and her puppies, though. With not looking at what you don't want to see, putting it off until you are face-to-face with something unspeakable.

And tonight those nine puppies go to the bottom of the lake.

A Short History

"They ain't ever been no fits on neither side of the family. That's how the doctors knowed it was them licks on the head that made LeeRoy how he is." Minnie Yarbrough is LeeRoy's mother. She is seventy-six years old, and she's sitting on the couch in her living room, as far away from the yellow chair in the corner as she can get. That is where it happened.

It's an old house on Plymouth Street, in west Jacksonville, brown shingles, a bad roof, the porch gives when you step on it. An empty trailer sits rusting in the backyard. Inside it's dark. The windows are closed off and Minnie Yarbrough keeps the door to her room locked any time she isn't in it.

"I was born and partial raised in Clay County, Florida. Mr. Yarbrough was partial raised in Baker County. Both of us come from Florida families, Baptists, and there was never no fits on either side. Mr. Yarbrough died in 1974, but he'd of mentioned it if it was. We was together forty-three years . . ."

Lonnie LeeRoy Yarbrough was one of six children. He was the first son, born September 17, 1938, and named after his father, who ran a roadside vegetable stand.

Lonnie Yarbrough hauled the vegetables in an old truck and played penny poker with his friends to pass the time.

LeeRoy passed his time at Moon's Garage. He put his first car together when he was twelve—dropping a Chrysler engine into a 1934 Ford coupe—and wore the police out stopping him along the back roads of west Jacksonville. He quit Paxon High School after the tenth grade, and he won the first race he was ever in at Jacksonville Speedway when he was sixteen.

Even now, sitting in the Duval County Jail, waiting to be processed out to a state hospital, he can tell you exactly what he was running that day. A 1940 flat-head Ford, bored out 81/1,000ths of an inch, with high-compression heads.

He can tell you that, but he can't tell you who is president.

In 1956 LeeRoy married Gloria Sapp, who was sixteen, and became friendly with Julian Klein, who would later own the Jacksonville Speedway. "I been knowin' LeeRoy pract'ly all his life," Klein says. "He come right out on top in the old modified days, had it all in the bag right from the beginnin'. His impulses was sharp as a tack, but it got to his attitude. Sometimes he was cocky, sometimes he wouldn't say nothin'. He had a temper, but not too much for a dirt-track driver.

"I carried him to Daytona with his first car. It was obsolete, and we was too ignorant to know it, but he come in thirteenth anyway. After that we won about every race we went to. But he was gettin' too big too fast, tryin' to race too many races, and his wife was already out in the bars on him. Got to where he wouldn't even be on time.

"We was comin' back from South Carolina one Sunday, stop at this place in Jesup, Georgia, called The Pig—that's where we'd settle up—and I looked at him and made up my mind to change drivers. I'm sixty-six, been around racin' all my life, and in his day I haven't seen nobody any better. But it was time. I didn't tell him right out. Knowin' LeeRoy, I thought I'd space it out. I didn't get through sayin' it till we was back in Jacksonville. He didn't seem to mind, like it didn't matter.

"He never come back out to the track after he got big. He went on fishin' trips. He didn't care, but it didn't make you feel better seein' him these last years, walkin' up the street in a daze, pickin' up soda bottles to turn in for a quart of beer down to the store.

"Nobody who was ever LeeRoy Yarbrough oughtn' to end up like that."

LeeRoy Yarbrough entered his first Grand National race in 1960, won his first one in 1964. It was two more years before he won on a super speedway, the Nationals 500 at Charlotte.

Three years after that, driving for Ford in Junior Johnson cars, he had the greatest year that any stock-car driver had ever had.

He won seven NASCAR Grand Nationals, all on super speedways. His winnings were almost $200,000. He kept about half of that, along with a regular salary from Ford and fees for tire and engine tests. He bought a seventeen-room house on Lake Murray near Columbia, South Carolina, an airplane, a boat, cars. When a reporter asked that year about his early days, he said he'd been a juvenile delinquent. "I don't let myself think about some of what I did," he said.

For half a year, every other banquet south of Indiana named him man of the year. The papers were full of pictures of LeeRoy in the winner's circle, sometimes holding a trophy, sometimes his son LeRoi, getting kissed on the cheek by Gloria.

And by that time Gloria was called "Sweet Thing" in big racing towns all over the South.

Even though he was its top driver in 1969, Ford never used LeeRoy much for personal appearances. He stayed to himself, and Ford let him. He was quiet, but every now and then he'd hit somebody, usually without much warning. He would brag to the newspaper writers, or not talk to them at all. Or tell them he was sick. Nineteen sixty-nine was the year LeeRoy Yarbrough began to get sick.

Paul Pruss, who handled public relations for Ford racing, said, "I suppose you could say he was respected. He didn't wrestle bears or anything."

The year after that, in April 1970, LeeRoy crashed at College Station, Texas, during a Goodyear tire test at the Texas International Speedway. He came out of it unconscious. Later he wouldn't remember the flight home, or Cale Yarborough (who is not related) picking him up at the airport and driving him to the next race in Martinsville, Virginia.

That whole year LeeRoy won only one major race, the Charlotte 500, and at the end of the year Ford pulled out of racing. LeeRoy and Junior Johnson split up.

In May 1971, driving a Dan Gurney car, LeeRoy went into the wall during practice for the Indianapolis 500. His hands and neck were burned, and he took another serious crack on the head. It was the sixth or seventh major accident in his career, and probably the worst.

Cale Yarborough was the first person after the doctors to see him in the infield hospital. "His color wasn't good, like he'd seen . . . I don't know what. It was a bad crash, a terrible one. He was frightened, and he should have been."

LeeRoy spent the rest of the year in the minor leagues, winning thirty-seven late-model sportsman-class races, mostly in the Carolinas, because he couldn't find a car to drive on the Grand National circuit.

He was in and out of hospitals from June to November, and toward the end of the year he began telling people that the doctors had traced his troubles to a case of Rocky Mountain spotted fever.

The year after that he was back on the Grand National circuit, driving a Bill Seifert Ford. His best finish was a third at Dover, Delaware, but he was fourth twice, fifth at Charlotte and Atlanta, sixth in the Firecracker 400. Respectable.

And then he was gone. Gone from racing, gone from the house on the lake in Columbia. He took his family back to Jacksonville and disappeared.

He lost his money in a business deal with his uncle, Willie Lee Yarbrough, lost his children—LeRoi and Dawn Nichole—in the divorce settlement in 1976, the court placing the children with Willie Lee and his wife, Ernestine, setting conditions that neither LeeRoy nor Gloria was allowed to visit the children "within a period of 12 hours of either party consuming alcoholic beverages."

He went back to live with his mother in the brown-shingled house on Plymouth Street. LeeRoy and his mother and a house full of racing trophies that never got polished.

"All his life, he was a momma's boy," Minnie Yarbrough says. "When somethin' got to eatin' on him bad enough, he always come to me for what he needed."

Sweet Thing and a Two-Dollar Part

Junior Johnson is sitting on a tractor in fresh overalls and a starched T-shirt, arms big enough to lift an engine block and there's not a hair on his head out of place.

The tractor is sitting nose up on the bottom of the creek that runs through twenty-six acres of land that Junior owns at the foot of Engle Holler in Rhonda, North Carolina.

Besides the twenty-six acres, Junior has seventeen fulltime employees, fifteen coon hounds, thirty-nine cows, 92,000 automatically fed, climate-controlled chickens, and three or four businesses connected one way or the other to his racing cars.

All that and a tractor stuck in the creek bottom. On the bank above him, two of his employees, eleven of the cows, and a dog named Red watch him try to get out. He kills the tractor engine twice, shakes his head, and whistles.

As soon as Junior does that, one of the men scrambles to help him up the bank, the other one goes for the jeep. The cows change positions, and in the distance, a fight starts in the dog pen. Junior just waits for the jeep, and when it gets there he climbs in to be the one to pull the tractor out.

Junior Johnson runs things personally.

You get the feeling that it must half kill him when he sends somebody else out to drive the cars he puts together.

The tractor comes out on the second try. Junior leaves the cleaning up to the help and walks across the road toward his office, scraping at the mud on his boots. A man meets him at the door with his lunch.

In the office he unwraps a hamburger, folds the paper before he puts it in the wastebasket. "LeeRoy," he says. He thinks it over, nods.

If you believe Junior Johnson's reputation, this is already a long conversation.

"I liked LeeRoy," he says finally. "Didn't talk much, he was a great driver—good as Cale or Donnie [Allison]—best I ever had at goin' from one kind of car to the next. He was universal that way, like A. J. Foyt is. I like him, but I don't make a family association with drivers.

"By LeeRoy's time, they wasn't a lot of hard drinkin' and partyin' goin' on anymore. If you done that you got caught up with. Oh, they went to dinners and parties and such—a lot of them boys even had airplanes. I never cared too much for parties or airplanes myself. I know too much about mechanical malfunctions . . ."

Three days before, at Atlanta, Johnson's Chevrolet—with Cale Yarborough driving—had problems with a bad rotary button twenty laps from the finish. That is a two-dollar part in the distributor, and the way the race was going Junior figures it cost him forty thousand dollars.

"Chickens," he says, "now that's a reliable thing. Controlled conditions. But racin'—any little thing can happen and throw it all out the door.

"When I heard what happened to LeeRoy, it surprised me, but maybe not so much as others. When Ford pulled outta racin', I couldn't afford to keep on at the same level. Me and him never had a formal split-up or nothin', we just went our ways. But the last time I saw him, I seen trouble comin'. You could sort of tell he was changin', his appearance weakened.

"No, I got no idea what caused it. The doctors says it was mental damage. I'll believe that. LeeRoy, he stayed to hisself, except for his family. That's what he had. You take somethin' complicated, say like a race engine, push it to its stress limits, sometimes a two-dollar part is goin' bust and take you out the race . . ."

They called her Sweet Thing.

She was married to LeeRoy Yarbrough twenty years, a little blond girl who drank at the races and put her hands on the men when she laughed.

"It was the booze that put the pressure on his brain," she says. "It had to be somethin' more than a lot of licks on the head. I can't believe in my mind seven or eight years had to pass before any of this would of showed up. I wisht I could of helped him. I wisht I could help him even now, but I got a life of my own to live.

"Up until 1970, I never saw LeeRoy drunk but on Christmas. Along about that time he took to drinkin' Monday to Thursday, but he was proud, you know, didn't want nobody to know it. So he'd say he was sick. That was his way of coverin' it up, sometimes he'd go to the hospital.

"That's how that story about Rocky Mountain tick fever got started. He was in the hospital with alcoholic seizures—he'd grit his teeth and shake all over—and the man settin' in the next bed says, 'LeeRoy, maybe you got Rocky Mountain tick fever,' so he come out and that's what he told everybody." (The Medical University of South Carolina refuses to release the medical records.)

"For LeeRoy's whole life," Gloria says, "when he done somethin' bad, he'd always say he didn't remember it. He thought people didn't know if he didn't know. He'd get drunk and bad-dispositioned, but people'd want him around anyway. He is a private person who was never allowed no privacy.

"When we lived out to the lake in Columbia, he'd go off on the boat sometimes in the mornin' and wouldn't come back till after dark. Just take him some half-pints out and sit in the middle of the lake all day. He always bought booze in half-pints. I ast you, what could you be doin' sittin' in the middle of a lake when you got a family and a beautiful home?

"Either that or it'd rain and he'd lock himself in the office upstairs. He had an office filled with them hot-rod books. He'd go up there all day and read them. Later on, back in Jacksonville, he'd buy him a quart of beer at the Majik Market and just go out in the woods and sit in a tree.

"When we left Columbia, we had $200,000 in cash. Miz Yarbrough never liked me, and she and Willie Lee always tried to get me and LeeRoy apart. What for? You figure that out. The only thing I brung out of that divorce was fifteen hundred dollars, and nine hundred of that went for the lawyer.

"After we split up, sometimes he'd call up on the phone and wouldn't say nothin'. I always knew it was him, and one time little LeRoi answered and I took the phone and said, 'I know it's you, LeeRoy.' He started cryin', said his momma was gone, and he was lonely. A grown man.

"Look, I'd like to help, but I got a new husband and a new life . . ."

Ask a little about the old life, and she won't talk about her problems, says there weren't any problems with the law. "I thought this was s'posed to be onto LeeRoy," she says. "I think the less said about me the better."

Dan H. Stubbs, Jr., has been the Yarbrough family attorney for thirty years, and some of the sorrows and failures of those years are collected in his files. One of those folders is for Gloria.

He shuffles through it now. "The last time I kep' her out of jail was 1976. Charge of disorderly intoxication. On a *Monday*." The police report says Gloria Yarbrough was drunk and belligerent and abusive to the staff at the hospital detoxification center. It also says Gloria is five feet, three inches tall and weighs 188 pounds.

A year and a half before that was drunk driving on a suspended license, and she only weighed 142.

He goes through more papers. "She remarried," he says. "I guess she's got the kids now." He shrugs, closes the folder.

Sweet Thing is about to turn forty years old and has a new life, a new husband, and a job at the electric company. "I only wisht I could of done somethin' to help," she says.

Wicky-Wacky

By February of 1980, LeeRoy Yarbrough had lost contact with his wife, saw his children only at Christmas. Of his four sisters, three of them— Libby, Lillian Sweat, and Evelyn Motel—still lived in the area, and he'd see them once in a while when they came to visit Minnie. There were no old friends from the racing days—there weren't really any of them even then. And there was his brother Eldon, a dirt-track driver who never made it beyond that.

"Eldon, he don't think about LeeRoy." Terry Sweat is LeeRoy's nephew and lived in the house with him and Minnie Yarbrough. He is seventeen, and it was up to him to stop LeeRoy from killing his grandmother. He is in the house now, waiting for her to come home from the store. A radio is on too loud in the kitchen. "Eldon," he says, "is only interested in his cars.

"Here, let me turn off that nigger music so we can hear . . ." He gets up and walks into the kitchen, the music stops. "My daddy done more for LeeRoy than Eldon ever did. Whenever LeeRoy was beat up, laying in a ditch, it was Daddy who went with Grandmother to get him. When the police had him and called, it was always my father who went with her down there to the station.

"All the kids around liked him. They'd holler, 'LeeRoy, LeeRoy,' and he'd go over if he was sober, play with them half the afternoon. The neighbors liked him too, he was famous. A lot of them, though, they'd give him liquor.

"One neighbor lady, she saw LeeRoy walkin' back from the Majik Market with a quart of beer one day and she ast him would he like a drink. He says yes, and she says what would you like?

"She had three different kinds of liquor, and he took every one and poured it into the quart, and right there in the yard he drunk it down. He says, 'Thank you,' and goes on his way, gets on my motorcycle and runs it into a ditch.

"People ought to know better but they don't. When LeeRoy drinks he just gets . . . radical. This hurts me so bad. If nobody's around him, he's all right, but you got to leave him his distance."

By February of 1980, LeeRoy Yarbrough only had one person left. That doesn't mean there weren't others who cared about him. And whatever else there is to say about it, the night LeeRoy tried to kill his mother he was strangling the last person he had left in the world.

Minnie Yarbrough is a long time coming home. She says the Winn-Dixie was crowded. "Some day I maybe can live this out," she says, "but it hurt deep. If he'd had al-kee-haul was what caused it, I could understand. But he hadn't had nothin'." She stops, confused. "I can't talk on it no more right now.

"There was nobody ever really knowed LeeRoy's background," she says. "Maybe even me. But I know this: a woman can make a man or she can break him, and Gloria put LeeRoy to the dogs.

"Onct she called me up to South Carolina, she says I got to come and sober LeeRoy up. So I got in the car and drove up to their place on the lake and throwed all the liquor out the house. I walked right over and took them out. The house was disgraceful messy. LeeRoy was out settin' in the boat. I said, 'Gloria, this here is a ruin-nation.'

"And I got right back in the car and drove home. After they'd broke up I tol' her, 'When I was tryin' to show you your points, nobody could tell you nothin'.' She said that she resented me, and she jus' wisht she could live it over, it'd be different. I tol' her, 'No it wouldn't, but that's water done run under the bridge.'"

After LeeRoy came back to Jacksonville, he went into business with Willie Lee and Ernestine.

LeeRoy put up the money. Nobody is sure now what happened to it. Some lots were bought, but they are gone. So is Willie Lee. Ernestine is dead, and LeeRoy thinks his Social Security check comes from tenants in his houses.

His mother says, "LeeRoy and me, onct he come home here we never had no argument, no hard feelin's. If he saw that red sign board outside that says STOP, if he says it was black, I'd say it was black too. If you know somebody's disposition was set, it don't do no good to argue.

"We lived here together. I knowed I couldn't comfort him like a wife could. I tol' him, 'I can cook for you and be kind to you and keep your shirts clean, but that's all a mother can do.' I tol' him, why didn't he go git hisself a girlfriend. He'd just laugh, ast me how come I didn't go get me a boyfriend, me livin' forty-three years with one man.

"I don't know what got into him," she says, "but I know when his mind collapsed. It was early 1977, I can't give you no date but it was a Monday morning. He was stayin' with Willie Lee, and his sister and me had been by the day before, he was jus' fine as anything.

"The next day Ernestine called, said LeeRoy'd been sick all night with headache. I went over and by then his head hurt so bad he couldn't get his socks on, so I did it. I said, 'We is goin' to the hospital,' and when he didn't make me no answer, I looked at his face, and it was all changed. It was like he was lookin' at the devil.

"Then his body drawed to the left. I got him out to the car and blowed the horn for Ernestine to hurry—Ernestine was always slow as Christmas—and when she got in I didn't know if I could drive. She says it was better than sittin' in the backseat and lookin' at LeeRoy like he was.

"So I went to blowin' the horn and flashin' the lights and I never got my foot out the carburetor the whole way to the firehouse. They looked at him there and give us one of them paddles to keep you from chewin' your tongue, and I drove on to the hospital. By the time we got there, LeeRoy was drawed up into a knot—like his face was tryin' to meet with his knees.

"Next mornin' we come in and he didn't know nothin'. We couldn't even tell him he wasn't in jail. And he was wicky-wacky from then on. The doctors said it was them licks on the head and the liquor. They said it was that if it didn't run in the family, so it must of been, but you don't know.

"I can't sleep no more, worryin' on it. I don't know why it happened, maybe God never intended us to know such. I know they is things God didn't intend us to see."

LeeRoy Yarbrough has been examined twice in the last three years at the psychiatric center at University Medical Complex in Jacksonville, both times at the request of his attorney, Dan Stubbs.

The first examination was in March of 1977, after LeeRoy had been sentenced to 120 days at the county farm for two different assaults on the Jacksonville Police Department.

"A lot of times the police would see LeeRoy out walkin' around in a daze and take him home," Stubbs said. "The older ones, they knew how to handle LeeRoy. The younger ones, they got him stirred up. And you stir LeeRoy up, you got your hands full."

LeeRoy got six weeks for kicking a police officer two weeks before Christmas, and another six weeks for tearing up the insides of a police car six days later.

Stubbs said, "All this time LeeRoy thought he had a lot of money in the bank, but he couldn't remember where. He said he owned three or four houses and an airplane and kept a hundred thousand dollars in his driving helmet. And if you'd tell him to go to the store he was likely to end up in South Carolina."

On March 25, while LeeRoy was still in the county farm (eventually he was released after serving six weeks), Judge John Cox, on the basis of the psychiatric report, ruled him incompetent to handle his own affairs. By that time there were almost no affairs left to handle.

No guardian was ever appointed. "His people were afraid of him," Stubbs said. "His mother felt she was too old, so it just sort of never got done."

After LeeRoy attacked his mother in February, he was examined again. While that was going on, Stubbs allowed the charges against him to be increased from aggravated battery to attempted murder. (There was also a charge for punching Officer W. T. Weaver in the nose.)

"The bond on the first ones came to a little over twenty-three hundred dollars," Stubbs said. "That means he could get out for two hundred and thirty, and I knew damn well what he'd do."

The doctors sent the court a two-page report saying LeeRoy was insane at the time of the attack. They put the condition down to brain damage.

They called it "organic brain syndrome, non-psychotic, secondary to cranio-cerebral trauma." Too many times into the wall. The report also noted that in cases of brain damage, alcohol can "precipitate violence and other types of distressed behavior."

The report said something else too. That LeeRoy probably wasn't going to get any better. "[It is doubtful] hospitalization would accrue any substantial change," it said, and recommended a nursing home where LeeRoy could be under constant and close supervision.

On the basis of that report, LeeRoy was judged incompetent to stand trial and eventually will be handed over to the state's Department of Health and Rehabilitative Services.

LeeRoy

They bring LeeRoy Yarbrough down from the third floor in slippers and checkered pants. It takes a minute for it to register that it's the same man in all those pictures holding trophies with Gloria mashing in his cheek. He could be fifty-five years old.

"I don't like bein' touched," he says. "Basically, I don't know 'xactly what's goin' on, but one of them police and me fell into a little bit of an argument, I know that."

He looks himself over, a swollen stomach, arms that have lost their tone. He flexes his hands. The outline of bone-thin legs show in the wave of his trousers.

The guards at the Duval County Jail all know LeeRoy, some of them grew up wanting to be drivers too. They find a room where he can sit down to talk and get him a paper cup of cherry Kool-Aid.

Before he shuts the door, the captain says, "He's lookin' much better now." As soon as the door is shut the room gets close, you feel the walls.

LeeRoy leans back in his chair and smiles. "I can't basically tell you what's goin' on," he says. "Basically, I don't know about that." He looks around the room. "Don't nothin' worry me about here. Nobody says much to me, and I got very little to say to them. We watch television . . ."

Outside somebody slams a steel door, LeeRoy smiles. "Jail is noisy, ain't it? I always like it quiet, out on the lake." He shrugs. "Ain't no sense braggin' about it, but I can get out any time I want. I been here about five or six days, you know."

It is March 15, and LeeRoy has been inside since the middle of February. He doesn't know how old he is, how long he has been divorced, who is president. He pulls the hair up off the back of his neck and bends forward to show a patch of skin about the color of a coated tongue.

"I got myself on fire at Indy," he says. "Gordon Cooper and Gus Grissom owned the car. [Grissom and Cooper owned a car LeeRoy drove in trials at Indianapolis five years before his accident there.] We all got along jus' fine. I didn't talk about what I did, and they didn't talk about what they did. I know they made a dollar a mile goin' to the moon, though."

Leroy sips at his Kool-Aid. "The first I knew I had somethin' out the ordinary was when I was fifteen. I was the biggest hot-rodder in west Jacksonville. Won my first race in a 1940 flat-head Ford, bored out 81/1,000ths, with high compression heads . . ." He taps the back of his head. "That's somethin' that stays with you," he says.

"After that I basically married a real stinker. I kept the children, but then me and my uncle . . . well, sometimes things don't work out. But I still got my houses and my airplane."

He looks across the table and suddenly everything in the face changes. "Is the plane in some kind of trouble? If somebody's got my plane I don't 'preciate that, hear? When you got somethin' of your own it's always dif-ferent from usin' somebody else's. If I was up there, I'd just walk in and tell him to give me the keys to the plane, and if you didn't I just come over the desk and git them from you." He is coming up, more on the table than his chair, when suddenly his face changes again.

"It's somethin' goin' on," he says and sits back. "I jus' don't basically know what it's about, but it'll come back. I know me too good." He is quiet a minute, looking into his cup. "I bet my mother's worried. I bet she's real upset not knowin' where I am."

LeeRoy pulls the hair away from his neck and shows the scar there again. He talks about the crash at Indianapolis, suddenly stops. "Basically, I had a beautiful life. I married a stinker, but I kept the children. Racin', it don't scare you. At Indy I got on fire, and it damn sure hurts, but it don't scare you or you wouldn't of got there. What it is, if we know one of us is gonna be dead when we come out this room, you try to fix things on the outside first, before you come in."

He stops and thinks again. "I could still drive," he says. "Just clear up whatever this is all about first."

February 13

Terry Sweat started sweetening up about five in the afternoon. "When I'm goin' to a party I get sweetened up all the way," he says. "Some-times it takes me two hours."

When he came out of the bathroom, it was after six-thirty. His grand-mother was sitting on the couch, LeeRoy was in the chair near the door. "They was just watchin' television," he says, "and my grandmother ast me to go down to the store to get her a pack of cigarettes."

According to what Minnie Yarbrough told police, Terry was gone about five minutes when LeeRoy stood up, went into another room, then came back and locked the front door. He said, "Mother, I hate to do this to you," and threw her into the yellow chair in the corner and began to strangle her.

"I heard her screamin' my name clear out to the street when I come back," Terry says. "I run up to the front door. It was locked, but I could see in through the little window up on the top. What I seen was LeeRoy bendin' over the chair. All I seen of grandmother was her leg.

"She was screamin' for me, and he was yellin' too. He said, 'That little sumbitch ain't gettin' in.' Well, a lot of people don't understand how close me and my grandmother is. I ran around to the back door, and he'd forgot about that. I come flyin' through there like a bullet and tried to knock him off. He was like a brick wall. He was screamin', 'Leave us alone, goddamnit.'

"I tried to git him off, but I couldn't. So I did what I could. I got a jelly jar out the kitchen and hit him over the head. That hurt me so bad to do it. It stunned him—it never knocked him down—but it was long enough that I got my grandmother out of there. I took her next door to Libby's, and they'd already called the police.

"When the first cop got there, LeeRoy about knocked him over the fence."

Patrolman W. T. Weaver already knew LeeRoy Yarbrough. He'd picked him up the week before and taken him home. "I found him sittin' on a porch, lookin' lost, so I talked to him. I got him in the car and all of a sudden he grabbed my microphone, took five minutes to wrestle it away. Anybody else, I probably would of taken him in, but he seemed so frustrated, you know? I felt sorry for him."

Weaver was the first cop to get to the house on Plymouth Street. He was followed by a backup car and the fire rescue squad. Minnie Yarbrough and her grandson stood in the next yard and watched. LeeRoy came out of the house with a glass in his hand.

"He walked to the edge of the street, and I grabbed the glass," Weaver says. "I got that away, and he hit me in the nose."

It took a while, but a little at a time Weaver and the other cop and four or five firemen wrestled LeeRoy down and got handcuffs on him.

Terry says, "They took him away and my grandmother just stood there in the grass, holdin' her neck, until he was gone up the street."

Minnie Yarbrough can't talk about that night yet. She still feels what happened when she walks into her house, she won't stay there alone. "They is things God didn't intend us to see," she says.

And LeeRoy sits downtown in the Duval County Jail, shut off from what he has done, all that he has lost. And shut off from whatever it is you see going into a wall at 170 miles an hour, or at the moment you have to kill your mother.

Time slides by unnoticed, like a day on the lake. Somewhere under the surface, though, it's all there waiting for him.

"It's somethin' goin' on, I don't know basically what it is," he says. "I'm just layin' up, rollin' with the punches, and it'll come back to me. I know myself too good." He sits up suddenly, his eyes narrow.

"It ain't my plane in trouble, is it?"

78

Thursday afternoon, Fields' house burned down. He took his wife out to lunch and when they came back the streets were blocked off by the fire department. He stood and watched it while the firemen cut holes in his roof. He lost everything he had in there—furniture, clothes, paintings, three dogs. One of them slept on his head at night.

I caught up with him eight hours later at the Four Seasons Hotel. He came into the Swan Room in muddy shoes, needing a shave. He'd been drinking scotch, which is a reasonable thing to do after your house burns down, and we sat down and he drank some more.

"That dog," he said, meaning the one he'd had the longest, "she'd come to bed with me every night, check my hair for fleas, lick my eyes, and sleep on my head. Who's going to check my hair for fleas?"

Did I mention he'd been drinking?

"Listen," I said, "try to look at this in a different way. The dogs are gone. You can't get them back, but that won't hurt as long as you think it will. The rest of the stuff—rugs, paintings, clothes—all that can be replaced. This can feel like a new start if you let it."

"You can't replace my Desi Arnaz, Sr., bongo shirt," he said.

And the truth was I hadn't thought of that. The shirt in question is—was—the ugliest thing ever made of cotton. It had collars like donkeys have ears. And ruffles, and leafy sleeves. Fields wore it about every nine days during the summer, and he was absolutely right when he said it couldn't be replaced.

"See?" I said, "you're already making the best of what's happened."

Fields ordered another scotch, which the Four Seasons declined to serve him. The manager suggested we go up to his suite to finish drinking, which is what we did. I wouldn't presume, incidentally, to tell the Four Seasons Hotel how to run its business, but I will just say that if Fields walked into my hotel in that condition, I would much rather have him in the bar, where I could keep an eye on him, than in the eighth-floor suite.

Anyway, we all went upstairs. Fields, his wife, Andrea, two of her friends, and me. There was more scotch in the bedroom, and wine in the sitting room. "I don't know how I'm going to get to sleep tonight," Fields said. "I'm used to that dog lying on my head."

I fixed him a drink, a nice brown one. There was a table of vitamins and various kinds of pills on the table. They smelled like a burned house. Sometimes Fields takes pills to go to sleep.

"One thing you shouldn't do is take any of those," I said. "You've got too much alcohol in your blood."

"It's the strangest feeling," he said, "to drive up to your house and find the fire department blocking off your street. You don't even think it might be your own house, and then you walk up there and see it burning, and everything you've got is inside there, and there's not a thing you can do. It doesn't feel like anything else you know of."

He finished the drink and began to nod off. "Everybody get the fuck out," he said.

"All right," he said, "everybody stay the fuck here." Nobody can ever say adversity affects the man's manners. A few minutes later, however, he finished the drink and went into the bedroom. He got undressed and lay on the bed, coughing hard and having trouble breathing.

I sat in the next room and listened. He began to snore, then he called out in his sleep, something about dying. I think he was dreaming about the dogs. I went in there and his eyes were half-open behind his glasses. "You all right?" I said.

He said, "I need a . . ." and then his voice seemed to disappear.

"What?"

"I need a . . ." I stood in the room five minutes, waiting for him to tell me what he needed.

Finally I said, "Tell me what it does, and I'll figure it out."

"I need . . . I need it to be colder."

I opened the window and he thanked me. "Just stay away from the sleeping pills," I said.

Fields opened his eyes all the way. "Dexsser," he said, "you known me a long time. Am I suicidal?"

"No," I said, "but tonight you're accidental."

And hearing that, Fields' whole face changed. He smiled and stood up on top of the bed. "What a wonderful line," he said. "A wonderful, wonderful line."

"You can have it," I said.

He reached out and we shook hands. "You just proved your class beyond any question," he said. Then he fell straight backwards, his head landing on the pillow. It was quiet a minute. "I wish the dogs had gotten out," he said.

I said I did, too.

Fields is somewhere around fifty years old, and he has lived out of a suitcase most of his life. That house was the first permanent thing he ever had. The dogs—and, in a different way, the art and rugs and furniture—were security he'd never had before. God knows what he saw as he watched it going up.

79

The woman was heavy and had on too much makeup, and came in the door with her own stick. The men at the bar looked at each other when she came in. The bar was in Nye County, Nevada, sixty miles north of Las Vegas, and it had been twenty minutes since anybody but the bartender had said anything.

"How you been, Helen?" the bartender said. "We was sure sorry about little Crystal." He filled a glass with ice, filled it with red wine out of a gallon bottle. There were half a dozen dusty cowboys at the bar, and some of them nodded when the bartender said they were sorry.

The woman didn't seem to hear it. She took a swallow of the wine, spit ice back into the glass and took the stick out of the case. She left a lipstick mark on the glass. The pool table was through the doorway. It was a hundred years old, hand-carved legs, and probably worth more than the building.

"I should've never gone down there to live," she said. "I should've stayed where she was used to, but you never know . . ."

The bartender filled her glass up without waiting to be asked to. He said, "No, you sure never know. No sir."

She screwed the two ends of the cue together, took a quarter out of her purse and went into the next room and put it on the table. The man shooting said, "Hey, Helen, I ain't seen you in a while."

She said, "Well, I'm back now," and sat at the bar to drink the wine and wait for her turn.

The game was eight-ball, and the man who had spoken ran four small-numbered balls, then scratched on the eight. He put two dollar bills on the table and said, "Shit." The man he was playing picked them up and watched Helen rack the balls.

As soon as she had gone into the other room, the cowboys began to whisper. One of them said, "You don't know what to say." I'd been there half an hour and it was the first sign anybody knew anybody else in the place.

The bartender nodded his head toward the door. "Used to whore out of here part time," he said. "Get a trucker sometimes, or somebody drivin' through from Vegas or Reno. Had a twelve-year-old daughter who wasn't right in the head. Always wanderin' off someplace, tryin' to get into a truck. Helen'd get mad if you said it, but the child was a retard, and 'bout May or July she left for Vegas, she says to put her in school.

"They was gone a while and the child disappeared. They come by here lookin' for her, thinkin' maybe she'd found her way back, but then they found her body off the airport. They didn't put it in the papers 'cause it wasn't murder."

In the other room, Helen was lining up a shot. A cigarette was hanging from her lip and you could see cleavage halfway to Mexico. She took a long time getting ready. She didn't understand how to make a bridge, and the stick came at the cue ball from a slightly different angle every time she stroked.

She missed a six-ball into the corner, and came back into the bar to watch while the man she was playing ran out the table. The bartender gave her a handful of fresh ice and poured more wine. "You gonna be around here, Helen?" he said.

She looked around the room for customers. "I'll probably starve to death," she said, "but I don't know what else I want to do. Sometimes I think I feel cut loose."

"We was gonna send flowers but . . ."

"Sometimes I don't know what I feel like. She was just always wantin' to go somewhere, like she had some idea that she got on an airplane, it took you someplace like she saw on television."

The man in the other room finished shooting and came out of the smoke like a ghost. She handed him two dollars as he walked past. She looked up and saw the men at the bar were watching her. She checked her lipstick in the mirror, pulled in her stomach. "You think I need to lose some weight, Roy?" she said.

The bartender shook his head. "You look jus' right for me, Helen." The cowboys smiled and nodded, but there was something polite there that didn't belong. She put two quarters in the jukebox and looked out the window. "Let's get us a customer," she said.

She waited at the window and when the truck finally came by it was going seventy-five miles an hour. She watched it disappear to the north. She put another quarter on the pool table and drank wine and waited for her turn to play.

And a long time later she said, "You know what, Roy? Sometimes I know what got into that child's head."

80

The man sits behind a table in the jockeys' room at Aqueduct in a coat and tie. He is soft-faced and middle-aged, too big and too soft to have ever been a jockey himself but hard enough and small enough for what he does. And whatever he does, he's got all the authority in the room.

It's not just that he's the only one wearing a tie. He's got a clipboard too, and he makes notes as the jockeys holding their saddles and whips step onto the scales before each race. He is impatient with the jockeys, not interested in talking to them. As much as he can, he just nods or points.

For an exploited minority (if you empathize with women who are wanted only for their bodies, consider being loved only for a borrowed horse), jockeys seem like happy people, especially when you consider growing up to weigh 108 pounds. Some of the ones here are still kids, some of them have faces that have been almost erased, like old statues.

Most of them have come to the track for one or two races. They are paid $35 a race, $45 if they finish third, $55 if they finish second, and 10 percent of the purse if they win. This is Aqueduct, and these are some of the best jockeys in the world.

One of them—he looks sixteen years old—steps on the scale now, laughing at something a valet has said. The man in the bow tie is suddenly furious. "Who told you to do that?" he says.

The kid has done something out of order before he got on the scale. I don't know what, and I'm not sure the kid does either.

The man in the tie cuts him off. "Shut your ugly mouth," he says, "and do what you're told." And the kid shuts his mouth, and looks down at the saddle in his hands until the man in the tie has finished making his notes and walks away.

Ten minutes later, in ten-degree weather, the kid will finish out of the money on his only ride of the day and make $35. On the way back in, somebody in the stands will call him a crook.

And that's what it can be like riding horses for a living.

A day later, December 28, Angel Cordero, Jr., is getting ready for the seventh race. The temperature outside is still around ten degrees, and everything is either frozen or wet. He puts black-and-white silks over a white sweatshirt, fits his small, arthritic hands into his gloves, and steps onto the scales, singing a Latin love song.

He has a romantic voice for a man with congested sinuses.

Angel has a cold or the flu six months a year. "My daughter," he said earlier, "she don't have no immunity system, you know? She catch everything out there. She's seventeen already, but when she get sick she still want to come to bed with Mommy and Daddy. Very strong-headed girl, so what she get, I get . . ."

I don't think the man in the tie and coat appreciates music, but he nods at Angel, then smiles. He looks at Angel even while he writes notes in his pad. He does not tell Angel to shut his ugly mouth.

With three racing days left in the year, the horses Angel Cordero has ridden in 1983 have won more than $10 million. No other jockey has ever done that. He has wins in forty-eight stakes races, the most any jockey has ever had, and—on the same pay scale as the other riders—he will make close to $900,000 before the year is over.

None of that is why the man in the tie is nice to him, though.

To understand that, I think you can go back to this year's Belmont Stakes. In that race, Cordero, on the favored Slew o'Gold, was coming down the stretch in first place on the outside of a horse named Au Point, who was ridden by Gregg McCarron.

There was a small opening between Au Point and the rail, and as Cordero looked back—you will never see another jockey spend as much time looking back as Cordero—he saw Caveat trying to come through. Caveat, the second favorite, was the best horse in the race on that day, and from the move he was making Cordero had to know it.

Cordero looked back once, then again, timing it, and then crowded Au Point, who rode into Caveat. Caveat hit the rail hard and bounced off, losing stride, and then, refusing to be cut off, he gathered himself and came back through the hole between Au Point and the rail and won the race. Just as easily, Laffit Pincay, Jr.—Caveat's jockey—could have gone over the rail. As it was, Caveat was found to have torn a muscle—and there is still some argument about whether it happened in that race or later, during training. He hasn't raced since.

The lesson in that, of course, is that given the right reason, Angel Cordero will kill you. And somewhere along the line the man in the coat and tie has noticed that and decided to work around it.

The horse Angel is riding in the seventh today is a three-year-old filly with a history of bad behavior in the starting gate. Her name is Last Word Susie.

The gate is probably the most dangerous place on the racetrack for a jockey; there is no question that it is the scariest. All kinds of things can happen in a race—Cordero, for instance, went down in front of the whole field earlier in the year—but on the track the jockey has some control, he has places to move. In the gate, he is packed into a narrow space with an eleven- or twelve-hundred-pound animal, the purposeful distillation of six generations of anxiety, and he has nothing to say about what happens until the starter opens the front door.

Because of the weather, the horses go straight from the paddock to the gate. Cordero coaxes Last Word Susie halfway in, where she stops. It takes two people to push her the rest of the way. Because of Last Word Susie's reputation, once she is in the gate somebody usually wraps her tail around the bar in back of her and then holds it there until the gate opens. It gives her less room to move.

In the bad weather, though, the man in back can't get her tail around the bar. It slips out of his hands as he tries to wrap it, slapping his head, and in the end he gives up on that and bends her tail over the rail at a right angle and tries to hold on to it that way.

He might as well be holding on to a truck by its tailpipe. The horse jumps forward and then back, Angel's head moving the opposite directions, and as she moves back she also throws her head, as far as it will go, and the top of her skull comes up to meet the right upper quarter of Angel's face.

"You canna 'magine nothing," he will say later, "as strong you bump heads with a horse. That's a big head, man. I hear the noise, next thing I know, I'm on the ground and all I see is horse legs. I think, 'How many legs this sonuvabitch got?' Then I hear them screamin', 'Get him outta there, get him out.' And then somebody is dragging me out by the feet, people still screamin', 'Get him out.'"

The horse jumps up, trying to get through the opening at the top of the gate, and catches her front hooves, which may be what saves Angel's life. Fighting to get loose, she falls back, loses her balance, and then she is on the ground too. What Angel sees when he comes around is Last Word Susie struggling to get back on her feet. It all happens in four or five seconds, and then she is standing up again, somehow facing the opposite direction, and the men in back are pulling Angel out by the legs.

"Angel come home that night," his wife says later, "he don't say nothin' about it, but he got this terrible-looking eye. He don't complain to nobody, but ever since Angel broke his back, he can't find no place comfortable to sleep. Tossing and turning all night. He sees some things in his sleep, it all comes out at night."

Her name is Santa, and she has been married to Angel for twenty-one years. She comes from Puerto Rico too, where his family is famous. His father and both grandfathers were jockeys, and all his uncles on both sides were jockeys or exercise boys or trainers. In twenty-one years of marriage her husband has ridden more than five thousand winners.

He has also broken his back, both of his legs, his arms, his collarbones, his wrists, his hands, and all his fingers. He is forty-one years old and beginning to curl into himself.

Last Word Susie is scratched and taken back to the stables. Cordero gets to his feet and is taken back to the jockeys' room. He is not angry at the horse. "She's a nice horse," he says, "once you get her out of the gate." The bruise around his eye is swelling now, leaking blood here and there where the skin has split.

He covers it with an ice bag and lies down. Then, a few minutes after the riders have come in from the seventh race, he changes silks, picks up his helmet and his whip and his saddle, and steps onto the scale—not singing now—in front of the man in the coat and tie.

And then he goes back out onto the track and wins the feature.

Even in the stands, where they know everything, they are surprised to see him. Winners turn to losers and say, "I don't care what anybody says, it takes balls coming back out here after what happened."

The losers stare into their *Racing Forms* and say, "What else has he got to do?"

So the racetrack is not the place to look for love, and that's not what Angel is doing there. For love, he goes home to his wife. He tosses and turns at night, she says, and sees some things in his sleep.

81

The gas station was sitting off the highway a couple of hundred yards, a few miles past Abbott, Texas, the hometown of Willie Nelson. There was an old man inside, wearing a green shirt with the name "Miles" written in longhand over the pocket, trying to make sense of one of those four-colored cubes that have taken over America, now that everybody's gotten tired of the Medfly.

Outside there was a Doberman pinscher chained to a Chevrolet pickup. It was ninety degrees in the sun, but the dog wouldn't move under the truck to the shade. He jumped against the chain over and over, turning circles, making vicious, foamy snaps at something only he could see.

He didn't make much noise—it was a fight to the death now, past the bluffing and growling. Every now and then the old man would hear him and shout through the door, "Shut up, Rem!"

Rem was short for Remington.

Besides gas, the old man sold beer, Dr Pepper, and rifle shells. All self-service. He worked a ten-hour shift and only moved to get himself beer or use the bathroom.

"My wife don't think I work," he said, "but look at it now, I got two customers at once, and it ain't like it's air-conditioned." One of the customers was me, the other one was a van with Colorado plates, and four people riding in it who said they'd spent all morning in Abbott, taking pictures of the town and getting the feel of Willie's roots. They said they needed gas and they needed to stretch their legs.

"You spent the morning takin' pitsures?" the old man said.

One of the women had said there was an understated dignity to the place, that the little houses and the flat, bare landscape were a throwback to the country's hardest times. And that's why it had produced its greatest musician. She handed him an American Express credit card.

The old man shook his head. "Don't take American Express," he said. She looked through her purse. He read her, though. "Don't take Visa or Mastercharge, neither," he said. "Too much damn trouble workin' them machines."

While she looked for cash, he said, "But that's Abbott all right, understated dignity." As soon as she walked out of the office he smiled. "That place got as much dignity as the shithouse blowin' down on you," he said.

The people in the van were still stretching their legs when the first motorcycle came down into the station. It was big and black and extended four or five feet in front, and it made a horrible noise. There was a man in a leather vest driving it, and a girl in a leather vest behind him, and you could see they were horrible too.

Another motorcycle followed him in, and then there were two more, and inside of five minutes there were nineteen bikes and maybe thirty-five people walking around the station, drinking beer, using the weeds for bathrooms. The men who couldn't get dates were staring at the girls who had been taking pictures of Willie's roots.

The first biker came into the station and he and the old man studied each other. "I don't take American Express," the old man said.

Outside, the van was pulling out of the driveway before all the doors were shut. "No problem," the first biker said. "All we want is gas and some beer . . ."

As he finished saying that, the girl who had been on the back of the motorcycle came into the office. "Spider, you got to see this dog," she said. She led Spider outside to the pickup, where Remington was tearing at the air with his teeth.

The bikers were beginning to fill up their tanks, running up one bill.

On the way to see the dog, Spider told them he needed cash, so they all went into their pockets for gas and beer. The old man didn't seem worried that they might steal anything; he didn't even get up out of his seat to keep an eye on them.

The one called Spider came back into that office fifteen minutes later with a handful of cash. A couple of the other bikers were with him.

"That's a righteous dog," he said. "That dog's fuckin' crazy."

The old man nodded, began counting the money. "You had him a long time?" Spider said.

The old man nodded, without losing his count.

"You want to sell him? I pay anything you want, man." All the bikers were smiling. The old man counted out $122, gave the rest of the money back.

He looked up and said, "You go 'head and take him. No charge."

Spider and the others went back outside and stood around the dog for a minute or two, then an engine kicked over, then the others, and then the motorcycles were headed, two by two, out of the station toward the highway. Blowing dust, making noise. And then it all settled.

And in the quiet, you could suddenly hear the dog again, still out there snapping at the air, fighting something only he could see.

The old man put the money in his cash box and picked up his four-colored cube. "Shut up, Rem," he said.

82

The kid was big, but he was a kid.

He was standing beside the drive-in window at Church's Fried Chicken on North Broad, asking the people who came by for money. "Do you have some change so I could get somethin' to eat, sir?" He said it like it was memorized.

It was early last week, the weather was catching up with the season. He had taken his arms out of his shirtsleeves and put them underneath, trying to stay warm, so when he tapped on the window I figured he had at least a machete under there.

"Get the fuck out of here," I said. I did that without thinking about it, the same way you check for cars before you cross the street.

He looked at me, I looked at him. He took his hand off the car and put it back underneath his shirt. He began to shake, then he moved away. I turned on the radio to put the kid out of mind. If there is anything you have to know in a city, it's how to put things out of mind. If you can't do it, you better not be here.

I have been in Philadelphia more than six years. It took a while, but I can do that now.

The kid moved back to the corner of the building, stared at the car. I could see him in the side mirror. He looked like he was seventeen or eighteen, but you couldn't tell. He looked cold in every way there is to be cold. I put him out of mind again, but every time I looked in the mirror, he was standing there, black and cold and angry, and he wouldn't move away.

I don't know exactly when it happened, but somewhere along the line I got tired of victims in groups—women, blacks, Puerto Ricans, gay, and all the self-promotional bullshit that went with it—then I got tired of victims in person. I didn't want to see the mother and father nodded out on heroin at the Fox Theater Sunday afternoon while their four-year-old kid tried to wake them up anymore.

I didn't want to see old people who had been mugged, or fourteen-year-old alcoholics or abused children.

So, as much as you can in the city, I quit looking. At least I tried to only look once. There is too much of it to carry around with you.

And to do that, you have to forget that you have been hungry too.

The kid moved again, slowly across the parking lot to the garbage bin. He began going through it a piece at a time.

I was a couple of years older than this kid, but I went about a week once without anything to eat. In Minneapolis, in the coldest winter, I was hungry enough to go through garbage, but in the morning it had passed and what replaced it was just an empty, weak feeling, and later on a dizziness when I stood up. And much later, something inside that kept saying I was getting myself in serious trouble.

I wondered if the kid had heard that too. If he knew what it meant. I turned around and watched him a minute. He held the garbage close to his face, then put it back in the bin. A piece of paper stuck to his hand, and suddenly he was throwing things. Picking up cans and bags out of the bin and throwing them back, over and over. A beat-up gray cat with milk in her nipples jumped out of the other end of the bin.

He stopped and sat down, exhausted. He put his face in his hands. I said it out loud, so I could hear how it sounded. "Get the fuck out of here."

I ordered two chicken dinners and drove back around the lot to where the kid was sitting. I don't think he recognized me because he got up, tapped on the window and asked for a quarter to buy something to eat. There was garbage stuck to his chin.

I gave him one of the chicken dinners and said I was sorry. "I didn't see you were hungry," I said. The kid was looking at a two-dollar box of chicken with something close to love.

"Thank you," he said. "Thank you very much, thank you . . ."

"I've been in the city too long."

He studied me a minute. "Me too," he said. Then he took the chicken and walked over to his spot near the garbage and sat down to eat it.

The cat came out of the weeds toward him, a step at a time. The kid looked up and saw her. He tore a piece of meat off the breast and stroked her coat while she ate.